MW01147012

Third Button

A Journey from a Boy to a Man

Beset with the troubles of an engineering college, a boy, who, like a frog in a shallow pond, is afraid to swim in the deep ocean, takes the plunge. He submerges at one time and emerges at another, faces his fears and embraces the tears to finally learn an important lesson. The lesson of life.

Rohit Dharupta

.

Thank you, Dad, for the title, *Third Button.*

— Rohit Dharupta

Contents

THE JOURNEY

CHAPTER ONE

BANG! BANG! BANG!

At the stroke of midnight, loud and incessant banging at the door woke all four of us. Jay opened the door.

Through the fine holes of the mosquito net that hung right over my bed and added to my already blurred vision from being half awake, I saw a boy at the door. Clad in formal wear, he looked terrorized.

"Himachal Electronics! Who is Himachal Electronics?" he shouted, his voice trembling.

"That's me. What happened?" I replied, shoving aside the annoying mosquito net, fully awake and confused by now.

"They are calling!"

"Who?"

"The seniors! Seniors are calling! Go to the main entrance quickly!"

"What seniors? Who? Why? What's the time? Is something wrong?" I was confused.

"Don't waste time! Make it fast!"

I quickly got up from the bed, almost had a head rush, reached out for my sandals, and slid them on.

"Hey! Are you nuts? Going in these shorts and chappals? Wake up! Get dressed! Quick!"

I quickly looked for my formal wear in the cupboard. It was futile to enquire to this panic-stricken boy who was simply not prepared to explain anything further. His sole aim in the middle of the night was to take me with him, all dressed in formals like him, which made me very nervous.

Shirt. Pants. Belt. Necktie. Socks. Shoes. Done!

The boy stormed out. I followed him.

I could hear a loud noise as I quickly walked down the stairs. As soon as I reached the lobby near the entrance, the noise reached a deafening level, and the view in front of me was horrifying.

I spotted fifteen or twenty boys, all dressed in formal wear like me, standing at the grill gate of the main entrance. All of them stood close to the gate with their heads bowed down.

Some thirty-forty people were on the other side of the locked gate. They yelled, hurled abuse, and banged the gate from the outside, like a flock of bats squeaking at the highest decibel level. Some of them slipped their hands through the grills and pushed the guys who bowed their heads. Others climbed one or two steps of the grill gate to get a better grip and kept screaming and hounding them.

It felt like a terrifying scene from a *Planet of the Apes* movie, when those aggressive apes went wild and took control over the civilized and helpless citizens. I had never witnessed such madness in my life. They were going delirious, and I stood there with my legs trembling with fear, like a deer caught in the headlights.

What the hell am I doing here? Where have I landed? Is this place for real? For human beings?

Three days ago, I could not have imagined a remote possibility of such a view, even in my dreams, let alone in real life!

Three days ago, my heart was heavy, yet full of hope.

It was July 31st.

No, wait... the 31st was Tuesday, and I met my friend on Tuesday. It was Wednesday, so it must have been August 1st.

Or was it August 2nd?

Ok, let me confess to the reader my difficulty in remembering dates. Probably the reason why I found history the most boring subject back in school.

Who on earth would be fascinated by the date when the Battle of Panipat took place? As a schoolboy, I sometimes wondered why people engaged in those mutinies, revolts, and battles and left the dates for us to remember. Did they even care that some four or five hundred years after, schoolboys like me would be obligated to write those dates in our exams?

And not one, not even two, but *three* battles of Panipat! I mean, c'mon, that's three different dates!

Yes, I wished for no wars, but not because millions of innocent lives were lost, but due to my discomfort in keeping track of them!

This was not much of a challenge for my elder sister, though.

Didi, as I called her, was a living encyclopedia. Historical events, details, dates were no big deal for her. In fact, she once helped me memorize the names of Mughal emperors in chronological order, which I did so well that it was still ingrained in my mind.

Babur-Humayun-Akbar-Jahangir-Shah Jahan-Aurangzeb. See? No chance of a mix-up!

Back then, events and dates were not one Google search away as they are today. I am talking about the nineties here, when "the Internet" were lesser-known words than "mosquito net," and all dates were to be found in those heavy textbooks. I wished they had at least put in bold letters, or underlined those dates, or documented them in the appendices, for that matter.

Speaking of Didi, another talent of hers which I remember vividly was that she was very fond of idioms, and wasted no opportunity to use them to pull a joke on me.

There is a popular idiom in Hindi: "*Bandar kya jane adrak ka swad,*" often used for someone incapable of appreciating the value of something good. Literally, it translates to: "Monkey does not know the taste of ginger." So, she would offer me ginger to eat on purpose. Tell me, who would want to eat a piece of ginger? I did not even eat those ginger candies, let alone ginger alone. It's not even a snack!

My memory of eating tangy ginger chunks went back to only those rare nights of severe coughing, when Mommy would offer it to me as a substitute for cough syrup.

I would refuse, and promptly came Didi's reply: "*Bandar kya jane adrak ka swad.*"

Unable to handle the bantering again, I made it a point to accept those chunks of ginger every time she offered them to me, as I did not want to be referred to as a monkey again. Yeah, yeah… it's not a snack. I didn't care.

Back to the topic. Let's say August 1st, 8:30 p.m. A fine evening in Shimla.

Dad and I were sitting in a Volvo bus stationed at the bus terminus and waiting for a very important person. Yes, the VIP. Who else? The driver of the bus. Our lives, along with forty-odd passengers on the bus, would be in his hands for the next nine hours. Who the hell could be more important than him at that time?

The medical profession held high stature in our society because doctors were regarded as intermediaries between life and death. Drivers, in my view, commanded equal respect as the slightest error of judgment could risk innocent lives.

Oh, before I forget, let me introduce myself. I am Aahan Sharma.

Why Aahan? Well, that's the exact question I asked Dad once. The answer lies within the meaning of Aahan. As my dad very proudly explained, Aahan is a Sanskrit word for "early morning" when you witness the first ray of light.

There you go. Early morning. So, my name is Aahan because Mommy brought me into this world at the first light of the dawn.

Yes, exactly. That was my follow-up question too. What if I was born at noon?

Time for my dad to boast about his research in the field of the naming database. "Well, in that case, you would be called *Madhyahn*, a Sanskrit word for noon."

Ok, let me try again. "What if I was born in the afternoon?"

"*Aparahn*," came his prompt reply.

Ok, I gave up. I am glad that Dad settled with Aahan only. Also, I am so relieved that he did not limit his research to a month of the year or day of the week and went on further to drill down to the time of day between sunrise and sunset. Imagine people calling me *Friday* on a Monday or *April* in every month of the year!

Ok, so Dad and I were sitting in a Volvo bus. A few minutes of waiting, and then entered the important person. No, not the driver, the other important person, the bus conductor, the IP. The VIP was still to come.

After a cursory glance at the passengers, he looked outside to a busy, lively place with many colorful buses parked in no order. Organized chaos. A swarm of people, ranging from kids to the elderly.

Teenage boys were roaming here and there with a kettle and screaming, "Tea! Tea!" That was a routine day at the bus terminus.

At the main door of the bus, holding the bar for support with one hand and one foot resting firmly on the threshold, our conductor leaned forward with his upper body, one leg almost hanging out in the air, and shouted at random people, "Anybody up for Chandigarh, Delhi, Chandigarh, Delhi? Anybody?"

I looked around the packed bus to reassure myself that there was indeed no seat available on the bus. So, where was he going to accommodate another passenger?

Amused, I looked at Dad. Reading my mind at once, (telepathy, you see!), he winked at me and, pointing towards the driver's seat, said, "I guess he is calling somebody to drive this bus!"

We laughed.

Monotony leads to carelessness, I thought. *That's the reason why the bus conductor's brain had become wired in such a way that he stopped paying attention to the details. Wow! That observation adds another fact to my theory of human behavior.*

As the people outside paid no heed to his shouting, the conductor got out of the bus and disappeared.

9 p.m. The wait was finally over. The conductor arrived, along with the

VIP of the bus. *Ustadji* (that's how they are addressed respectfully), a tall, well-built man wearing a mustache pointing upward on either side of the nose, took his seat and pressed the horn. That was his signal to the passengers to get ready. He then blew the horn multiple times, signaling drivers of the buses close by to make way for him. After engaging in some playful banter with the other drivers, *Ustadji* was all set to go.

Chnnnn. Chhnnn. Vroom. Vroom.

And we started.

As soon as he left the Bus terminus and took to the main road, *Ustadji* struggled with a slow-moving car right in front of him.

Irked, he screamed at the driver of the car, "Hey! Get your soap bar out of my way!"

The funny analogy made everyone inside the bus burst into laughter. The soap bar moved swiftly to one side, and *Ustadji*, who was visibly beaming with the pride of driving a big vehicle, cruised ahead.

Lights off, and we were finally headed for New Delhi.

I closed my eyes, and the image of my mother appeared in front of me. Tears had rolled down her cheeks like pearls as I had left her at the doorstep today. When we had hugged, strong emotions welled up. My legs had frozen as if heavy rocks had been tied to them, making me motionless. I knew she wasn't going to eat this evening. She wouldn't sleep either.

Dad had looked at our faces while wiping his tears off his spectacles with the handkerchief. Nobody spoke a word, but our eyes said it all.

I wished Didi could have accompanied Mommy, but she had a brand-new family to take care of, post-marriage.

I remembered vividly when I left for Delhi the first time to get coaching for entrance exams, and Mommy had broken down.

Hugging her tightly and weeping herself, Didi had tried to comfort her, "Mumma, don't worry! I am here for you."

Dad had told me that Didi changed after that day. She hardly spoke, did not joke or throw tantrums, and did not chant her favorite idioms either. In a nutshell, she had stopped being a girl.

I opened my eyes and looked around. I was still on the bus, sitting beside dad, cruising into the darkness. I noticed the rings on my fingers—three of them glowing in the dark.

Mommy got me the rings a year ago after consulting my *janma kundli* (birth chart) with various pundits. She had explained to me with a sparkle in her eyes, "An iron ring made of a horseshoe to bring peace and tranquility, a white pearl ring to bring fame and name, and a red coral ring to remove obstacles in the way of your fortunes."

"Really!" I had laughed at her innocence and asked, "Three rings are going to make me successful and solve all my problems?"

Deep inside, I had faith in her belief. I threw the rings away once in a fit of anger and frustration after failing to pass an exam. Mommy had patiently collected the rings and persuaded me to wear them again the following day.

Mommy. Like an endearing alarm clock, she would wake me up in the morning with a glass of milk. She would never use an alarm clock, yet woke me up as early as I wanted during my exams and then stayed awake the rest of the morning, doing household chores while I studied.

Strange, I never asked her why she sacrificed her sleep all those years.

She would always slip a portion of her omelet into my plate at the breakfast table, even though she knew that my share was enough. It was pointless to tell her not to do so as she wouldn't change. What satisfaction did she get by giving me her share of my favorite food? I never gave it a thought.

She would inquire if I ate something every afternoon when I returned from school. Strange, I never realized why my every meal was so important to her.

Why? Why had she prayed all these years endlessly for my better future only to see me off, being separated from her?

Selfless and unconditional. I had heard those words many times, but it had not occurred to me before that they were perhaps discovered only to describe a mother.

As the emotions welled up, I didn't remember when I fell asleep.

CHAPTER TWO

5:45 a.m.

"The bald one is mine!" screamed one man.

"The foreigner is mine!" yelled another.

"No, you always take foreigners," retorted a third one. "She is mine!"

"Fat man is mine, fat man is mine! I saw him first!" announced a fourth one.

Loud yelling woke me up. I saw a few men gathered outside the front door of the bus. The bus was stationary, and some of the passengers were queuing up to get off.

We were at Delhi bypass, the final stop for some of our fellow passengers. Those men outside were the taxi and auto-rickshaw drivers looking to offer pick-up. By peeping inside and yelling, they declared their choice of passengers to their fellow taxi-men. Such was their shamelessness that they did not shy away from name-calling based on the physical appearance of the passengers, which, by the way, all the passengers could hear clearly.

I turned to Dad, who was already awake. "It's strange that after offending the passengers, these people approach them without any hesitation!"

"Perhaps they don't even realize it. For them, physical appearance is the only way to stake their claim on passengers, and each of them ends up settling with at least one passenger. They even help each other, a classic example of a self-governing body. Even the passengers do not seem to take offense. They are simply thinking of their destination," Dad replied.

I nodded my head in agreement.

As those men got busy negotiating with their respective passengers, one of them entered the bus and addressed the remaining passengers,

"ITO… Airport… Shahdara… Jamuna-Paar! Come, come! Anybody? Anybody, please?"

"Please? Really? Are you asking or begging? Man, if you could manage passengers just by begging like this, you would be rich by now!" the ever so witty *Ustadji* took a potshot at him.

"*Ustadji*, how come you know so much about beggars? Any beggars in the family?" returned the man jokingly.

"Hey, no jokes on my bus. Get off my bus and go back to Jamuna-Paar all by yourself," *Ustadji* snapped at him.

We could not control our laughter this time. The man got off the bus.

We carried on. The next stop was the New Delhi Inter-State Bus Terminus (ISBT), and, finally, the last stop was Mandi House, Himachal Bhawan.

Mandi House was a former estate of Raja (King) of Mandi in Delhi and had been later sold and divided. Now there were modern buildings and offices in place of the old palace. Himachal Bhawan, an all-stone building, was the state house of Himachal Pradesh. In simple words, an affordable guesthouse for the people of Himachal.

As we prepared to get off at Himachal Bhawan, along with two or three remaining passengers, Dad thanked the conductor and the one and only *Ustadji*. I was expecting another one-liner, but *Ustadji* just acknowledged us with a smile this time.

Dad had booked a room in Himachal Bhawan, and we proceeded to our room to catch some sleep and freshen up for the remaining journey.

12:05 p.m.

Delhi Hazrat Nizamuddin Railway Station was alive with a flock of people. Some passengers were ready to board, some queued up at inquiry counters, some curiously looking at the seat charts, and some waited at the platform with their dear ones who had come to see them off. Coolies roaming here and there offered their luggage services. Stalls on the platforms sold tea, coffee, water, newspapers, and magazines. Small shops at the corners sold samosa, bread pakoras, and soft drinks. Trains honked and announcements were made for arrivals and departures.

A typical day at the train station.

Platform two, Kalinga Utkal Express, ready for departure.

The AC two-tier coach was sparsely occupied. There we were, in the compartment near the entrance. The luggage was already tucked under the lower berth.

The train started with the familiar horn as an indication for departure. Dad turned to the newspapers that he had bought at the platform from one of those stalls, and I stretched my legs to relax.

2:15 p.m.

Mathura Junction. A brief halt for a few minutes. More passengers boarded. Most of the empty berths were taken by now. Our berth was near one of the entrance doors of the compartment, and I could easily spot people hopping in or getting off.

I observed people. That's how you pass the time on a train journey. I saw two young boys jostling near the entrance in a bid to enter first. They must have been six and eight. Then entered a girl, I guessed ten years old, and another one, probably twelve. A lady in her forties followed, and…

Oh, wait. What is that?

A bag! A kind of big round cloth bag from what I could see. Someone was pushing it through the entrance.

Oops! I see now!

It was a man with a big belly struggling to enter. Wow, I thought that belly was a big round bag. I mean, I had heard those jokes about the tummy arriving first and then the rest of the man but had never seen one!

The big man with an even bigger tummy who was in his late forties or early fifties, accompanied by his large family, approached our compartment.

The man verified his berths with the tickets, and the family took time to settle down. The man and his lady took the berth right in front of us, while all four kids took the side berth. The two boys now jostled for a side seat.

I took a guess in my head—a cliched one, judging by the man's appearance—that he might be a *halwai* (a sweet maker).

After a greeting and exchange of pleasantries, Dad started a conversation. "Where are you going?"

"We are going to Jhansi for a relative's marriage."

"You live in Mathura?"

"Yes."

"You look like a businessman."

"Yes, I do. We are in the business of sweet making," the man replied.

*And h*alwai *it is,* I thought. *I am getting better at this.*

"That's nice. What's the specialty? Is it *peda?*" Dad asked, referencing a sweet made from milk. "Mathura is famous for it."

"Yes, it is. *Kesar peda, malai peda, prasad ka peda.* Our *kesar peda* is special. Have you heard about Nathulal-Atmaram sweets?"

Dad shook his head. "No."

"That's our famous sweet shop. I am Nathulal, by the way. You see, the art of sweet making runs in the family," said the man, visibly beaming with pride.

The art of sweet making runs in the family, I repeated in my head. *But does anyone run in the family? Forget running. Does anyone jog or even take walks, for that matter?* I looked at the big round stomach with the navel peeping out of the shirt, which I had almost mistaken for baggage.

Does he eat all those pedas himself? I wondered if he was making any profit in his business at all!

Ok, enough of fat-shaming. Now I feel like a hypocrite, no different from those name-calling taxi drivers I saw at the bus station this morning who irked me.

"What about your relatives in Jhansi? Are they sweet makers too?" asked dad.

Nathulal nodded. "Yes, have you heard of Gaindamal-Agyaram sweets?"

As an Indian tradition, we brought sweets when we visited relatives or friends' places. I wondered what *halwais* brought when they visited another *halwai*.

Sweets, really? That would be like a barber bringing a pair of scissors to another barber friend. Fruits could be an option. Or maybe something special or exclusive from their sweetshop. But that would be something a halwai would surely want to keep away from another halwai for fear of his secret recipe getting revealed.

"Where are you from, Delhi?" asked Nathulal.

"Not Delhi. We are coming from Shimla."

"I see. Shimla is a beautiful place. We had our honeymoon in Shimla." He winked at his wife, took a slight pause while she smiled, and continued, "And where are you going?"

"Rourkela."

"Rourkela in Odisha?"

"Yes, my son cleared NCE," Dad replied, pointing at me.

"NCE?"

"National College of Engineering, Rourkela."

"Engineering college," I tried to help, looking at the blank expression on his face.

"Ya, ya, I know engineers," returned Nathulal. "My sister's son is also an engineer. He has a big workshop in Mathura. He repairs all types of scooters, motorbikes, and cars too. He is a diploma holder, a very brilliant chap, you see."

"I think you are confusing a motor mechanic and an engineer. The engineer would be the one who designs or builds a machine or some structure. You have to clear a tough entrance exam to get admission. You see…" and dad made an effort to clear his concept of an engineer, which I felt would be in vain. I would have rather let him live with his impression of an engineer.

Dad had always been like this. A proud father who loved to boast about his children in his friendship circle. But then, which father wasn't? Perhaps dads thought that they made an immense contribution to the betterment of society—or the planet earth, for that matter—by bringing up their super talented children and thought that society needed to acknowledge that.

I often told Dad, "I get embarrassed when you praise me in front of your friends. After all, why would they be interested in me?"

"Why won't they? They should. I am all ears when Sharma Ji tells me about his painter son, or when Verma Ji talks about his school topper daughter."

Well, there you are. I tell you, if all the dads are to be believed, we have a generation of legends in the making in every field.

Ok, to say I get embarrassed is not entirely true. I must admit that it feels good whenever dad brags about me, even if he exaggerates. That's a simple human behavior; appreciation feels good, and criticism feels bad.

What's with people saying, "constructive criticism is always welcome"? Let me tell you: appreciation is always welcome, but criticism is hardly ever appreciated.

"…and those big corporate companies and MNCs hire those engineers. They offer handsome pay packages."

My chain of thought broke as Dad finished explaining what an engineer was and how well they got paid (emphasizing the latter part).

Nathu *halwai* nodded his head. I didn't know how much he understood, but Dad made sure that he learnt something new, whether it mattered to him or not.

I knew one thing: for him, the difference between kesar peda and malai peda mattered more than that mechanic-engineer crap.

Dad often had his friends over for drinks. After three pegs down, the appetite for entertainment needed to be fulfilled, and watching Doordarshan surely would not help. Why go far when Kishor Kumar was sitting in the adjoining room doing nothing?

So, yours truly would be invited to demonstrate his singing talent. I felt like a rock star performing in front of a small audience at a private concert. Praises would be showered, and I was compared to the likes of legendary singers Kishor Kumar and Mohd Rafi. I felt wonderful.

I particularly remember one of Dad's friends, an IPS officer and another proud father who would say, "Beta, my daughter is very witty. I told her that she should study hard, that no one has ever died of hard work. She says, 'Papa, I know nobody ever died of hard work but then, why take the risk?'" His story left us in splits.

Having him at our place was a lot of fun. One evening after a few drinks, he discovered that his service revolver was missing. He told Dad, "I may have dropped it while parking the van. Let's go and find it."

It was winter season, and Shimla had witnessed heavy snowfall. So, around 9:30 p.m., the two tipsy men started the hunt for the revolver that freezing cold evening.

Shimla, the Queen of Hills, became the center of attraction during snowfall. Just like a lady on her wedding day, the white gown of snow, embellished all over with stars up in the sky, made the outside view picturesque.

Didi and I giggled as we observed them from the balcony. Mommy, standing next to us, instructed us to go inside, but we would not budge. Who would want to miss the fun?

We could see dad and uncle wobble while walking down the sloped lane. They held the railing for support to avoid stumbling. Believe me, walking down a steep lane covered with two feet of snow for our men was like two amateurs wandering cluelessly on the ski track.

With great effort, they arrived at the parked van. Uncle did not find the gun in the van, and they started looking around.

"Careful. Watch your step!"

"Here it is… No, no, that's a stone!"

"What color is it?"

"Black!"

"Not the stone, I mean the revolver!"

"Black! Ah… I got it. Got it!" Uncle confirmed with a quiver in his voice. "Bhabhiji. Look, I found it! I found it!" Raising his hand and flashing the revolver from where he was standing, Uncle exclaimed in a slightly pitched voice that quivered under the influence of either the severe cold or alcohol (or both).

"I am glad you did. Now please come back. And for God's sake, don't shoot!" said Mom, panicked, fearing the policeman Uncle might start celebrating by shooting in the air.

Back on the train, Nathu and family kept binging on wafers, peanuts, and biscuits at almost every other stop, and the two boys remained busy jostling, pushing, and snatching from each other. I understood that families that eat together stay together, but that was over-eating.

Around 7:30 p.m., we arrived at Jhansi Junction, and the sweet Nathu family bid us *adieu*. The two boys now jostled in a bid to exit first.

A few more passengers hopped in.

It seemed like the momentum of my train of thoughts was more than the moving train itself.

It had never occurred to me before that life is like a train journey. The trains are in constant motion, heading for a destination, and so are the people chasing their goals in the persistent desire to fulfill their dreams.

We face challenges that decide the course of our life, like the web of railway tracks which may give momentum to the train or slow it down. Or sometimes there is a bad track which leads to an accident, putting the whole journey to a complete halt.

Passengers hop on and hop off the train like people in our lives, some for a brief period and others for longer. Some make us laugh, some make us cry, and there are others who do not make a difference at all.

We were served a nice dinner from the railway pantry, then it was time to sleep. Dad took the lower berth, and I took the upper one.

"And those big corporate companies and MNCs hire those engineers. They offer handsome pay packages." Dad's words kept repeating in my head.

Is this what I want? Is this going to make me happy? If not this, what else will? Is this the best career option for me?

I didn't know. I never had.

We were all bound by social conventions. Doctors, engineers, or civil services were believed to be promising career options, and the grades and marks in high school were considered the benchmark of capability.

Per society's norm, if you were good at studies, the obvious step was to opt for science subjects, which would open the doors to a job. Parents pushed their children to score high and clear entrance tests.

Peer pressure was sweeping the children and their parents equally—children competing to score better than their peers to prove their mettle. Parents wanting a bright future for their children and to keep up their pride in society.

Which one was more important, the former or the latter? I had no idea.

Sports, music, dance, or other art forms were largely thought of as extracurricular activities that wouldn't earn bread for you. This perception was changing in big cities, but small towns were still behind the times.

Could I have pursued my interest in music beyond entertaining Dad's tipsy friends? I used to paint well. I had many inter-school prizes to support that claim.

Could that be a career option for me? Would Dad be equally proud if I opted for those options? Of course, he would, I reassured myself. *Engineering seemed to be a more promising prospect, and he knew that I had the potential to nail it. Forget about passion; it often takes a backseat in the real world.*

The express train carried on the track, and so did my train of thoughts, which did not keep track of the time. Sometime around midnight. I finally fell asleep.

CHAPTER THREE

8 a.m.

"Tum to thehre pardesi, saath kya nibhaaoge! Subah pehli gaadi se tum to laut jaaoge!"

The high-pitched frequency of the popular Bollywood song woke me up. Rubbing my eyes, I saw a little girl who was singing at the top of her voice and profusely clobbering the two stones, one in each of her hands, to create the background score. It was amazing to see just a pair of stones (not drums) in those little hands producing such accurate beats that accented her song perfectly.

I had heard before that necessity leads to invention, but I was witnessing for the first time that poverty could lead to innovation.

She was wearing a worn-out frock and absolutely no footwear. She must have been six or seven. She was accompanied by her little brother, who was wearing a clown hat with a fur ball tied to a thread on the top. His clothes were also in tatters.

The boy was dancing around and shaking his head incessantly to keep the furball in a circular motion in perfect sync with his sister's stone music. The boy, who was barely four, also tried his hands at acrobatics.

After a brief halt at Pendra (in the state of Chhattisgarh), the train continued. The two kids quickly collected the coins on the floor thrown by some generous passengers—meager earnings for an astounding performance—and hopped off the slow-moving train.

Everyone around looked delighted with the entertainment they had just had, but I was sad.

I had been pondering over the apt career option for me last night, and there were kids for whom the struggle for survival was the only option. I often contemplated my career choice, and there were these kids who could not even afford a meal of their choice. I thought about my future, my goals in life, and those poor kids had only one goal—to arrange their next meal.

We often take our privileges for granted, I thought, *but God has a way to remind us now and then.*

I saw Dad enter the compartment, fresh from his morning wash, with a brush and shaving kit in his hands. We greeted each other, and another day on the train began.

Around 3 p.m. in the afternoon, the train halted at Jharsuguda (in the state of Odisha) for ten minutes.

Sipping tea served in *kulhar* (a disposable clay pot), Dad reminded me that we had traveled all the way to the east part of India, after starting in the north.

We counted eight states and one union territory that we had covered—starting from Shimla, in Himachal Pradesh, Haryana, Punjab, Delhi, Uttar Pradesh, Rajasthan, Madhya Pradesh, Chhattisgarh, Odisha. Wow! That was like one-third of the states of India.

We arrived at Rourkela Junction in another two hours, at approximately 5 p.m. Our twenty-nine hours of train journey had come to an end, and we were in the steel city of Rourkela.

We got off. The train carried on to its destination, the final stop Puri, the holy city famous for the Jagannath Temple. We got in a cab and headed for NCE.

We arrived at the college fifteen minutes later. As our cab entered the huge gate where "National College of Engineering" was engraved in bold letters on a brass plaque, my heart was filled with pride. The plush campus spread over more than one thousand acres was going to be my home for the next four years—my *gurukul.*

Before leaving for Rourkela, Dad had requested via the registrar on the phone for a temporary stay at a guest house, and he graciously obliged. We checked in to the guest house, which was a short distance from the main entrance.

We freshened up quickly, and Dad relaxed with a drink. After enjoying a scrumptious dinner, we took a casual stroll along the guesthouse lawn. We met a young boy and a lady (who must have been dad's age).

Dad, curious as always, initiated the conversation. "Hello! Are you also here for admission?"

"Hello, Uncle. No, I am a student of the fifth semester. My name is Vijay," replied the boy.

I quickly did the math in my head. *Ok, that would be a first senior in college. The fifth semester means a third year student.*

"Meet my mom."

"Hello, have you come for the admission of your son?" asked Vijay's mother.

"Yes, we will commence joining formalities tomorrow morning," returned Dad.

"Great! I am here to take care of Vijay. He has just recovered from typhoid. We have been staying at the guest house for the last fifteen days. You see, the kids don't take care of themselves properly in the hostel."

"Yes, you are right. Where are you from?"

"Palampur, Himachal Pradesh," said Vijay.

"HP! We are from Shimla. Wow! What a small world," replied Dad, elated.

"Good. Which branch?" asked Vijay, smiling at me.

"Electronics," I replied.

"Well, you are supposed to say the whole thing, 'Electronics and Communication Engineering,'" said Vijay, and his smile turned into a grin.

I just smiled and chose not to respond.

Dad enquired more about college, and I was all ears. Vijay explained that the college had students from almost all the states. Odisha, being the home state, had the maximum share of seats. He added that the students from five northern states—Jammu and Kashmir, Punjab, Haryana, Himachal, and New Delhi (UT)—had a loosely organized association to help each other. They were addressed as *Northees* in the college.

"So, here's your new *Northee,*" Dad said.

"Yes, Uncle."

"Tell me something about the ragging in the college."

"Yes, ragging is common in NCEs, Uncle."

"Do they abuse or get physical?"

"Yes, many seniors do. I don't indulge in any form of torture. Personally, I am not in favor of ragging," said Vijay.

"Yes, he tells me, 'Mumma, my friends hit the juniors.' I don't like it and try to stop them," Vijay's mother chimed in.

"Madam, your boy is kind-hearted. No wonder you are from Himachal. Himachalis are peaceful by nature. I am relieved. My son is in safe hands," returned Dad.

What a gentleman, I thought. *I wish all the seniors were like him. He has a gentle voice.*

Back in the guest house, Dad was in all praises for Vijay. "If you need anything in the hostel, go to Vijay. He will take care of you. I am glad we met someone from Himachal."

I nodded in agreement.

We went off to bed as we needed to get up early for the big day. Yes, the admission day.

It did not occur to me that some uninvited guests were waiting. I had hardly dozed off when an incessant buzzing sound close to my ears woke me up. My uninvited guests were the thankless mosquitoes who would suck on my blood and annoy the hell out of me.

I never understood why they announced their arrival by buzzing around the ears. That was like poking fun at my helplessness. Why not just suck the bloody blood quietly and fly off? Imagine the audacity of the burglars who formally announced their intention first and then broke into your house!

I looked at Dad, who was sleeping peacefully in the same room, despite the jarring buzzing music. Now *that* was the magic of alcohol.

Wait a minute, did those mosquitoes sip leftover drops from Dad's empty glass tumbler?

I had heard somewhere that the bloodsuckers tended to bite people who consumed alcohol more than teetotalers. I guessed the love of alcohol was not just limited to humans. Even bugs were addicted to it.

I was in no mood to let those mosquitoes celebrate over my dad's booze. I found a mosquito repellant that was enough to spoil their party— probably the last one of their lives.

Finally, I slept.

CHAPTER FOUR

8:45 a.m.

Admission Day. The administrative building. Ok, "The admin block," short and sweet.

The building appeared like a cinema hall, with three small windows at the ground level like ticket counters that were yet to be opened. The boys and girls queued up in front of the counters and waited patiently. Everyone was here to collect the admission form and pay the fees for the first two semesters.

The counters opened at 9 a.m. sharp, and the officials started distributing the forms. I collected the form on my turn and sat on the steps of the stage-like area near the admin block.

I looked around. Some of my fellow batch mates were busy filling in the form. Dad was interacting with the other parents and guardians. I started working on my form carefully.

"Hey! New joiner?" A brusque tone broke my concentration. I looked up to find a lean boy with moderate height standing in front of me. "I said, are you a new joiner?" he repeated.

"Yes, I am," I replied.

"I am your senior. Come with me. I will introduce you to the other seniors."

"Sir," I responded very politely, "I am almost finished with my form. I request you to let me submit it first, and then I will come with you."

As I was speaking to him, Dad approached us.

The lean boy respectfully greeted Dad. "Uncle, I am a second year student. My name is Ravinder, and I am from Phagwara, Punjab," he said.

"Oh, you are a *Northee*! We are *Northees* too," returned dad. "We are from Shimla. We met another of your *Northee* friends in the guest house yesterday—Vijay. Do you know him?"

"Yes, Uncle, I know him. He is our senior from the third year."

As they talked, I completed the form and submitted it to the counter. Soon my joining formalities were completed, and I was relieved. Dad was now socializing with other parents and children. I spotted Ravinder in one corner and went up to him.

"Sir, I am back. You wanted me to meet other seniors?"

"Yes, come."

He took me to the backside of the admin block. A secluded place where hardly anyone came. Before I could sense it, he snapped at me.

"Why didn't you come with me before?"

"Sir, I told you—"

"Shut up, you F$!%&R!" He raised both his voice and a hand.

Sensing that he would slap my face, I moved my head away as a reflex action.

He did not hit me.

"Don't you dare disobey senior's orders!" he roared.

I chose not to respond.

"Where is your third button?" Ravinder growled again.

I looked at him with a blank expression.

"Third button of your shirt, you idiot! Look at your third button!"

I could not fathom why he asked me to look at the third button of my shirt, but I did it anyway.

"Ok, come with me, you can look up now."

I was appalled by Ravinder's behavior. Who the hell treated people like this? And on my very first day. Did he expect me to leave my joining formality and meet his silly friends instead?

Ravinder now took me to the entrance of the admin block. I saw four boys passing by; one of them was holding a notebook, another one playing with a pen in his hands, and the other two carrying absolutely nothing.

Ravinder shouted enthusiastically, "Hey! Look, I have *butru* with me!"

Butru? Had he referred to me as *butru*? So, the lean boy had given me a name! What a silly name. God... I hated this guy.

The boys approached, seemingly exhilarated to meet me. One of them, a well-built boy, put his heavy arm around my shoulder. The other one kept grinning. I felt very uncomfortable in their company. They asked me questions and kept joking. I was careful this time and kept my responses short and to the point.

Dad stood some distance away and did not take his eyes off me all this time. He clearly sensed my discomfort but did not interrupt. Perhaps he wanted those guys to get well acquainted with me and wait until their excitement settled in.

After a while, Dad joined us, and Ravinder introduced his friends. All of them greeted him respectfully.

Ravinder invited us for lunch at the hostel as part of a tradition that the *Northees* followed, and dad graciously accepted. So, we headed to the hostel with the lean boy Ravinder and the well-built boy Samar for lunch while the other three parted, saying they had a lecture to attend.

Why did dad accept Ravinder's offer for lunch? He could have made some excuse. We could go back to the guesthouse. I wish I could tell Dad how Ravinder treated me. Now there will be many more overexcited boys in the hostel.

And the other three? Did they attend the lecture? Really? What's with that notebook he was carrying? Even a fifth standard boy has a bigger notebook! I would guess it had twenty-five pages or less. Does that even qualify as a notebook or is it just a file cover?

And that other guy who was continuously rotating his pen with his thumb and two fingers? Does he only play with it, or write too? Or does he just scribble on the classroom table?

And the one who did not carry anything to the college? Does he ever attend the classes or just accompany his friends?

Why am I a center of attraction? It's as if they spotted an alien from the planet Mars! Ok, but in that case, they would be terrified, not excited.

"Are you also a *Northee*?" Dad asked.

"Yes, Uncle. I am from Sonipat, Haryana. We are in the second year," replied Samar, walking with his bicycle.

"So, your juniors are joining. You must be excited."

"Yes, Uncle, Our *butrus*."

"*Butrus*!" Dad repeated. "What's that?"

"Uncle, here we call the juniors *butru*."

"I see, so Aahan is your *butru*?" asked Dad, pointing at me.

"Yes, Uncle. And like every *butru*, he has a family too. Since he is from the state of Himachal and has joined the Electronics branch, his seniors are also from Himachal and are in the Electronics branch. Those from the second, third, and final years will be referred to as his *baap* (father), *dada* (grandfather), and *pardada* (great grandfather), respectively. Like a state and branch family tree!" explained Samar.

"Great! See, your father and forefathers are already here in the college. I do not think you are going to miss us!" Dad said to me jokingly, and I smiled in return.

What a ludicrous attempt at fake relationships! And what for? To establish the authority of the seniors?

Ironically, I never met my real great-grandfather, but here I will meet one thanks to this illogical family tree.

I guess if the senior is a female, then they must be called mommy *(mother), dadi (grandmother), or par-dadi (great grandmother). I hope their family chart does not make the girls of my batch my sisters or cousins.*

In any case, I was glad that *butru* was common terminology and not used for me only, as I had previously thought to be the case.

As we walked, I got to witness the grandeur of the college for the first time. Departments that were on either side of the road had distinctive architecture. I also noticed a basketball and tennis court as we walked further.

We arrived at the final stretch in a few minutes, where I could see five hostels in a row, all named "Hall of Residence" followed by the numbers one to five, respectively.

Samar told us that Hall One was for the first years, Hall Three for the second years, and Halls Two and Five for third and final year boys, respectively. These halls were allotted to students doing their Bachelor of Technology. All the boys pursuing their masters were accommodated in Hall Four.

I did not understand the order of allotments of the halls, but I did not really care. What I really cared about was the girls' hostel. I could not muster the courage to ask this important question, but Ravinder was proactive enough to tell us.

"The ladies' hostel is on the other side of the college building and is called LH," said Ravinder, sharing the useful information, perhaps the only good thing to come out of his mouth since we had met. This further strengthened my belief that all boys thought alike when it came to girls.

As we walked past halls One and Two, I noticed a big playground on the other side of the road. Samar and Ravinder took us to their hostel, the Hall Three messroom, where we had lunch with the boys.

As expected, I was the center of attention in the hostel. After lunch, while Samar talked to Dad, Ravinder showed me to a room. Soon I found myself surrounded by a group of fifteen to twenty enthusiastic boys in the room.

"Do you have a girlfriend?" a fat boy with long, messy, uncombed hair and wearing thick spectacles enquired. I wondered when the last time he had shampooed his hair was. He was sitting on a chair seemingly too tiny for his size.

"No, sir."

"Why are you wasting your life?" said another one, a tall guy who had somehow managed to find a place on a single bed shared by his ten other friends.

I didn't know how to answer that question.

"Ok, let me calculate the probability of you finding a girl in your batch," The fat boy continued, "You see, there are five boys' hostels and one girls' hostel. That means the ratio of girls to boys is one to five. So in your batch, for every 100 boys, there will be only twenty girls. Forty percent of the girls are those *fundu* ones, who are here for marks and not for boys."

"Yes, they do not get enticed by boys. They only get turned on by quantum mechanics and Bernoulli's principle," interrupted Ravinder, and everyone laughed.

"So, forget them. Now, twenty percent will be those popular ones, the so-called hot girls. Since half of the college boys will be after them, they will act as high-headed divas. You are a good-looking boy and likely to fall into the trap of trying luck with the divas, but I highly doubt your chance of success as you will face tough competition from sixty to seventy percent of boys of the college starting from the first year to final year. The truth is that even those divas will end up alone as they will always look for a better option. As yours truly Baba Kamdev says, so many options leave you in a state of indecision," said the fat boy as he referred to himself as Baba Kamdev.

"Wah, wah! Words of wisdom from his holiness Baba Kamdev!" shouted the tall guy.

"Thank you, thank you. So how many girls are left now? Forty percent, which is just eight. These are the girls you need to focus on. But, like everyone, it will take at least two years for your high standards to come crashing down. By the time you become *despo*, those eight girls will also settle down with average guys who have been pursuing them since day one. Eventually, you will become *frustu*. In a nutshell, your probability of a link-up in your batch is zero," concluded Baba Kamdev.

What a self-proclaimed connoisseur of matchmaking, I thought. *Talking about probability! What about the probability of that poor chair holding him for another ten minutes? Does he know that? If that chair could speak, I am sure it would be begging him for some fresh air. I bet this self-professed love guru Baba Kamdev is a desperate, single, ready-to-mingle kind of guy with no luck so far. His theory is stupid, and so are those slang words that he uses...* Fundu, despo, frustu.

"It's not over yet. After rejection from your batch girls, you will eagerly wait for your junior batch to come," continued Baba Kamdev, "By the time you reach the final year, your benchmark of beauty will drop to such a level that every girl in the college campus will look like Aishwarya Rai to you."

"Yes, beauty queens! All of them!" said Ravinder. "Even those who do not study on campus! Yesterday, a final year guy told me that he found the mess contractor's daughter hot. See the level of his desperation."

"Who?" asked Baba Kamdev.

"Kumar."

"Kumar? Really? Kesto's daughter?" His laughter boomed around the room.

"Yes, Kumar has already paid his future father-in-law for the meals at least six months in advance. He calls him Kesto, sir. Imagine! No one in the history of this college has ever called that guy 'sir'!"

All the boys in the room burst into laughter.

"Take my advice. Ask out the very first girl you meet in your batch. Don't go after external beauty, think about the inner beauty, like Kumar. I repeat the golden words, 'Ask out the very first girl you meet,'" advised Kamdev.

Ask out the very first girl I meet? I repeated those words in my head.

As a regular boy who had attained their knowledge and wisdom of love interests through watching Bollywood romantic movies while growing up, this was certainly not how it worked. The process worked in basic steps like, you met a girl, fell in love, and then asked her out or proposed to her.

But here was a guy jumping straight to step three, leaving aside the "meet a girl" and "falling in love" parts altogether. That was like skipping almost a half of a Bollywood movie and starting from intermission, a perfect formula for a flop.

If the recipe does not work in a romantic film, how will it work in real life? I do not buy into their advice, though I must admit that their playful banter is amusing.

I kept a straight face all this time without reacting much to anything. I only spoke when asked something and even then, I kept it short. After the rough experience with Ravinder that morning, I was not sure what to expect.

Dad came looking for me, and all the boys greeted him respectfully. I must admit that everybody in the hostel was very courteous to my dad.

We thanked everyone and started for the Hall of Residence One. Samar and Ravinder showed us to the hostel entrance.

SEMESTER ONE

Rohit Dharupta

CHAPTER ONE

Back in Hall One, we met the warden at his office and commenced the formalities of the room allotment. The hostel was abuzz with a lot of energy and excitement of other new joiners like me.

Room B36 was allotted to me. The three-floor hostel building was divided into three wings: A, B, and C.

Following the signboard, we quickly figured out where the B wing was and took the stairs that led to the first floor, where my room was located.

It was a large room with four corner sections, one for each person, which contained a wooden cot, a table with a table lamp, a chair, and a cupboard. Those were the valuable assets for each of the four occupants.

I met my other three roommates, my roomies, for the first time.

I did not have a choice in my section as the other three were already occupied. Besides, the furniture in all the corners looked old, with chairs and tables equally scribbled with compasses and ballpoint pens.

The room was well lit with large windows, and that was the only thing I liked about it.

Jay, Chandru, and Vibhu were my roommates, and they all greeted me with a smile. Jay and Chandru were lean, while Vibhu was a bit bulky. These simple boys, who were natives of the state of Odisha, appeared to be from humble backgrounds. Vibhu was accompanied by his father while Jay and Chandru had traveled alone.

I initiated a conversation to know more about them. They spoke little, only interested in enquiring about ranks and percentage marks of entrance and secondary board exams. Vibhu was the topper of the senior secondary board exam, and his father proudly shared the feat with Dad and me. Another proud father.

Soon they carried on with the task of organizing their respective corners. I also got busy juggling with the task of mounting the mosquito net over the bed and the arrangement of books and clothes. Dad talked to

Vibhu's father and stayed for a while to oversee my arrangement of the stuff before he left for the guest house.

My first evening without Dad, or my first evening with my brand-new roommates, so to speak.

Once we were finished with organizing our sections, we proceeded for dinner. At the hostel messroom, we talked about jobs, subjects, ranks, and marks. Again, ranks and marks were the prime topics of discussion. My super focused roommates aspired for top grades and the best jobs and talked about future prospects.

At one point I thought about bringing up the topic of the funny matchmaking probability analysis that the seniors did for me that afternoon but then changed my mind. Though I felt the topic of girls could qualify as "future prospects," with these boys, it was perhaps out of the scope of the present theme.

Perhaps these were the *fundu* people that Baba Kamdev mentioned; those who get seduced not by girls but by the idea of quantum mechanics! Did that mean Baba Kamdev's probability theory of the pursuit of the significant other was not entirely trash?

No, no. How can one be convinced with his golden words, "Ask out the first girl you meet"? Anyways, good to have studious roomies. I hope I will benefit from their company, I thought.

Back in the room, I crashed out under the protection of the mosquito net. A long, tiresome day was over.

But was it over yet?

BANG! BANG! BANG!

At the stroke of midnight, loud and incessant banging at the door woke all four of us. Jay opened the door.

Through the fine holes of the mosquito net that hung right over my bed and added to my already blurred vision from being half awake, I saw a boy at the door. Clad in formal wear, he looked terrorized.

"Himachal Electronics! Who is Himachal Electronics?" he shouted, his voice trembling.

"That's me. What happened?" I replied, shoving aside the annoying mosquito net, fully awake and confused by now.

"They are calling!"

"Who?"

"The seniors! Seniors are calling! Go to the main entrance quickly!"

"What seniors? Who? Why? What's the time? Is something wrong?" I was confused.

"Don't waste time! Make it fast!"

I quickly got up from the bed, almost had a head rush, reached out for my sandals, and slid them on.

"Hey! Are you nuts? Going in these shorts and chappals? Wake up! Get dressed! Quick!"

I quickly looked for my formal wear in the cupboard. It was futile to enquire to this panic-stricken boy who was simply not prepared to explain anything further. His sole aim in the middle of the night was to take me with him, all dressed in formals like him, which made me very nervous.

Shirt. Pants. Belt. Necktie. Socks. Shoes. Done!

The boy stormed out. I followed him.

I could hear a loud noise as I quickly walked down the stairs. As soon as I reached the lobby near the entrance, the noise reached a deafening level, and the view in front of me was horrifying.

I spotted fifteen or twenty boys, all dressed in formal wear like me, standing at the grill gate of the main entrance. All of them stood close to the gate with their heads bowed down.

Some thirty-forty people were on the other side of the locked gate. They yelled, hurled abuse, and banged the gate from the outside, like a flock of bats squeaking at the highest decibel level. Some of them slipped their hands through the grills and pushed the guys who bowed their heads. Others climbed one or two steps of the grill gate to get a better grip and kept screaming and hounding them.

It felt like a terrifying scene from a *Planet of the Apes* movie, when those aggressive apes went wild and took control over the civilized and helpless citizens. I had never witnessed such madness in my life. They were going delirious, and I stood there with my legs trembling with fear, like a deer caught in the headlights.

"Himachal Electronics! Hey! Come here, you M@#$%R F@#$%R!"

"Where are you looking?" I heard one of them crying out loud amidst the deafening noise.

I ran towards the gate with my head lowered down. I could see the third button of my shirt. The memory of the lean boy Ravinder making me look at the third button flashed in my mind for a moment.

"Here! This side, you Bastard!" roared the guy again.

I tried to follow the direction of the sound of the abuse the loud guy was screaming, but with my head lowered, all I could see was my lower body and the floor tiles, which were probably made of granite.

A hand reached out to the collar of my shirt, pulling me so forcibly that my head almost banged the gate.

"What took you so long?" The boy smacked the gate with his fist. I recognized the voice. It was the lean boy Ravinder with whom we had lunch that afternoon. I guessed Samar would also be around.

SLAP!

I closed my eyes momentarily as a reflex action, but soon realized that

I did not feel pain and opened my eyes. I realized that it was not me but the boy standing beside me who had been slapped hard around his face. He shuddered as if he had almost fainted from the forceful slap.

"Wow, that was tight. How did you manage to do that?" Ravinder, who was still holding my collar, asked the boy next to him outside the grill gate.

"Easy. I slipped in my whole arm and brought him close to the grills. That way, you can apply more force. Think of my shoulder as an axis of rotation and the tip of my finger as the distance from the axis. If I slip in my whole arm, I can manage maximum torque in the slap."

"Cool, what about the angle? The sine theta in torque calculation?"

"90 degrees! For sine theta, even if theta is not 90 degrees, he will still get a wide *sine* on his face!"

"Haha. Like cosine? Good one!"

The other boy was not Samar, as I remembered his voice vividly. As Ravinder and his friend were busy discussing the physics behind the slap, all I could think about was how the geography of my face would change shortly, given the visibly good chemistry between them.

Who says that the subjects that we study at school do not have any use in practical life?

Now that Ravinder knows the trick, I am going to be hit next, I thought.

"Here! Take this!" Releasing my collar, Ravinder handed a piece of paper to me.

"Do you know what this is?"

"No, sir," I replied, a mild relief flowing through me at realizing that he had not hit me.

"It's a north *funda* list! You must carry it all the time. Find your other north-mates and share it with them. Make sure that every *Northee* has a handwritten copy of this! Everyone is supposed to memorize it by heart. I am assigning you this duty. If you fail, I will beat the shit out of you! Understand?"

"Yes, sir," came my prompt response.

"Now get lost!" said Ravinder, yelling at the top of his voice.

I turned around and ran away from those maniacs. As I took to the stairs, the noise slowly faded away. What remained was trauma and confusion.

"What happened? Why did they call?" asked Chandru as soon as I entered the room.

"Are you alright?" enquired Vibhu.

My roommates were awake and scared.

"Yes! Yes! I am alright!" I gasped for breath.

Why can't I, for once, say it as it is?

Two minutes ago, Ravinder asked me if I understood, and I said yes.

Pulling my collar and stifling me, guys getting slapped around me, the belligerent boys banging the grill gate violently, and 125 decibels of background noise... that's a lot in just a few minutes to startle you! How could I have understood him?

Now my terrified roommates ask if I am alright, and I again said yes. How can I be alright? Look at my crimsoned face and ears. Look at the goosebumps running down my arms. Look at my roughed-up shirt. Despite all this, I am trying to put on a brave front.

Why can't I, for once, say as it is?

"What did they ask?"

"Nothing much. They gave me a list; said you must memorize it."

"What list?"

I unfolded the piece of paper, and all eyes went straight to it.

North Funda list

Final Year

Jammu and Kashmir.
1. *Mr. Kamal Kumar – Computer Science Engineering*
2. *Mr. Sumit Kaul – Mechanical Engineering*
....
Punjab.
1. *Mr. Karan Singh – Electrical Engineering*
....
Haryana
....
Himachal Pradesh
....

Delhi
....

Pre-Final Year
....

Second Year
....

"These are names! You need to memorize all of them?" asked a confused Jay.

"Yes, I guess so. That's what the senior said."

What the hell? Some fifty-sixty names of the seniors of three batches from the northern states! Also, the branch of each one of them. I need to remember all of this? I don't even know these seniors! I only barely know Ravinder and Samar. Oh yes, and the Himachal boy Vijay—the good senior we met at the guest house from my dear state. Dad liked him so much.

I tried to forget what had just happened, like a bad dream. I lay in bed and closed my eyes, but the thing about unwanted thoughts was that the harder you tried to avoid them, the more they popped up in your head.

Have you ever wondered who shares the most treacherous relationship routinely, the relationship full of deceit with no loyalty whatsoever? Well, it is the relationship between your eyes and sleep.

There may appear to be a truce between eyes and sleep for a while, but there are times when sleep is like an uninvited guest. It knocks at the door, but your eyes do not want it and refuse to budge. There are other times when your eyes are begging for it, but sleep maintains a safe distance, refusing to cave in.

That night, sleep had decided to betray my eyes, like a dominating partner in a relationship who would have her way in the end.

There is this love-hate relationship between eyes and sleep, with sleep having its way most of the time while the eyes are rather docile.

I believed in a general rule that "the effort you make is directly proportional to the success you achieve." But sleep is a good exception to this rule. The more you make a conscious effort to sleep, the higher the chance you might end up wide awake.

Dad said, when you find it hard to sleep, you should paint a mental image of a green garden full of roses. But tonight, all I could imagine was a jungle full of beasts.

Another solution for sleep that Dad often suggested was to count numbers. I tried that too, but all I could count was the number of lunatics outside the grill gate or, for that matter, the names written on that *funda* list.

CHAPTER TWO

6:30 a.m.

I got up reluctantly from the bed. No enthusiasm was left in me after what had happened last night. But as someone famously said, "The show must go on."

In my case, the show had just begun.

The common bathrooms of my wing were already occupied, so I went up to the second floor to perform my ablutions. As per the warden's instructions, all the boys were required to be ready by 7:45 a.m. and assemble at the main entrance. Yes, the same place where the nerve-wracking scene had unfolded last night.

So, 7:45 a.m. by the clock, and all the boys assembled at the main entrance. The gate was already unlocked by this time, and a few boys near the gate saw three seniors approaching the entrance. Panic broke out among the boys, and everyone bowed down.

"Queue up!"

"Everybody will walk in a queue! Remember, do not break the queue until we reach the college!" shouted the guys. These seniors were here to escort us to the college.

Wow, very thoughtful of you, Mr. Warden! What a foolproof arrangement! At night they torment us from the other side of the locked gate, and in the morning, the gates are wide open, and they come to take us to the college! The saviors of mankind! What, are they going to protect us from other seniors?

Ok, they may protect us from the other seniors, but who will protect us from them? It's like cats deployed to protect mice from the other cats!

One boy passed through the gate. Another one behind him. Another one, and so on.

Imagine 150-odd boys walking in a queue with their heads lowered. This queue was complete chaos as it was not easy to match the steps and judge the speed with our heads bowed down. While some people banged their heads on the backs of the boys walking right in front of them, the others stepped over their ankles, almost taking shoes off.

"Hey, *butrus*! Where are you guys looking? Third button! You bastards!" Seniors who were passing by yelled at the human train.

The herd of the boys quickly matched up with the queue.

"Himachal Electronics!" I sensed somebody approaching me. "Hey, Himachal Electronics! Remember me?" the boy who was now walking next to me asked.

The same gentle and soothing voice. Yes, I recognized him. It was Vijay, who met me in the guest house with his mother. I had been so busy looking down and matching up with the queue all this time that I had not realized one of the boys who was escorting us to the college was Vijay.

"Yes, sir, I remember," I quickly replied.

"All is well with you?"

"Yes, sir."

"Has your dad left?"

"No sir, he will leave tomorrow morning."

"Ok!" He said, and walked past me.

What a nice gentleman Vijay is, I thought. He had clearly indicated his disapproval of ragging when we met in the guest house, and now he was escorting us to the college. My respect for Vijay had enhanced. His little gesture of inquiring about my wellbeing helped to bolster my morale.

The human train took around ten minutes to arrive on the first floor of the college corridor. By now, I had noticed the finer details of the third button of my shirt, my shoes, my shoelaces, the shoes of the boy in front of me, *his* shoelaces, the concrete road directly beneath my shoes, and the steps leading to the first floor of the college building.

The seniors left us in the corridor. Finally, I raised my head, and so did the others.

Wow, what a feeling! Only today did I realize the potential of my neck. It can hold, support, and move your head according to your wishes.

We found our classrooms and quickly settled down. Since it was the first semester, the subjects were common, and our batch was accommodated in three or four classrooms.

As per my rough count, there were around seventy-five to eighty students in my class, with fifteen or sixteen girls. That made a ratio of one girl to five boys. I must admit, the analysis of the girl-boy ratio done by that senior boy Baba Kamdev had been spot on.

A few minutes later, a man entered the classroom. He had grey hair and big, thick spectacles on his nose. He must have been in his late forties.

"Good *mohhhrning* class! *Whhelcome* to NCE! Isn't it?" he greeted the class. (No spelling mistakes; this is how he laid stress upon the letters.)

Isn't it? Is he asking or telling? Maybe I was not attentive enough or missed something due to his heavy accent.

"I am P.K. Maangelal. Your Mathematics teacher," he continued. "This is my first class. Isn't it? So, I am telling you what I have pointed out *prevhhiously*. Whatever I teach you is for your benefit and not my botheration. So, you don't bother the botheration and ask your doubts! It is bad if you ask your doubts *nehhver*, but it is also bad if you ask *forehhver*. Isn't it?"

The man clearly butchered the English language. Be it grammar, pronunciation, or enunciation; he was unbeatable.

"Let us take your attendance first of all!" Mr. PK opened the register that was lying on the table.

"Roll number one!"

"Present!" one of the boys responded.

"Roll number two!"

"Present!"

"Roll number three!"

"Present, sir!"

"Roll number four!" There was no response. "Roll number four?"

Mr. PK raised his arm up in the air such that the tip of the pen that he was holding pointed towards the ceiling, as if begging for some ink from the Gods. Then the hand came down in a projectile motion, landing directly on the register to put an absent mark for roll number four.

After two or three more roll calls, he stopped again and began to address the class. "Ok, this will take a long time. I have an idea. Those who are absent, please raise your hands!"

Almost everyone was giggling in the class.

Quickly realizing his gaffe, Mr. PK smiled and said, "How can absent people raise hands? You should consider my *prevhhivous* statement as a joke. Isn't it?" And he switched back to his original projectile method of roll call. Well, the time taken would have been a lot lesser had he avoided the takeoff and landing of his pen in his trademark style for every absent he marked.

As soon as he was done with the attendance, Mr. PK turned to Vibhu, who sat right next to me.

"Stand up. *Whhat* is your name?"

"Sir, Vibhu!"

"Open the window! Let the atmosphere come in!"

I almost fell off my chair. The whole class was chuckling by this time.

"Let the atmosphere come in!" Did he just say that? So, according to him, is the atmosphere waiting outside the window? Or is it rather knocking on the window requesting him to let it in? Does he expect the

atmosphere to be in motion? Well, why not? When eighty-odd students can be let in through the door, why leave the poor atmosphere outside? Of course, he did not think any of that. The poor man is struggling with the usage of the right words. I guess the word he is looking for is "air." Who knows, the next thing he will say is, "Let the air force come in."

Vibhu opened the window, and we could feel the morning breeze float inside the classroom.

So, as per Prof PK's instructions, the atmosphere was right in the room. I hoped all the atmosphere did not come inside because some of it had to be left outside.

Ok, I needed to stop, there were too many jokes playing in my head. I had this habit of holding on to something funny I saw or heard and losing all my focus.

That was fun. But why? I am no connoisseur of the English language myself. I think laughing at someone's poor English makes you feel so much better. It gives you hope that you are not the only one who butchered the language. There are others who not only butcher the language, but also bury grammar ten feet under the ground. So, the takeaway from Professor PK's class is a deficiency in communication but proficiency in the subject.

We had a smile on our faces thanks to Mr. PK, who brought some life into the otherwise gloomy atmosphere.

See, that was the atmosphere he talked about.

A few more professors delivered lectures, but Mr. PK was undoubtedly the star of the day. The human train was escorted by the "good Samaritans" to the hostel for lunch and then back to the college again. The seniors kept yelling and hurling abuse on the way. We had a few more lectures post-lunch, and then we were done for the day.

Around 4:15 p.m., when we were about to head back to the hostel in the "third button" position, Dad came to meet me.

Dad and I had a good time together. We went out for dinner. I decided not to tell him how I was roughed up the previous night. It was our last evening together as he would be leaving the following day, and I did not want to upset him.

Dad dropped me at the hostel, and with a heavy heart, we bid *adieu.*

I had always been very close to my parents. In fact, I had no shame in being referred to as a mamma's boy or Dad's boy.

Just like a frog finds comfort in a small well with its kin, I was content in my small world with my family and friends. It never occurred to me that there was a life beyond this.

I remembered, back home, when I broke the news of my selection at NCE to my elderly neighbor. He asked me, "Are you going to stay in the hostel?"

"Yes!" I replied promptly.

"A new city and hostel life! Congrats! Your life is going to start now. Get ready to learn the lesson of life."

I could not understand what he meant by that, neither did I ask as I felt it would be rude.

Does he mean that my eighteen years of life so far do not count? Or has it not been a life at all? Then what was it?

I did not comprehend the statement of this man, who was well respected in society and believed to be wise. I thought perhaps he was trying to be philosophical, like one of those people who made insightful statements. People his age did not miss any chance to pass on wisdom that you couldn't understand.

Dad attempted to break it down for me in these words: "What he meant was that you are entering a new phase of your life; the most significant one. The phase which will carve your path as an independent individual. From now on, you will manage your day-to-day problems independently. You will deal with people from all walks of life and make decisions almost every day. Your mummy and I will have less involvement in guiding you at every step. We will not lay the tiles anymore for you to walk on; you will lay them yourself. You will make mistakes and correct them."

"Ok, I understand. I will do all those aforementioned things, but mistakes? Really? Do you think I will make them?"

My reply made the moment lighter, and we had a good laugh, but the thought that I would be on my own was scary to me. The idea of laying tiles on my own had not cemented in my mind until my dad left me at college.

CHAPTER THREE

My roommates Jay, Chandru, and Vibhu, were glued to their books under the table lamp back in the hostel room. As per seniors' orders, no lights were allowed in the rooms, and hence the hostel was scarcely illuminated.

"Your *Northee* friends came looking for you. They are waiting for you in Room B56," informed Chandru without taking his eyes off his book.

"Oh shit!"

"What?"

"I was supposed to find the *Northee* boys and share that *funda list* with them. How could I forget? That senior boy Ravinder will kill me!"

I quickly rushed to the top floor. Room B56. The last room of Hall One.

I entered the dimly lit room and spotted some fifteen or sixteen boys, all dressed up in formal wear. I found a few of them occupying chairs and writing on paper while others were seated in groups and reading something. I quickly realized that they had received the *funda* list, and some of them were copying it. So, here were my *Northee* batch mates.

"Hello, everyone! I am Aahan. Himachal Electronics," I introduced myself to the group.

SMASH!

Just as we were greeting each other, something, (a pebble, I guess), hit the windowpane, breaking it into several pieces of glass, scattering them in every direction.

"Turn off the lights, you bastards!" somebody yelled from outside, perhaps on the street.

Apparently, some seniors who were passing by could spot the illuminated room from the road. Those boozers didn't even care for the poor boys inside who could get hurt from the pieces of glass of the windowpane. Boys quickly turned off the table lamps, leaving the room in absolute darkness. Further introduction with the *Northee* batchmates was of no use as we could hardly see each other in the pitch black.

"Himachal Electronics and Jammu Computer?" A figure emerged at the door.

"Yes! Tell me!" I replied.

"Seniors calling outside B5! Go fast!"

I ran along with Jammu Computer. Fortunately, we were in our formal dress already. Room B5 was on the ground floor, where the corridors were fenced with metal grilles.

"Come here! Come to this side!" cried one of the two guys from the other side of the grilles.

Both of us drew closer to the two seniors with our heads bending as usual. My heart was pounding hard.

"Jammu Computer! Your name is Ganjoo, right? How are you?"

Wait! I know this voice. I have heard the same soothing voice before. I could easily make out it was Vijay. How come Vijay is here? He probably wants to talk to us. But what could be the urgency now? He could have spoken to us this morning as he is one of those guys who escorted us to college. He might have some advice for us.

My mind was clogged with mixed thoughts, but my heartbeat had returned to normal due to some relief from Vijay's presence.

"Yes, sir! I am fine," replied Ganjoo, my Jammu Computer companion.

SLAP! SLAP! SLAP!

"Now you won't be fine," said Vijay, while the boy with him giggled. Ganjoo's face turned red hot from the drubbing.

Oh my God! Vijay slapped Ganjoo! Three times! How could he? But he disapproved of ragging. He told Dad that he was against physical abuse. Did he lie to us? He was the senior I so looked up to. I feel betrayed.

Wait, Vijay called him by name. He might know him. Did Ganjoo misbehave with him? Let's not jump to a conclusion so fast. There could be a reason for Vijay's violent actions.

My heart was beating hard, and my mind clogged with thoughts.

"You know, Raja, why I slapped him?" Vijay turned to his companion, who gestured enquiringly.

"Because when I met his mother at the guest house, she requested I protect him from ragging. She said, 'My son is homesick, so please take care of him. Please see that seniors don't beat him,'" Vijay clarified.

"Haha, did you ask her, 'Lady, what are you saying and to whom?'" replied Raja with a wide grin. Both were in splits.

I bet he would have qualified for a Bachelor of Hypocrisy had there been such a degree. A living example of the pretense of moral standards.

I had liked this guy a lot, but what a disappointment. Dad was so proud of him and had attributed his etiquette to his origin from Himachal, my home state.

The poor mother, anxious about her son's safety, pleaded with him and our brave senior Vijay decided to teach him a lesson!

Dad had also enquired to him about ragging, I thought, *so going by Vijay's bizarre logic, I am going to get slapped next! The smile on his face which I mistook as a mark of humility, was a sign of deception!*

"Himachal Electronics, come here!" Vijay cried again from the other side of the grilles. I moved one step closer while Ganjoo stepped back. "How are you?"

Now, how would you respond to this question? The real response in my head was that I was not fine with this situation. But then I knew he would slap me and say, "You will be fine now." Another answer could have been, "I am fine," but Ganjoo had said this a minute ago and got thrashed. If I chose not to respond, that would be rude, and beating was still guaranteed. Now, what was the point in putting so much thought into a question when the result of any response would be the same?

"Sir, I am fine," I replied, closing my eyes in anticipation of a slap.

"Ok! Step back. Jammu Computer, come here!"

I opened my eyes and stepped back in disbelief.

"How are you now?" Vijay enquired again, speaking to Ganjoo.

Ganjoo, after a brief pause, replied, "Sir, I am fine."

SLAP!

One more slap to Ganjoo.

"Get lost, both of you!" ordered Vijay and left with his friend Raja, who had been grinning all the while.

I wondered how my response to the question was escape-worthy, as opposed to poor Ganjoo's. But then, he would not have hit him in the first place had there been any logic in Vijay's actions.

Red-faced Ganjoo did not speak a word, and we both left for our respective rooms.

CHAPTER FOUR

6:30 a.m.

My head was reeling after the tumult of last night. I was in an absent state of mind where I almost applied toothpaste to my face and shaving cream to my teeth.

I feel like I am losing my mind. How could Vijay hit Ganjoo? He was the only boy in the college whom dad and I trusted equally. And why did he spare me? Is it because I am from Himachal, his home state? But there's no guarantee that he will spare me next time. Will he talk to me this morning when he comes to escort us to the college? Will he speak to Ganjoo? What will happen tonight?

Endless questions popped into my head, but my wisdom did not present me with any clues. My mind was clogged with confusion, blank and absent. All my morning ablutions took more time than usual as there was hardly any synergy between my thoughts and actions.

I grabbed a cup of tea from the messroom on the ground floor and took a stroll along the hostel corridor. I saw a boy sitting on a bench near the telephone room. This was the room where the wireline telephone was available for boys to use to receive or make calls. I quickly figured out that he was one of those *Northee* boys I had seen in Room B56 the previous night.

"Hey! Are you alright?" I enquired, as I noticed his wet eyes.

"Yes! Yes! I am good!" he replied, collecting himself.

"I am Aahan. I saw you in B56 last night."

"Yes, I know. I am Sushant," he replied, wiping away his tears.

"What happened?"

"Nothing, I just talked to my mom on the phone. She asked if I was ok, and I broke down. She kept asking. You know how moms are. They can just tell."

"I know."

"I told her that I was missing home badly. I don't like it here."

"Yes, I hate being here too. Take my advice, try not to share your misery with your family. They can't help much here, and your grief will only give them pain and sleepless nights!" I empathized with Sushant.

"I agree with you. I just could not control myself. Normally I am a tough guy."

I didn't know if my advice was for Sushant or a reiteration for myself that I needed to lay those tiles on my own.

Another routine day had started. The irony was we dressed up all dapper, like the top executives of some multinational company, but walked in a queue with our heads lowered like a herd of sheep.

I simply did not understand the intentions of the seniors for forcing us to dress up in formal wear all the time, only to be subjected to rough treatment at their discretion. Was this a fetish to inflict pain and suffering to the most spruce and elegant-looking lot in the entire college? Was it less exciting and arousing on their part to have us casually dressed and then treat us poorly? Or would the right to dress up casually be earned through a course of several thrashings and beatings?

Another morning. The human train headed for college, as usual, escorted by two seniors, but sans Vijay. I wondered if the fun he had slapping Ganjoo last night was much better for him compared to the dull and unexciting walk with our swarm of lame ducks that morning.

On the way, the boy at the front of the queue was stopped by a senior, bringing the whole human train to a standstill.

"Hey! Why are you leading the queue? Are you a leader? Shall I teach you a lesson? You F@#$%R!" the senior roared.

Now the nervous leader retreated, attempting to push the boys behind him to take his place, but they would not budge for obvious reasons. The herd of sheep had spotted a wild beast, and the ones at the front getting exposed had no choice but to jostle with the ones behind.

The irate senior's issue with the leader of the queue was inexplicable and perplexing to me, as how could anyone expect the queue to move forward if nobody was to take the front spot?

At one point, the panic-stricken boys at the front turned sideways, and the human train was at the brink of derailing, almost headed to the basketball ground.

The senior who was escorting us pacified the irked senior and suggested resuming in the afternoon as the boys were getting late for the morning class. To this he agreed, and thus left, and the human train was back on track.

Another day of lectures in the college. Another day when Mr. PK stood out among all other professors and managed to lift the otherwise dull and somber spirit unintentionally and unknowingly. I wished there were more sessions with him for new joiners so that they could cope with the stress. In fact, I would have loved to see him provide some motivational talk sessions in his trademark style, along with the regular subjects.

As usual, Mr. PK took attendance with his arm moving in projectile motion to connect his pen with the register for every absence that was marked. He was in the mood to tell us about his family today, and went on like this:

"*Childrhhen*, I have a small family. So, sharing information about them will not waste your precious time. I have only one wife, isn't it?"

That's what happens to you after years of teaching and asking students if they follow you every time. I think Mr. PK has never realized that his favorite expression, "isn't it" is not to be used at the end of every sentence, or else it will lose significance or even common sense, such as in the present situation.

Now here is Mr. PK telling us about his wife and asking students to validate, as if he is not sure himself. And did he say, "Only one wife"? I wonder if he is not content with the concept of monogamy or just trying to be funny. You cannot tell when he tries to be funny and when he is simply trying to speak, and is funny accidentally.

"And all of you are like my sons and daughters, but in reality, I have two sons! Both are boys!"

Wow! What a coincidence. Glad he clarified, I thought. *How else could anyone establish that both of his sons are actually boys? In fact, it would be unfair to the daughters if it is not mentioned that they all happen to be girls!*

I was pretty sure he was not joking this time, as men usually tried to be funny about their wives, but not about sons who, by the way, were boys. I didn't blame him. Even when proving an equation, a mathematics professor could not stop when it became obvious. In the end, he had to write, to eliminate the last possible doubt on earth: *Hence proved LHS=RHS.*

Well, a man who could make way for the atmosphere through windows could do anything. Incidentally, the windows were already open that day, but Mr. PK was in no mood to let in the atmosphere.

"Close the windows! I have winter in my nose!" said Professor PK to Vibhu.

Somebody stop me, or I am going to jump out of the window! This man is unstoppable. He has "winter in his nose"! Our Shakespeare of English language has invented an expression for the benefit of those who catch colds!

So, there was a professor in the class with winter in his nose and some eighty-odd students who had summer in their noses. The class was in splits.

That was not all. While teaching, Mr. PK also enlightened us with some facts that were unknown to mankind.

"Let me draw a circle...of any shape! It doesn't matter!" He demonstrated by drawing three circles of different diameters on the blackboard. Mr. PK's limited vocabulary perhaps found a replacement of "diameter" in the word "shape" and had never bothered to validate it, thanks to his nonchalance. So, for the first time, we witnessed the different shapes of a circle.

I wondered if oval and spiral shapes also qualified as a circle in Mr. PK's dictionary. And how did he imagine a semi-circle to be? Was it a circle of any shape cut into two halves of different shapes?

Ok, I submit to the unprecedented wisdom of Professor PK.

That was the only hour of entertainment in my otherwise miserable life, thanks to Mr. PK, who probably was not aware of the gift of entertainment that he bestowed upon the class every single day.

In the evening, after all the lectures, the human train was taken to the lecture gallery. What for? I had no idea, and nobody told us, as usual. I had even lost interest and curiosity to find out.

The lecture gallery (LG) was a big hall with long benches placed precisely in rows, each elevated by a step from the other. The side walls were neatly adorned with framed pictures of Mahatma Gandhi, Jawaharlal Nehru, Dr. Radhakrishnan, and a few other distinguished people who I could not recognize.

On the front wall at the stage area, there was a big banner made of cloth that read, *The Freshers' Welcome at NCE.* This was how we established that it was some kind of orientation program for the welcome of us freshers by the seniors.

Except, we were no more strangers to the welcome of seniors, for we had already witnessed a warm—in fact, red hot—welcome that radiated the cheeks and ears of many back in the hostel. But I think this was the official one.

We were seated on the benches. The senior boys, about fifteen in number, appeared to be friendly, maybe because of the presence of senior girls, and had arranged games like dumb charades and *antakshari* for us.

I was glad to have another dose of fun after Mr. PK's inadvertent lecture on entertainment.

Just when I had begun to enjoy the fun games, two seniors barged in from the back door and sat beside me on the last but one bench. I took a glance when they entered and realized one of them was Raja, the third year senior who had accompanied Vijay the other night when Jammu boy

Ganjoo and I were summoned at the hostel corridor near Room B5. I lowered my head at once and bowed to him.

"I like this guy," Raja told his friend with his usual grin, pointing at me.

This was enough to make me nervous. After the experience with Vijay, the words "like" and "dislike" did not hold opposite meanings for me anymore. They just meant the attention of a senior, which could only lead to trouble. Besides, there was this uncanny feeling that my every action or gesture was being observed. And that grin made me very uncomfortable. I wondered if Raja produced that grin all the time, or if it was saved for an occasion such as this.

"Raise your head! No need to bow here. Can you see that fair girl in the first row?" Raja asked softly but authoritatively.

"Yes, sir."

"Go to her and say, 'Mam, I've got to pee. Can I pee?'" said Raja.

His friend giggled and abruptly added, "Also ask her, 'Where do I pee here?'"

So, is this the price I pay for being liked by a senior? Ask an awkward question to a girl? I thought. What is he trying to do with that ridiculous question? Make the girl feel awkward, or make me look silly, or both? I can tell there is no toilet in the lecture gallery. What, does he think that the girl won't figure out who sent me? This surely cannot be an attempt by Raja to impress or woo the girl, for that would be a silly prank to play upon her. It might be some vicarious pleasure that Raja is looking for.

Amidst all these thoughts in my head, I rose from my seat and went to the first row, where the senior girl was sitting with her friends.

"Mam?" I addressed the girl.

"Yes?"

She had curly hair, an attractive face, confident, big eyes lined with kajal that clearly highlighted them, and she was looking right into my timid eyes. All of this was enough to make me nervous to say what I was going to.

"Mam, I—I have… I've got to sing. Can I sing? Where do I sing?" I asked, replacing "pee" with "sing" in a last-minute correction. I had no idea why I did that, but it felt much less awkward.

For the first time in the past few days, I felt smart. Clearly, Raja and his friend could not have heard me from where they sat at the second last row, so why not change it?

"You want to sing for me, or for the other girls?" she replied with a shine in her eyes, clearly amused. Her friends giggled.

I wondered if her reply would have been the same had I asked the original question, that I wanted to pee? That very thought put a smile on my face.

"Well, I can sing a little bit. But you see this girl?" she said, pointing to the girl next to her. "She can sing very well. Do you want to sing with her? Like a duet?"

Mischief was dancing in my head now. Every time the girl mentioned the word "sing," all I heard was "pee," and that changed the whole meaning. *Well, I can pee a little bit. But you see this girl? She can pee very well. Do you want to pee with her? Like a peeing duet?*

It turned out I was no different than Raja and his friend in terms of vicarious pleasure.

"In fact, I have a better idea! Come with me!" She went up to the podium and announced over the microphone, "Please welcome a budding singer in the first year batch. He is going to sing a song!"

I was glad that I had not asked the real question I was supposed to. What if the lady announced that in front of everyone? No glory in the public display of the mundane nature call.

Singing in front of three hundred-odd people? Why not? After all, I had many years of experience in amateur singing back home, mostly for my dad and the validation of my unprecedented talent from his tipsy friends.

Clearing my throat, I held the microphone like a professional singer. *"Chal udd jaa re panchhii ke abb ye des hua begaanaa..."*

It was my favorite song from the collections of sad songs from legendary singer Mohd. Rafi. Well, I had already become the epitome of sadness over the past few days, so the profound melancholy was vivid in my singing.

The audience clapped and applauded as soon as I finished—it was a feel-good moment.

The fair lady who had initially planned to embarrass me in front of the audience was now delighted to take the credit for her accidental discovery of my talent. Serendipity.

I went straight to my place where Raja and his friend were waiting eagerly for me.

"What did you say to her?"

"Same thing, sir. I've got to pee!" I replied sheepishly.

"Trying to fool me? I saw she was smiling at you and talking to other girls."

"Believe me, sir! She smiled and told her friends about it."

"She took you to the stage and made an announcement. So, don't give me that malarkey!"

"I swear on God, sir! I just asked her, and she took me straight to the podium saying, come and pee on the stage, and then announced that I would sing!"

Raja left with his friend, half convinced. I was quite confident that Raja was not going to check what really happened with the girl. Even if he did, what would he say to her? That he sent me to her to ask for a pee?

In fact, to me, Raja was not the kind of boy who would talk to any girl, let alone this super smart girl. He seemed more like a guy who, along with his idle friends, would tease, play a prank, or pass an unwarranted comment or two on girls, but from a distance.

CHAPTER FIVE

A few fun games in the lecture gallery, and the welcome program came to an end. As usual, we queued up and headed back to the hostel. As we approached close to Hall One in our usual heads-down position, a hand grabbed my arm and separated me from the queue.

"Both of you, follow me! Do not look up!" a short and stout boy ordered me and a boy who was standing beside me. The senior hastened forward, and both of us tried hard to keep up with his speed due to the additional difficulty of a lesser field of view, thanks to our lowered heads.

The tacit understanding or agreement between seniors was evident as the boys escorting the human train did not object to our separation from the queue.

We are clearly not going to Hall One, I thought. I realized, looking from the corner of my eye, that the other boy with me was Virender, one of my *Northee* batch mates.

As soon as we approached close to a hostel, everybody who saw us either yelled at us or blocked our way.

According to my rough estimation, we had most likely gone past two buildings, which could have been halls One and Two, and this one was Hall Three, though I was not sure, as the concrete road and the senior boy's legs were our only means of navigation.

"Hey, *butrus*!" yelled someone from a corner.

"Sandhu! Whose *butrus* are they?" shouted another one from the entrance gate.

"Sood and Mehta," replied Sandhu, the short and stout boy leading us.

"Oh, Himachal Electronics and Himachal Electrical?"

"Hey, Himachal Electrical, where are you looking?"

"Hey, Himachal Electronics, where's your third button? I don't see it on your tie!"

"Himachal Electronics" and "Himachal Electrical," that's how the seniors identified us. Or, as Sandhu mentioned, *butrus* of Sood and Mehta. No one cared that we had names. We were like those terrified sheep following the shepherd blindly into a den belonging to an army of wild beasts roaring from every corner.

Now I was sure that we were in Hall Three, and that these were second year boys. How? Applying correlation was the only way to gain and spread awareness. The seniors would not introduce themselves or explain what they were up to, for they only believed in commanding, demanding, yelling, abusing, and assaulting.

From the *funda* list, which I had barely memorized, I recalled that Vikram Sood and Susheel Mehta were the seniors from the second year batch. Both hailed from the state of Himachal and were in the Electronics and Electrical Engineering branches, respectively. In other words, Sood was my *baap* (father), and Mehta was Virender's *baap*, according to the *funda* list family chart.

Since Sandhu had mentioned Sood and Mehta and the others were quick to label us, I had no doubt they were all from the second year batch. Samar and Ravinder had mentioned on admission day that the second year boys resided in Hall Three, hence, I concluded that Hall Three this was.

I didn't recall Sandhu from the *funda* list, though perhaps he was not a *Northee* senior or that was not his real name.

Sandhu took us into a room on the top floor, and two of his friends joined us.

"Oh, Sandeep! Great! How did you manage to bring them?" one of them asked.

"I just separated them from the line." Sandhu chuckled with a sense of achievement.

I knew now that Sandeep was his real name, and according to the *funda* list, he was a second year senior from Jammu and Kashmir. Correlation.

"Both Himachalis?"

"Yes! And he is Himachal Electronics! The singer. I saw his performance at LG today," replied Sandhu in a sarcastic tone.

"Great, get ready for another performance! Narrate the *funda* list. You must have memorized it by now. Quick!" the boy ordered.

I started to narrate, "Final year, Jammu and Kashmir, Mr. Kamal Kumar, Computer Science Engineering. Umm... Mr. Sumit Kaul... Mechanical Engineering. Umm..."

SLAP!

I was completely engrossed in the list, head lowered, when a forceful slap came out of the blue.

The misjudged slap missed my face and hit my ear so hard that I felt acute pain. I could not hear anything they said for the next twenty seconds, due to the incessant ringing in my ear, which sounded as if somebody had tampered with the broadcast of the signature tune of the Doordarshan channel.

SLAP!

Before I could recover from the previous one, another slap almost cracked my jaw, and I felt as if I had a mild concussion.

"Yes! That's how you do it. The hand should be one-hundred-and-eighty degrees. Yours was ninety degrees," said Sandhu, thrilled by the impact of his hard slap. Apparently, the savage beasts were discussing the angle with which they should slap to achieve maximum impact. "Look, I'll show you babies how it's done. He will remember me for life," said the charged Sandhu.

SLAP! SLAP! SLAP! SLAP!

More slaps landed all over my face with the same intensity, but the sensation of pain had disappeared after the second one. My threshold soared to a level where perhaps a wooden block or an iron rod clobbering my face and cracking my cheekbones would have mattered more.

I could tell that all these blows came from Sandhu, who had probably discovered his monstrous side and felt very proud of it.

I started trembling. Not because of fear, but indignation. My fists were clenched, and my breathing became faster than normal. A part of my mind wanted to pick up the nearby chair and break it over his head, while the other part pacified me to stay calm.

One part wanted to see Sandhu crash on the floor with his teeth scattered all over, while the other part warned me that hitting back in a fit of anger would be like challenging the authority of one thousand seniors at the college.

My juxtaposition of thoughts was vivid through my body language, and the seniors became a bit cautious.

"Are you angry with us?"

"No, sir!"

"Why are you trembling? Do you want to hit us back?"

"No, sir!" I denied, though my red face, hot ears, clenched fists, and abnormal breathing suggested otherwise.

Just when the tsunami of my emotions was on the verge of an explosion, somebody who perhaps had been standing at the door for a while grabbed my arm and took me out with him.

I looked up to find Ravinder. The lean boy, the same guy who roughed me up on my admission day, who had given me the *funda* list that horrible night.

He took me to a room, seated me on a chair, and offered me water. I was still breathing heavily and drank all the water from the bottle.

Within moments, I started sweating profusely and sobbing convulsively. The dark clouds of exasperation that had clogged my mind did not result in the lightning of rage, but the rain of tears. It seemed that the water I had just consumed was oozing out of my eyes and sweat glands. My shirt was soaked in sweat, and I was not able to control the convulsive gasps.

Ravinder put his hand on my shoulder, trying to sympathize with me, but did not say anything. Another boy entered the room. I recognized him at once. It was Samar.

"Who?" Samar enquired with Ravinder, while looking at me.

"Jammu guys," Ravinder replied.

"Only him?"

"No, him and Himachal Electrical."

I could make out from their conversation that all three boys who had thrashed me were from Jammu and Kashmir.

"Here, have some." Samar drew his hand close to me, offering the peanuts which he had been munching all this time.

"Take them! They will give you energy."

I hesitated at first but took two or three nuts after he insisted.

"And be cool! This is no big deal. Those guys might become your friends for life after the ragging period, and you will forget all this stuff!"

I could not have disagreed more with him.

Friends for life? I thought. *I do not wish to see their faces throughout my life, especially that hideous Sandhu! How can I ever be friends with these cowards who hit a boy bowed in front of them mercilessly and discussed the technicality of their slaps? And believing a guy who offers peanuts after you are beaten up, saying they will give you energy?*

I had already lost trust in all the seniors.

"Ok, Samar, let's drop them at Hall One. I will get the other one. He is still with them," said Ravinder.

So Ravinder and Samar dropped Virender and me at our hostel. They appeared to be considerate, but I did not even dare or wish to form any positive opinion about them. Once bitten, twice shy.

I was dismayed to notice Virender's swollen, lifeless face and a black eye, and wondered if I looked the same.

Virender and I went straight to the messroom as it was dinner time already. We found most of the *Northee* group having dinner together. As per the seniors' directive, the *Northees* had to display unity by going for meals together.

People were startled to see us, especially me. It turned out that the drubbing had distorted my face to a noticeable extent, more than that of Virender's, and my grim countenance made me stand apart.

"I can see blood-red marks on your face! Do they hit very hard?" asked Jashan Jeet, one of the *Northee* boys.

"Yes, they do! That boy Sandhu was wearing rings with big solitaires on perhaps all his fingers. He rotated his rings so that the solitaires aligned in the direction of the palm of his hand, and then hit me. I think that's how I got red marks."

Jashan Jeet was appalled, and so were the rest of the boys at the dining table. I had not exaggerated at all. Sandhu did not have the slightest hesitation in displaying the utility of his rings in his cruel scheme. In fact, I believed that to terrorize me, he had deliberately made sure that I noticed what he was up to with the rings.

"Hitting with a hand full of rings? What the F@#K?"

"And rotating those rings so that the stones leave scars? That's disgusting!"

"What kind of jackass does that?"

"Why didn't you put those rings in his ass?"

I considered the responses from all the boys. "You think I could?"

"I wish somebody could put all the rings in the ass of that jackass!"

"And rotate them with the solitaires facing outwards!"

"You and your obnoxious imagination! And at the dinner table!"

"Boy, he would definitely discharge a keyring in the morning!"

"Wow! That's like a ring causing suffe'ring!"

Everyone around the table laughed.

A few more swearwords and some wild imagination (which did not stop at the guys' asses!) left everyone in splits. Everyone contributed with the expert comments. The guys who looked perplexed initially were now amused.

How cool is that about college life? I thought. *Guys always find something funny about an adverse situation. Moods can swing anytime from livid to timid and from timid to gleeful.*

I ate my dinner with some effort as my jaw was still aching from the drubbing.

In bed that night, sleep evaded me. I was somehow not coming to terms with reality. Yesterday Vijay (the senior from Himachal) had hit Jammu boy Ganjoo, and today, Jammu seniors had hit another Himachal boy and me!

Is there any connection? Well, what about that preaching of Northee unity? I thought. *Clearly, these seniors who are trying to teach us the lessons of unity need to revisit those chapters themselves.*

Should I retaliate when they beat me next time? They have already caused me physical and mental agony. How much more pain can they inflict without thinking I will hit back?

Or else I could complain to the authorities. But what am I going to achieve through reaction? Can I expect any cooperation from the seniors? Do I need their cooperation? And can I expect any support from my batchmates after that? Can I manage to survive alone without any support?

What do I do? Should I let it go, like it's just another phase of life?

I missed Mommy!

I missed Dad!

I missed home!

I missed my *sleep*!

CHAPTER SIX

7:30 a.m.

My scarce sleep the night before did not help in reducing my anger and repugnance for those senior boys, especially Sandhu, who had acted like a belligerent savage. I just could not get him out of my head, and my vexation only increased the more I thought of him.

Bloody animal! How could he hit me like that? I thought. *And then to condescend to his accomplices? What is he so proud of? Hitting harder?*

Just because he joined this college one year before me, does that give him the entitlement to subject me to such torture? Look at my swollen face. The cut marks from the rings. My left eye, which I can barely open! How can he get away with this? He should pay. Yes, he has to pay for it someday!

And in that moment, I firmly resolved to teach Sandhu a lesson. When and how, I did not yet know.

I was getting ready for college when a boy from the messroom informed me that a senior was waiting for me at the main gate. The news irked me.

"What now? Do they want to kill me? They won't spare me even in the morning?" I mumbled angrily to myself while walking downstairs.

In the lobby area, I glanced at the boy waiting for me for a second, and then lowered my head and went up to him.

"Here, this way! Look up, no need to bow. Do you know who I am?"

"No, sir!" I replied, raising my head a bit and looking through the corner of my eye—the one which was not black and swollen.

"I am Vikram Sood. Does that ring a bell?"

"Yes, sir! You're my *baap*, Himachal Electronics, second year!" I replied with a smile mixed with shyness and hesitation.

"Great! I guess you memorized the *funda* list already. Here, take this." He handed me a bag full of books. "You will find most of the books for the first and second semester in there, plus some key notes which I prepared which will be helpful. There are also exam question papers from the first and second semester for the last three or four years. I collected them from my seniors. A few questions get repeated every alternate year. Even if you only prepare those questions, you should be good for the two semesters."

"Thank you, sir!" I extended my gratitude, surprised.

"I know ragging period is tough," he said, looking at my black eye and bruised face carefully. "Some seniors do it for fun while the others do it because it happened to them, like a misplaced vengeance." After a brief pause, he continued, "I used to miss my home badly during ragging days, but don't let this affect you; there are many things to cherish! Also, remember, this is the time when you can say anything to any girl in the name of seniors!"

How sweet! I could not help smiling. I wanted to tell him how I had gone up to the senior girl the other day in the lecture gallery when Raja had sent me over. But I held back, as it was hard for me to trust a senior.

"Yes, it's true! The girls won't mind even if you kiss them. Tell them you are just following seniors' instructions! Okay...maybe don't try kissing. But you can definitely talk."

I nodded with an amused expression. I liked Vikram and felt an urge to tell him everything that had happened. But I checked myself, not wanting to get carried away. A senior being friendly was such an overwhelming experience that I felt terribly short of words.

A gentleman with such agreeable countenance! But then Vijay also had a noble appearance, and look what he did to Ganjoo!

"Okay! I'm getting late for college. I will see you soon!" His parting pep talk helped to cheer me up.

Another mundane and monotonous day had started.

The first half of the day in college began with lecture sessions, while the other half—post-lunch—concluded with practical sessions (popularly called *sessionals*).

In the evening, after the sessionals, we were, as usual, queuing up. Just as we were about to head to the hostel, a bunch of seniors arrived and started separating some of the boys from the queue. I was one of them.

Most of these seniors were familiar faces from the orientation program of the previous evening at the LG.

They separated around twenty-five or thirty boys and asked the rest of the boys to carry on. These seniors also relieved us from the bow-down state; the third button position.

We followed the seniors to a place that was like an open-air theatre with large semi-circular steps and a stage at the center. The big round gate at the entrance read, *The Student Activity Centre (SAC)*.

A few girls of our batch approached, along with the female seniors. They were probably picked from the ladies' queue. Whether the selection was random or intentional, I had no idea.

Some five groups were made, each having eight members. The groups were seated on the large steps of the SAC arena at some distance apart from each other. Finally, a boy from the bunch of seniors addressed us while the other seniors stood close to him at the stage area.

"Hello, all! You must be wondering why you are here and who we are. Well, we are your seniors, of course! And the Premium Club members of the college. The Premium Club promotes social values in society and carries out humanitarian activities inside and outside the college. We are associated with some prestigious clubs and organizations across the city. I am Divyanandan, the president of the Premium Club, and Shivani is the general secretary."

He pointed to the familiar face standing next to him, the same kajal-eyed girl who had made me sing the other day in the orientation program.

"You guys have been shortlisted from yesterday's orientation program, which was co-sponsored by the Premium Club at the LG. As you can see, you are in groups. We will hold group discussions and Q and A sessions within each group today for the final selection. Around ten people are going to make it to the Premium Club. And mind you, there is no need for a third button position here. Be comfortable and give it your best shot!"

Divyanandan cleared the fuss in a brief speech. Interestingly, nobody bothered to ask whether we wanted to join the club or not. It was assumed that a great opportunity was being bestowed upon us lucky people. There was no question of refusal, even if they had asked for our consent.

To his credit, Divyanandan at least disclosed the purpose of bringing us to the SAC before the final selection, something that seniors had not bothered to do so far.

So, the moderators for these five groups were finalized, and the task for our group was assigned to two girls. One of them was Shivani. I wondered if she was responsible for my shortlisting.

"Okay, so we will give you a topic, and you have to give your views. Right?" said Shivani, and we nodded in agreement. "What are the qualities that you look for in your beloved?"

Okay, so we were supposed to discuss the qualities of the lover that probably none of us in the group had ever had. Well, at least I was sure about the boys, though I couldn't tell you about the only girl participant in our group.

I had been expecting a discussion on poverty, child education, or something similar. The question we had been given did not seem to do justice to the mission of the Premium Club that Divyanandan had described. I wondered how that question served the humanitarian cause.

Maybe it did for social values, I thought. *Humanitarian causes begin with humans, an individual, and it is important to discuss an individual's love life to understand about society and humanity.* I concluded my thought with effort, trying to connect the question with the vision of the Premium Club, but in vain.

"In my view, the girl should be good nature-wise," said one boy. When he was met with silence, he continued, "Umm, I mean—"

"She should be decent!" said another one, cutting him short.

I did not understand what he meant by "decent," and nobody bothered to ask.

"I like tall girls!" the third boy jumped the gun.

"Well, I would like a good sense of humor in a boy; the one who can make me laugh is a quality I look for in a boy," said the girl of our group.

Her striking good looks and amiable charm managed to draw the whole group's attention as, for a moment, the boys who fancied qualities like a good nature, tall, decent, et cetera, became tongue-tied.

"Good sense of humor! That's nice. Rinki, right?" asked Shivani.

"Yes, mam. Rinki Chandra."

Okay, so Rinki Chandra is looking for a good sense of humor, and Shivani seems to be on the same page. Why do girls want someone funny? One who can crack jokes and make them laugh? Joke books would be a better option, as they can make you laugh anytime and expect nothing in return.

Okay, it would be good to have, like, an appetizer on the menu, but not the main course dish. And I am sure girls don't really mean it because then the comedians of the world would all be the sought-after Casanovas, which does not seem to be the case.

Imagine all the girls running after the comics and funny men and all others who do not possess the gift of joke-making ending up alone. And stand-up comedy shows organized for the benefit of women to find the funny man of their choice would be a common sight. Okay, maybe I am taking it too far...

Before my train of thoughts could enter unchartered territory, they were abruptly brought to a halt when a boy broke the temporary silence and said, "Well, the girl should have good looks and a great figure!" It was Bhupinder Pyare, one of my *Northee* mates, and a skinny boy who hailed from Punjab.

"What do you mean?" asked Shivani, a bit startled at trying to "figure" it out.

"I mean 36x24x36!" Pyare revealed the stats without any hesitation.

"Whoa, whoa! That's very tacky," said Shivani in bewilderment.

"Yes! It's gross! Who speaks like that?" declared the other senior girl who was not in the best shape and took more offense to Pyare's statistics.

Pyare did not utter another word, but his countenance showed no signs of regret or doubt regarding the clarity of his thoughts, despite the objection of the senior girls.

I must say that Pyare is honest and bold. Maybe more of the latter, I thought. *Physical appearance is indeed one of the driving factors to make someone's acquaintance, although not the only one. Once an acquaintance is formed, it's only then that the other qualities like nature and compatibility become apparent, and they might draw two persons closer or apart.*

He has the courage to say it like it is. But 36x24x36? Pyare has set the bar of his expectations right up there. What does he do, watch fashion TV channels with models walking on the runway?

The way he put it was funny. Oh, the sense of humor! So, is this the kind of sense of humor that Rinki is looking for? But she did not seem amused by Pyare's comments, either.

"What about you? You are not speaking. Do you have some views to share or is silence simply golden for you?" Shivani teased me, noticing that I was engrossed in my thoughts.

"I think it doesn't work that way!" I replied.

"What way?"

"That the qualities mentioned by my friends are necessary to like someone."

"What do you mean?"

I had no idea what I meant. I was just under pressure to say something different that could make me stand apart amongst my talented folks. I wished I had settled with something simple like their eyes, nose, or ears. But now I had to back it up with some reasoning.

I went on, "Well, to form a liking for someone is something natural and inexplicable. It is irrespective of the qualities. In fact, when you like someone, all the qualities that person has, from your point of view, are likable, even if they are most annoying to others!"

"Wow! That is deep! I am impressed by the way you think!" said a visibly impressed Shivani after a pause. Her friend nodded in agreement.

I breathed a sigh of relief.

Thank God Shivani was able to draw some deep meaning out of something that I spoke spontaneously. I hope she now settles and does not dig any deeper, for I would not be able to save myself this time from sounding stupid.

Some more viewpoints and justifications were put forth, and then the first round of discussion was over. The next and final round was supposed to be conducted by President Divyanandan. He soon joined us after finishing off with another group.

"Okay, I am going to give you a topic for discussion. You can speak for or against, as per your choice. Your topic is...flattery is an art of deception. Do you agree or disagree?" asked Divyanandan.

Wow! I have no idea what that topic means, whether it is an idiom, a metaphor, or plain English words that I don't understand. Whatever that topic means, it perhaps is consistent with the humanitarian values of the Premium Club.

But the problem is how to speak about the art when you neither understand the meaning of flattery, nor deception. Shall I ask them the meaning?

No, it is okay for others to figure out your poor English on their own, but you just can't expose it yourself. Okay, let's hope someone else in the group asks the meaning, or else I will simply listen to the other speakers and try to deduce the meaning.

Growing up in North India with a limited command of the English language had never been a problem, as Hindi was a spoken language at large, but this was one of those moments where I wished I had done better with my English.

Admittedly, my dad had tried to hone my language skills back in my school days by encouraging me to read English newspapers daily, but I did not pay attention. I reasoned, *What's the point of reading a newspaper when we already have news on the TV?* (Though I did not watch the news on TV either.)

I was not to be blamed entirely for not doing enough, as my friend circle influenced my choice of communication, which, in my case, did not show any inclination towards another language whatsoever. My occasional attempts at English phrases were met with jibes from my friends of, "The British left the country long ago, but forgot to take you along with them," or "Meet the last viceroy of British rule."

Back to the topic: *Flattery is an art of deception.*

"I think flattery is deceitful because it is not real. It's fake!" said one boy confidently, who clearly understood the topic.

Okay, that did not help me with the meaning of flattery.

"But what if it is done casually? In that case, flattery is harmless!" said Rinki, the girl in our group.

I still had no clue about flattery.

"Most of the time, flattery is done in self-interest! So, it's misleading and not honest," replied the guy.

Boy, they are not helping! I thought. *I can make out that one person is "for" and the other "against" the art of flattery, but what the hell is flattery?*

I looked at my friend Pyare, who I was sure neither understood nor cared. If mine was limited, his knowledge surely was poor. I was amused to see Pyare's reaction. He was simply nodding his head occasionally and saying, "Ya, Ya... Ya!"

It was funny that though he did not have any clue, he showed no bias to one opinion and agreed with both opposite points of view.

The relief for me, however, was that only two people participated in the debate while everyone else seemed to be struggling, like me.

Hearing the two points of view, I figured out that flattery had some connection with dishonesty, and I clearly knew the meaning of dishonesty. With that little clue, I decided to take a shot in the dark.

"I think flattery is deceitful because there is no honesty. If something is not honest, how can it be good? And we have all been taught since childhood that honesty is the best policy!"

I glanced at everyone and was relieved. Nobody was giving me a strange look. I could tell from Shivani's expression of raised eyebrows and an eclipsed lower lip that she was impressed this time around as well. Perhaps, through my innocent attempt, I was again able to bring some deep philosophy that only she could comprehend.

Pyare, as usual, nodded his head to acknowledge my point of view. (Let's just forget, for a moment, that Pyare acknowledged every point of view in the debate!) So, I assumed I made sense.

The debate lasted only a few more minutes with scant participation and without any conclusion.

Then the results were announced.

I was selected, along with Rinki Chandra in my group. Graceful and confident Rinki was a fair choice, but my selection was a pleasant surprise as I felt the others in the group were better.

I reassured myself by thinking, *Maybe I am underestimating the potential that these people clearly see in me.*

There was a round of applause for the twelve lucky ones who got selected for the Premium Club, and we all headed back to the hostel.

In the hostel, Pyare and I chatted. "Man! I found your views about girls bold and shameless! 36x24x36! Really?" I exclaimed.

"I just meant that the girl should be physically attractive! But then she insisted on elaboration, and I was already running out of English words, so, I gave the figures," said Pyare.

"Yes, and then the ladies became upset! Especially that Shivani's friend."

"No wonder she took it personally! She might have felt better if I said

40x40x40!" Pyare replied.

"Haha, boy, you are tacky!"

Both of us laughed. Pyare amazed me with his brazen wit and nonchalance.

I shared my observation regarding the girls of our batch who walked in a queue but did not lower their heads in the third button position as we boys did. "Perhaps the girls do not go through the physical torture of ragging by the seniors in their hostel as much as the boys do," I stated.

But Pyare had a different viewpoint. "Well, I think the third button position for girls is impractical. See, the girls wear those *kurtas*, which I believe have two or three buttons at the top. Even if they lower their head, I bet they can't spot the second button, and forget the third one, considering the intricacy of the female anatomy, if you know what I mean! After all, it is stupid for females to stare at their own breasts. It's something that is better suited for boys!" explained Pyare with a naughty grin.

I did not dare to engage him further on the topic as Pyare's raw humor seemed capable of venturing into the territories of profanity and vulgarity of language and thoughts with perfect ease.

That was funny, shameless, careless, and fearless Pyare. I did not see even a single wrinkle of stress over his forehead, despite the pressure of ragging.

CHAPTER SEVEN

A few days passed with the usual humdrum. As per seniors' directives of enforcing unity, the *Northees* would assemble in a room every evening and spend maximum time together, which was an opportunity for me to make their acquaintance and observe them closely (not that I wished for it, or that anyone cared for my wishes). Each of them had his own little idiosyncrasy.

Jammu boy Ganjoo had the squeakiest voice in our entire batch. Such was Ganjoo's grating high pitched voice that a donkey would feel euphony in its own braying and the queen of melody, the nightingale would literally die of cardiac arrest upon discovering the existence of that sound.

His normal pitch was at least thirty decibels higher than that of other boys. Ganjoo could be audible from any corner at any floor in the hostel whenever he spoke, and boy, when he laughed, it was like the noise created by a hundred vintage cars of the 1920s starting their engines simultaneously.

Incapable of whispering, Ganjoo would find it tough even to follow others who whispered in front of him. Though good at heart, he could easily be mistaken for being rude and arrogant because of his voice.

Then there was another boy, Jashan Jeet Singh, who had the most distressing and sorrowful countenance. If ever a tragedy needed a depiction, Jashan's face would be the perfect fit. He reminded me of a groom in aftershock whose bride had eloped with somebody on his wedding day. It seemed that his goal in life was to spread misery and frighten the boys in the group.

He often struck his fist with the palm of his other hand and say, "All of you are going to get f@#$%d!"

He came up with some bizarre stories of ragging atrocities to petrify the group. The candle dance story was one of them.

"Those seniors will make us do the candle dance!"

"The candle dance? What the hell is that?"

"There is a dense forest at the back of Hall Five. The seniors will take you there at midnight and make you dance nude around the bonfire with candles in your hands! They have done this with previous batches. I tell you...all of you are going to get f@#$%d!" said Jashan, striking his fist with his palm, twice, with an expression of deep melancholy enough to make the group nervous.

And then he elaborated on the maneuvers performed over the nude bodies with the candles, which I will leave to the reader's imagination.

Jashan had another story to tell, and I had doubts regarding its veracity. "You know! There will be a mass ragging very soon."

"A mass ragging?"

"Yes! The seniors from all batches will barge into the hostel past midnight. They will switch off the mainline electricity and charge in the dark!"

"Who told you this?"

"Everybody knows! They will pound us with fists, hockey sticks, bats, etcetera. The attack will be so sudden that you won't get the time to even hide under your beds!"

"I don't believe you!"

"You will when you have a black eye and swollen face! I am telling you...all of you are going to get f@#$%d!" said Jashan, striking his fist with palm thrice!

Jashan and Ganjoo were roommates. While Jashan scared us with his stories, Ganjoo would startle us by just stretching his vocal cords.

Then there was Dispensary. No, I am not talking about some clinic! I'm talking about Sambit Gupta, Delhi Electronics, who developed some allergic skin reaction, and had to visit the college dispensary.

Not a big deal. However, the poor guy visited the dispensary multiple times. During the evenings when the *Northees* assembled in Room B56, Sambit would often be missing, and when boys enquired about his whereabouts, they found out that he was at the dispensary.

So, "Where is Sambit today?" became one of those questions where the answer was presumed, and the question soon got rephrased to: "Hey! Where's Dispensary today?"

And Sambit got a new identity against his wishes.

It's funny how an act of going to a place could give you the identity of the place itself, an identity that might stay with you for the rest of your tenure in college, or even longer.

I observed more budding talent in the *Northee* group and will elaborate in due course.

The next evening, Pyare met me at the hostel messroom at the 5 p.m.

snack time and said, "Hey, finish quickly! Ravinder has summoned us in half an hour."

"What? Where?"

"Outside Hall One, at the main road!"

Lean boy Ravinder was Pyare's *baap* as per the family tree.

"Is he asking for you and me only?"

"Yes!"

"Ohhh, man! What the hell does your *baap* want?"

"Don't know! He probably wants a new mommy for me," replied an amused Pyare.

"Then he should take you only! Why am I dragged into your family drama?"

"You see, every drama needs an audience, my friend!"

"How come you talk so much without making sense even once?"

"That's called hidden talent!"

"Oh yeah? You better keep it hidden in front of seniors or else it will soon become forbidden talent!"

As per Ravinder's instructions, Pyare made a fake entry in the hostel main gate register, stating he was going out to meet his uncle, and we hit the road. Ravinder, joined by his friend Samar, met us at the main road near the hostel.

"Look straight up! Third button position only when a senior approaches closer. Understand?" instructed Ravinder, and we nodded in agreement. Samar was smiling at us.

For the first time in my life, I was uncomfortable walking along the road with my head straight and felt as if I would topple or move sideways. Apparently, over the past few days, I had become so used to walking with my head down, noticing the minute details of concrete road and watching the landing and taking-off of my every step, that it had settled as a natural and comfortable walk in my subconscious.

"Samar, let's take them to JAM," said Ravinder.

My heart started pounding. Now, what the hell was JAM? Was this some form of torture that these guys intended to inflict on us?

That's what ragging did to you. Even the mere mention of mouth-watering words like jam and jelly could leave your mouth dry and dehydrated.

Although Samar and Ravinder seemed trustworthy, my yarn of trust had snapped on several previous occasions, especially during that terrible experience with Sandhu, the memory of which was so fretting and enraging every time I thought of it.

"So, are you enjoying Mr. PK's lectures?" asked Samar.

"Yes, sir."

The mere mention of Mr. PK brought a smile to everyone's face. It was evident that Mr. PK had entertained all the batches with equal sincerity.

"The man is cool. You know, if you take notes on his lectures, you can end up writing a comic novel by the end of the semester! All you need is to write down whatever he says in class." Samar continued, "There is a famous anecdote that our seniors often retell. One day, Mr. PK went to a movie with his wife and saw two of his students in the theatre. The next day during class, Mr. PK asked those boys, 'Hey, yesterday, I saw you two boys in the cinema with my wife!'

"The boys almost fell off their chairs in shock, puzzled, thinking when had they taken his wife to a movie? Soon everyone realized that only his English was misplaced; his wife was in the right place, with whom she was supposed to be.

"Later, when Mr. PK found the whole class chuckling, he smiled and said, 'Actually, our wife is very fond of movies! So, I have to take the botheration of watching with her! But you don't have wives! What is your botheration?'"

Pyare and I were laughing by the time Samar finished his short story.

It felt good that they were trying to cheer us up, but the JAM thing was still bothering me (or should I say, it was my botheration!). We kept walking with them until we crossed the main gate of the college. About a hundred meters from the main gate, I spotted a small eating joint that read *The JAM Restaurant*.

I was relieved upon realizing that they had brought us to a restaurant, and not for some torture session.

"Hey, look, *butrus*! Come here!" yelled one of the four boys standing near the JAM restaurant entrance.

I quickly recognized two of them as Vijay and Raja. *This group must be a third year batch*, I thought.

Pyare and I lowered our heads and greeted them as we approached.

"You brought them for an outing?" asked Vijay to Samar and Ravinder, and they nodded in acknowledgment.

"Himachal Electronics, come here! Look up. No need to bow," said Vijay to me, while Raja and other boys grilled Pyare. "Do you see that hot girl in green?"

I looked in the direction Vijay's eyes were pointing. Three girls were sitting inside JAM. My eyes rested on the girl for a moment. Clad in sky blue jeans and a parrot green top with a black and white slip-on, she was casually sat on a chair, talking with her friends. A prominent dimple appeared on her cheeks every time she giggled, while her long dark brown hair rested elegantly on one side of her shoulders.

Trendy, bubbly, and graceful, I thought. *No wonder why Vijay and his friends are drooling over this attractive girl.*

"Do you see her?" Vijay tried to point out without using his hands.

"Yes, sir."

"Ok, go and talk to her!"

I found myself in an awkward place but to defy a senior's order was not an option.

"Remember, you have to stay there for at least for five minutes."

I remembered Vikram, my *baap*, telling me that I could say anything to girls in the name of seniors. So, I gathered my courage and went up to the girl.

"Yes! What is it?" The girl asked politely upon noticing me standing next to her.

Looking at my formal dress and necktie, it was a doddle to identify that I was a newcomer.

"Mam, seniors are bothering me. They have sent me to talk to you. Is it ok if I join you?" I said.

"Of course! Take this chair!" she replied, and I quickly grabbed the chair.

"You mean those guys standing outside?" asked the other girl.

"Yes!"

"Those guys always follow us, but they never talk! They just keep giggling and passing comments from a distance," she said.

Oh, silent channel! I knew that Vijay and Raja fell in the category of uniform approach! I thought.

The uniform approach was a fun theory invented by my friend Sunil back in my school days. Back then, inspired by Einstein's theory of relativity, Sunil had stated that just like the speed of light is the same for the observers in uniform motion, a girl's reaction is also the same for the boys who follow a uniform approach towards her. And that reaction is rejection.

Sunil called his research the "theory of rejectivity." In his view, the merit of his postulate was the fact that he had faced rejection from almost every girl he pursued in the school.

"What would a person who gets the girl know about rejection?" he proclaimed. "It took me years of patiently and persistently getting rejected multiple times before I discovered my theory of rejectivity."

His significant work into the uniform approach included stating three key approaches that the boys followed (what he called "channels") to pursue a girl that would likely lead to a rejection:

Indirect channel: Where the boy starts an acquaintance of the girl's best friend or sister in the hope of interacting with the girl and getting to know her better. This doesn't work well, as the girl's friends or sisters are never to be trusted.

Direct channel: The boy is able to make regular acquaintances with the girl but does nothing more than trying to impress each time and fails to open his heart to her before it's too late, and he ends up friend-zoned forever.

Silent channel: This channel is only in the boy's head as he thinks the girl understands his feelings. He either giggles or ogles, unable to muster the courage to talk to the girl, let alone share his feelings, and waits for events like a birthday or Valentine's Day to send a card or a letter, only to get a written rejection in response.

The uniformity in all these approaches was that the boy does not seize the right opportunity at the right time by the right means. I didn't know if the theory held any ground in practice, but it was much fun to discuss back in school.

My eyes were set on the noodles placed on the table, and my mouth was watering. I had not had noodles for days.

"Mam, those seniors also asked me to eat with you. Can I have some noodles?" I don't know why I said this but never had any dish looked so irresistibly yummy to me in my entire life.

The girls looked at each other and laughed as if they had caught my lie. The girl in green ordered another plate of noodles for me.

I don't know if it was simmering frustration of being deprived of delicacies for days, the company of sweet and welcoming girls, or the noodles itself for that matter, but those noodles tasted like heaven.

When I had almost finished eating, I looked outside at the sulking seniors from the corner of my eye. I was not worried about them finding out as I knew they, being the victims of the theory of rejectivity, would never talk to the girl in green.

As I relished in and finished my noodles, the girls kept asking me general questions about myself, which I gladly and humbly answered. After spending around fifteen to twenty minutes with the girls, I thanked them for their time and, of course, the noodles, and walked out of JAM.

I could sense that Vijay, Raja, and their friends were eagerly waiting for me. I noticed Pyare was wearing a boat-shaped paper cap and greeting girls at the entrance.

"Namaste, Mams! Welcome to India! Have you seen the Taj Mahal?" asked Pyare respectfully to a group of girls who were about to enter JAM.

The girls were amused. "We have not seen the Taj Mahal, but I see you are coming straight from Agra!" said one of them, and they all burst into laughter.

I chuckled at the joke I overheard, as aside from the Taj Mahal, the city of Agra was also famous for a mental asylum. Poor Pyare was not doing this on purpose but was the target of the seniors' appetite for entertainment through the preposterous act.

As the girls entered JAM laughing, I approached the boys waiting for me.

"Hey, I didn't send you to date her! Who told you to eat with them?" asked Vijay.

"Sir, I didn't ask! She placed the order herself."

"Wow, we have a Shahrukh Khan in this batch! Hot girls order food for him! Did they invite you to the ladies hall for a night stay as well?" Raja took a jibe at me.

I made no reply.

"*Butru* is smart, I like him! *Northees* are generally shy when it comes to girls, but he is cool," said Samar, and everyone smiled.

"Yes, he is! Take good care of him," replied Vijay.

I was not sure if any of those compliments had a tinge of sarcasm.

The boys turned their attention again towards Pyare, who was busy asking Taj Mahal questions to every girl who entered JAM.

"Hey, undernourished Shah Jahan, that's enough! Come back," said Vijay, mocking Pyare's lean figure, and his friends laughed.

Pyare and I walked back to the college with Samar and Ravinder. They took us to the playground entrance, opposite the boys' hostel, and had us sit on the steps.

"Do you guys go for your meals together?" asked Ravinder.

"Yes, sir," Pyare replied.

"Good! You see, all the *Northees* should be united. This is very important! If you guys remain together, other people cannot harm you. Also, you should help each other with your studies. Let me tell you an interesting incident which happened with Samar last year," Ravinder said, and Samar smiled, as if he knew what Ravinder was about to tell us.

"We were in the second semester, and the ragging period was over. The third year *Northee* seniors were fond of Samar and me, especially two of them, and often took us with them for booze. One evening when Samar and these two *Northee* seniors were returning to the hostel, all drunk, they engaged in an altercation with a group of four boys from other states, also from the third year.

"Within no time, the situation turned ugly, and our two seniors grappled with this group. When those four boys began to overpower our two seniors, one of them shouted, 'Samar! Forget the senior-junior thing! Just beat the shit out of these bastards!' Samar, dumbfounded until that moment, joined the fight on the senior's order.

"And he becomes a raging bull in the open ground under the influence of alcohol. He beat those guys really bad!" said Ravinder.

Samar laughed at his comparison. "After that incident, the situation became tense. A first year boy had beaten third year seniors, something that had never happened before in college," continued Samar. "Our seniors went to Aman, a final year boy who was also my *pardada*, and requested he protect me from the anticipated repercussions.

"Aman Singh, a Delhi boy, was unarguably the don of the college at that time, and guys feared him. Upon hearing of the whole incident from our seniors, he pacified those other seniors. He said that this matter should not be pursued further as everybody was drunk when the fight broke out and warned them against causing any harm to me, or they would face the consequences," exclaimed Samar.

Ravinder picked up the story, "Yes! And for the next three days, Aman camped outside Hall One. He would bring his chair in the afternoon and sit at the entrance of Hall One until late in the evening to make sure no senior barged into the hostel with the purpose of harming Samar. We heard those guys sulked, planned, and plotted as well, but did not dare to indulge in any altercation with Aman."

"See? That's the unity among *Northees* which protected me from getting beaten up. Always keep that in mind," advised Samar.

I could not understand the fuss about the whole protection thing that made Samar and Ravinder gloat over *Northee* unity. The seniors dragged Samar into their fight with their peers, and later requested Aman to protect him. If it were not for them, the whole situation would not have arisen.

To me, the third year seniors seemed more united as peers, as they were not fighting each other anymore, and the only person at risk of being beaten up was Samar. I gave credit to final year boy Aman though, who stood up for a junior.

I was confused about the whole concept of *Northee* unity. Though the ragging was prevalent in the college, only *Northee* seniors abused us physically. While on the one hand they condescendingly gave assurance of help and protection, on the other hand, they thrashed their own *Northee* juniors.

What kind of help would one like in exchange for the merciless drubbing? Was it some sort of license or entitlement that you got in exchange for standing by their side? Ok, they protected us from the seniors of other states, but who would protect us from *them*?

Protecting somebody was a trait of bravery, while thrashing an innocent person was the act of a coward. One could either be brave or cowardly, and not both.

Was this torture simply fun for sick minds, or had they wanted to gain respect? If the latter was the case, then I thought the concept of respect was misconstrued. Respect or admiration was not something that could be taught or learned; it could only be earned.

Samar and Ravinder took off after sharing more wisdom, and we quickly headed back to our hostel. As we approached the entrance gate of Hall One, we spotted Bholu—a *Northee* from Haryana, Electronics branch—going towards the messroom.

"Hey, *butru*, where is your third button? Come here!" Pyare yelled at Bholu.

Bholu quickly lowered his head and followed the orders without looking up even once in order to notice who was speaking to him.

"Where were you going?"

"Sir, towards mess."

"Why? What's there in the mess?"

"Sir, I am going for dinner."

"Why for dinner?"

"Sir...um, because I am hungry."

"You had your breakfast and then lunch, and now you want dinner too? You bloody hungry?" Pyare raised his voice again, and Bholu looked scared and confused.

"Sir...umm."

"What, sir, sir? You bloody cereal eater. Why are you always hungry? Look at me!"

Bholu looked up with a lot of hesitation, only to find his own batch mate pulling his leg. Pyare ran towards the messroom, and Bholu hurried behind to catch him.

"Stop, you scoundrel!"

"Hahaha! Catch me if you can, you ambassador of Hungary!"

I laughed and followed them to the messroom.

I was spending more time with my *Northee* pals. Assembling in one room every evening had become a routine, and we enjoyed each other's company. Being a keen observer, I noticed the distinct qualities of everyone.

There was this boy Vivek, disinterested in most of the activities, to whom engagement with the group was perhaps an unwanted obligation. He often whisked in and paid a visit every now and then, only for fear of seniors.

He would appear arbitrarily at the doorstep of Room B56 and stand there quietly. Since lights were forbidden in the room, we would often get scared by the black shadow emerging out of nowhere in the dark. He would stand at the doorstep and listen to our conversation, stay if he deemed any information to be useful, or else take off without speaking a word.

On one of the rare occasions when he came in the room and joined the group, I said, "We are so lucky today that our friend took some time off from his highly busy schedule! Thanks, Brigadier Saab!"

The casual reference I made resonated so much with everyone that henceforth he was only called Brigadier, and his real name, like that of Dispensary's, faded into oblivion.

Then there was Sushant, the boy I had met in the hostel on the first morning, sitting on the bench, teary-eyed, near the telephone room. He had the most strikingly unpleasant laugh in the entire college, so much so that it would be denigrating even to the hyena community if their howling was to be compared with his laughter.

He laughed and laughed out loud at every joke, whether funny or lame, whether logical or dumb, whether sensible or senseless.

Sushant's laughter was so annoying to anyone who was being made fun of, that they would be offended more by his laughter than by the person who made the joke in the first place.

The boys admitted that they could handle jokes about them, but Sushant's laughter was like rubbing salt into the wound. They would chase him around the hostel corridors for his laughter, and upon his defense of only laughing but not making the joke, they would say, "We are ok to be the butt of jokes, we don't mind being made fun of by anyone, and we are also fine with other boys laughing, but *you cannot laugh!*"

Sushant, who hailed from Punjab, would often switch from Hindi to Punjabi without realizing or caring that the people around him who did not speak the Punjabi language had no clue what he was saying.

The boys from Southern India who understood even Hindi with great difficulty would be mystified when Sushant launched Punjabi words and sentences at them like unguided missiles, leaving them dumbfounded.

He bantered playfully with them by suffixing their names with the common Punjabi surnames like "Kumar," "Singh," or even "Kaur." For instance, "Hey, Muthu Singh! How are you? What's up, Ramalingam Kaur!"

Though Muthu or Ramalingam would hardly understand anything Sushant spoke in Punjabi, they had much fun talking back in their native language, making a perfect situation for two people talking in Punjabi and Tamil, respectively, and assuming they understood each other well.

Ramalingam would even respond to his name banter, "Oh, I am good, Sushant Narayan Murthy!"

Another boy in our *Northee* group was Subhash Ranga. He was tall, dark, and handsome (well, at least some thought so!), and originally from Hyderabad, he had lived in Gurgaon and joined the Haryana Chemical Engineering branch.

Ranga had an interesting view, backed by logic, on every topic we discussed, which kept everyone engaged and engrossed. Something even more interesting than his views and logic was his name. Not Subhash Ranga, but his full name.

"Rangaswami Murthy Vankat Subhash Chandra Bose!" he announced.

"Wow! That's a long name," I said.

"Yes! We inherit the father's name, too. Subhash is my name, and Venkat is my father's," said an enthused Ranga.

"In what way is Subhash Chandra Bose connected to you? Last time I checked, he was a great leader who fought for India's independence! How come you inherited his name?" asked Pyare.

"No, no, Subhash is my name."

"Subhash only is fine, but why is it Subhash Chandra Bose?"

"Well, that was already there! You don't get it," said Ranga reluctantly.

Though he had sounded logical in every other debate and discussion, Ranga would find it hard to explain his complex name, and when the logic failed, only jokes prevailed.

"Boy! How can you steal a leader's full name, even his title?"

"No, not steal, he calls it *inheriting*!"

"Do they let you do that? Do they make you fill in some form when you inherit those leaders' names at random?"

"And why leave out other leaders? Inherit their names too!"

"Actually, his name should be 'Rangaswami Murthy Vankat Subhash Chandra Bose Chandra Shekhar Azad Vallabh Bhai Patel Mohandas Karamchand Gandhi!'"

The group was in splits, and everyone contributed to the super long name with their knowledge of the names of important people.

"Add Akbar and Birbal too," said Sushant with convulsive laughter.

Like I always did, I enjoyed observing this dysfunctional group. It was like a scene from a daily soap, where they momentarily flashed to everyone to capture the expressions.

Pyare enjoyed every bit of the moment by improvising his jokes.

Sushant, as usual, annoyed everyone with his hyena-like laughter.

Our tragedy king Jashan Jeet Singh did not say a word or even smile. Looking at his sinister expression, he was perhaps thinking, *Laugh as much as you can, but all of you are going to get f@#$%d!*

Ganjoo's laughter sounded like the incessant high-pitched shrill of a broken radio.

Brigadier stood there at the doorstep. I could not see his face clearly as it was dark, but I guessed he was enjoying himself, since he stayed for a while.

And sitting in a corner and scratching his leg to get some relief from the usual allergic reactions, Dispensary chuckled at the jokes.

CHAPTER EIGHT

With every passing day, ragging, which had initially made us emotionally charged, became a mundane event, more so a new way of life. My keen observation led me to classify ragging into three broad categories:

The first type of ragging was light-hearted fun. The seniors did it to get acquainted with the newcomers. I didn't know if they were interested in passing our time or their own, but it did not matter as we had as much fun.

The *baaps*, *dadas*, and *pardadas* often hung around with their *butrus*. They made us sing, dance, and do fun activities. They showed interest in knowing their juniors better. We longed to meet those seniors in the otherwise boring evenings and would be elated and delighted whenever they summoned.

This form of ragging had its perks. The seniors were like our access to outings (as going out alone was far too risky), and free tickets to eating joints. Yes, at times, they delivered undesired lectures on unity and discipline and passed banal wisdom, but that was harmless. Samar, Ravinder, Raja, my *baap* Vikram Sood, and Vijay were the fun people. (Well, at least for me, not so for Ganjoo, though.)

The second category involved the angry ones, the beasts who perhaps used torture to vent their own shortcomings and frustrations. They had no sympathy towards their juniors nor any desire to know them better. They only enquired about the score, which was the total number of hard-hit slaps to date, which each of us had to remember and disclose when asked. They would make sure that our scores increased before they left.

Some of them were pathetic sadistic devils who simply derived pleasure by inflicting pain on innocent, helpless juniors by slapping forcefully. Sandhu was one of those. A wrathful bull.

One night, well past midnight, Sandhu summoned me to the main entrance gate. He waited with his friend, a senior from Rajasthan, at the other side of the locked main gate, both heavily drunk. They had a wicked and rather cruel idea to have fun, an idea that could only be a scheme concocted by good-for-nothing intoxicated losers throughout several rounds of alcohol.

Like Sandhu, the Rajasthan senior also called his *butru*—another prey in the game—who stood next to me, also in a third button position.

"Slap him hard! Did you hear me? Slap this guy, I said!" Sandhu ordered me.

SLAP!

I slapped my poor batchmate from Rajasthan after a lot of hesitation.

"Now your turn! Slap him back!" ordered the other senior to his poor *butru*.

SLAP!

The guy hit me harder than I hit him. Well, the poor guy did not have any choice but to follow the orders as I did.

"Ok, your turn!"

SLAP!

This time I hit him even harder, and almost felt a crackling of his jaw. Sandhu was exhilarated.

So, the prey at one side of the locked gate kept slapping each other while the thrilled predators at the other side kept pushing, and the filthy game of who slapped harder went on for a while until blood accumulated under the skin of our faces.

I felt like one of those helpless roosters in a cockfight, forced to fight until death while their masters become delirious with excitement at witnessing the bloodbath. I hated Sandhu more than anyone, and my every encounter with him (which went from bad to worse) strengthened my desire to avenge all the suffering caused.

For all those angry people in the second category, ragging was perhaps a way to avenge their own past circumstances. Some resorted to physical torture only because they had also gone through the same situation once, while the others hit the poor guys to prove themselves as hard-hitters and gain petty popularity amongst their lame friends.

The third form of ragging was the most terrible in nature. It was like the third degree of torture, a slow death. Only a few selected ones became the victim of this form as it required a special skill set that not everyone possessed, and that led them to the point of no return.

They were given the task of writing and copying files and registers and drawing complicated and time-consuming detailed graphs, charts, and diagrams for the seniors—the personal work they were supposed to do themselves.

It was not as easy as it sounds. A senior would suddenly summon you to the entrance gate in the middle of the night and give you his file or chart to be completed and a source to copy from (usually a file belonging to one of the good guys who had finished their work on time and, of course, all by themselves).

Since those lazy people always gave this task at the last minute, when the submission date approaching near, it meant a cumbersome, intricate, and arduous job which took long hours and resulted in several sleepless nights.

As I mentioned, some skill was required for this work, particularly good, neat, and legible handwriting. Poor boys with great handwriting— Virender (Himachal Electrical) and Vikas (Haryana Electrical) being two of them—became victims thanks to their talent. They soon became popular among all lazy seniors and spent endless hours completing seniors' work in addition to their own. They got some reprieve from physical torture (in comparison to others, at least!), but in exchange for what?

As Vikas pointed out, "It is a thankless job, like a slow poison that kills you."

I was spared, and it was one of those occasions when I was thankful to God for my ordinary (in fact, poor as per one of the senior's remarks) handwriting.

Necessity is the mother of invention. The third form of ragging gave birth to a new technique of copying the drawings and sketches that would save hours of laborious work, not only during the ragging days but the forthcoming years too.

What was needed to realize this technique? A rectangular panel of glass, a candle, and some bricks or wooden blocks.

The rectangular glass panel was placed on the bricks which supported each of its ends to make a short glass table. In the dark room, a candle was lit and installed under the table, right in the center. A blank sheet and the original sheet were placed on the glass table, such that the blank sheet was right on top of the original one. The sheets would illuminate due to candlelight, and the drawings on the original sheet would be clearly visible on the blank sheet, so much so that mere outlining produced an exact replica.

Hours of labor saved.

Days turned into weeks, and weeks turned into months.

Leg pulling was the favorite pastime of the group. Every evening, one boy or another would be the target who would be made fun of. Or—in the words of Pyare—the one on the hot seat. (Of course, there were few who became permanent incumbents of the hot seat!) There was never a dearth of topics to talk or make jokes about, followed by a series of improvisations with someone or other always ending up on the hot seat.

Pyare would always be charged up with his vulgar jokes and Sushant with his infectious and annoyingly loud laughter at just about anything. Ganjoo did not make jokes; only his shrill voice would be enough to create laughter and vexation equally. Dispensary, scratching his leg, and Brigadier (or his shadow!) at the doorstep would be, as usual, the silent spectators.

Jashan Jeet would not miss any chance to terrorize the group with his imaginary theories concluding each with his trademark expression, "You all are going to get f@#$%d."

I was not sure about others, but Jashan's theory surely made an impact on Bholu. Everything, just about every little thing, could distress Bholu and make him shake his head mournfully and say, "What is this? What am I going to do now?"

Waking up in the morning, sleeping at night, and everything in between frustrated him. Nothing could relax him. In fact, his whole existence made him anxious.

Pyare sometimes wondered if he even asked his mother when she delivered him, "What is this? Why have I been born? What am I going to do now?"

Then there was Dhanjeet Singh. Tall and a bit bulky, Dhanjeet would apply balm on his ankle every morning and then wrap it up neatly and gently with a plaster tape. He would not walk in the queue (the human train!) but next to it, with his slippers (as per seniors' orders, formal shoes were required to be worn all the time). Upon inquiry from seniors on the way to college, he would say that his ankle bone was brittle, and doctors had advised him to walk slowly.

Pyare and Ranga believed that there was not any disease or disorder in existence called "brittle ankle bones," and that it was just a lame excuse.

Ranga called him "Fake Ankle Singh" and bet those plaster tapes were there only to fool the seniors.

Pyare often predicted jokingly, "Forget walking slowly. Our friend Dhanjeet Singh will sprint like the Olympian athlete Milkha Singh once the ragging period is over."

Finally, the date of the IG session arrived.

"IG session? What the hell is that?" someone asked.

Everybody was confused as the seniors mentioned it often, saying that the ragging period would come to an end after the IG session. So, this was some sort of final hurdle which the boys were supposed to clear.

Would it be like a final exam in the toughest subject—ragging—after which we would become eligible for ragging-free status? One thing was clear: that there would be no ragging after the IG session. But the session itself remained a mystery.

Lack of information is the mother of speculation! And the mischievous sister of speculation is a rumor!

There was a slang term commonly used in college for the word rumor—*gulli*. Why *gulli*? I had no idea. Perhaps a brainchild of someone who did not put any logic behind it.

Gulli could have been derived from a local sport usually played in rural areas called *gulli-danda*, played with two sticks, the smaller being the "gulli" and the longer one, the "danda." The gulli, when hit forcefully by the danda, followed a projectile motion.

Just like the gulli was in the air for a short while, rumors were also short-lived, and hence the analogy, perhaps. So, people spread rumors like the danda hit the gulli. And by this logic, those people spreading rumors could have been called *danda*, and that was my theory.

Speaking of slang words, there were more. *Chamak* (literal meaning: glitter or flash) was another such word. Seniors used this word many times and often asked, *"Chamak raha hai ki nahi?"* Initially, I would get confused as it literally meant, "Is it glittering or not?" I wondered what was that glittered so much and so often for those seniors.

The word "understand" was the real interpretation for *chamak*. So *"Chamak raha hai ki nahi?"* meant "Are you getting it or not?" Perhaps the seniors meant that understanding a point was as good as a flash in the brain. That's the best logic I could find to relate the two words.

Another funny or rather a sleazy term was *chaat* (literal meaning: lick). The seniors used the term *chaat* for being bored. The irony was that those seniors would turn up at the hostel gate at odd hours, call for one or more of us, talk for hours, at times not even making any sense—mostly preaching at us and hardly letting any of us speak—and, in the end, say, *"Mein chat gaya,"* ("I am bored"), or *"Tune chaat liya,"* ("You are boring me").

When the term was initially introduced to me, I would get confused when a senior said, *"Chaat mat mujhe,"* which literally meant "Don't lick me." I wondered, *when did I lick him and why on earth would I, or anyone for that matter, want to lick him?*

One of the seniors used the term *chaat* so often that I sometimes wondered if he had really scaled the heights of boredom or if he actually *wanted* to be licked all over.

Back to the IG session, which had become a matter of conjecture. Boys used their half-baked theories and questionable information to unfold the suspense around the IG session.

Jashan Jeet Singh, who would not miss another opportunity to terrify the group, explained the mystery of the IG session with his evergreen theory of the naked candle dance, "See, I told you! It's going to be a candle dance for sure. All of you get ready to dance at midnight around a bonfire, all naked with candles in your hands!"

"How do you know for sure? The seniors did not say so. Who told you that, the candles?" asked an amused Pyare with his usual nonchalance.

"I know you don't believe me, but we cannot be ragging-free without the candle dance!"

"I am sure I will. But they won't free you unless they stamp your naked butt with the hot wax from the burning candle!"

The whole group was in splits, particularly Sushant and Ganjoo.

"Make jokes, you cheap comedian! I know you will be the first person to get f@#$%d!"

"Hey, Jashan! Why are you so obsessed with candles? Just because we can't have electricity in Hall One does not mean they have candles ready for us," said Ranga, trying to control his chuckle, but in vain.

"Hey, since you insist so much, have you practiced the candle dance?" asked Sushant, bursting with loud, convulsive laughter, even before finishing the question, as if he had made the best joke.

"Hahaha! He must be practicing the candle dance naked on the hostel's terrace after we all go to bed! I bet he will be the best performer. Those seniors will honor him with a certificate as well!" said Pyare.

"Yeah," said Ranga, "the certificate will read something like: *Dear Jashan, congratulations on winning best performance in the ancient dance form, the candle dance. As your winning prize, we honor you with the candle that you held while you danced naked. Please take it. Thank you.*"

The guys in the room burst into laughter. Pyare stressed upon the words "Please take it," followed by, "Where will you take it?" alluding to his well-known vulgar propensity.

Sushant could not help his roar of laughter. Brigadier and Dispensary, who were usually quite somber, also giggled.

"And this Mr. Fake ankle," said Pyare pointing at Dhanjeet, who was busy applying balm on his ankle, "he will be the worst performer. They will present him with a blank certificate and a bottle of balm."

"Shut up, you *seeti*!" replied Dhanjeet, frowning irritably. Due to his lean and skinny figure, Pyare was nicknamed *seeti* (meaning "whistle").

Jashan tapped his fist with the palm of his other hand and said, "All of you are going to get f@#$%d!"

Bholu, who, as usual, was not amused, plunged into a deep melancholy, as he believed everything that had even a little trace of pessimism. Who better than Jashan to fuel despondency and negative thinking? Bholu, with his droopy eyes and sunken face, shook his head with dejection and uttered, "What is this? What am I going to do now?"

Almost every conversation in that room ended in laughter. They said laughter is the best medicine. Then this room, B56, where we all gathered every evening, was a pharmacy that was never short of samples of the laughter medicine.

One more thing that would never be missing in that room was the odor of the balm that the allegedly brittle ankle of Dhanjeet consumed every day.

A date for the IG session was set for the first week of January, and we were told to be present at IG Park. The park was a few kilometers away from the college campus. As the date approached nearer, us *Northees* became more and more jittery. Though everybody tried their best to exhibit a cool exterior, the anxiety could be sensed.

CHAPTER NINE

IG Park, 5th January, 4:30 p.m.

The description at the entrance of IG Park read: *Indira Gandhi Park is spread over an area of about forty acres. Lush green lawns, gardens with seasonal flowers, rides for kids, picnic spots, and a small zoo are some of the features.* Of course, a splendid park that was hitherto unknown to us.

We reported on time. About fifteen of us, the first year batch *Northees* from the states of Jammu and Kashmir, Punjab, Haryana, Himachal, and Delhi, had gathered in the garden, waiting for the seniors. After about fifteen minutes of waiting, we spotted them approaching. A second year batch of *Northees*.

"Oh boy, so many of them! Are they here for a wedding?" Pyare whispered, but his efforts did not make the moment any lighter. All of us stood still, afraid and expressionless.

Moments later, the senior boys were standing in front of us, Sandhu, Samar, Ravinder, my *baap* Vikram, Virender's *baap* Susheel, and others, all geared up for the big event.

"Hey, guys, everyone's here!" said Sandhu with a conniving smile, as if leading a pack of wolves.

"You're going to be free today…you must be happy!"

"Hey, don't look down. It's a public place; no third button position!"

"Come, follow us!"

We followed them submissively. They took us to a sparsely populated area, probably to keep away from public attention.

"Ok, make a circle and sit down. Relax! Look, we brought you snacks!" Samar opened a large plastic bag and took out three small plastic bags, each with *pakoras*, *samosas*, and *wadas*, stuffed and carefully covered with newspapers. There was also a small plastic packet filled with red chutney and tied carefully with a thread, but that went unnoticed by Samar. Vikram helped Samar to serve the food.

"Eat! We've got the best *samosas* from MANDAP for you guys," said Ravinder.

"Yes, yes, we have a lot of work to do today! This will give you energy," said Sandhu with a wicked grin.

Who could eat under so much stress and mental agony? I found it hard to chew and swallow every bite of *samosa* that I took. It felt like I was simply stuffing the whole *samosa* in my mouth and shoving it down my throat with a painful effort. I knew we were not there for a picnic, and Sandhu's remarks had only aggravated my anxiety and nervousness. I felt like a lamb who was being fed well before the slaughter.

My fellow friends were not comfortable eating either, but the seniors were hardly bothered. They waited for a few more minutes and started with their actual agenda.

"Ok, Jammu Computer, come with us! The rest of you wait here, and we will call you one by one," said Sandhu rudely. Ganjoo followed the orders as we watched him disappear into the bushes with the seniors.

"What's with the *samosas* and *pakoras*? What are these guys up to?" I asked.

"No idea, yaar. I did not enjoy eating for the first time in my life!" replied Sushant, who was such a foodie that while having dinner, he would discuss the menu for the next day's lunch.

"I got it, I got it! Since they fed us, they will ask for us to return their food," said Pyare.

"What the hell? This *seeti* has gone mad! Everything is a joke to him," said an annoyed Dhanjeet.

"No, no! I mean it! I am sure Ganjoo is putting his finger down his throat right now to return the *samosas*," Pyare replied.

"You are silly, they won't ask Ganjoo to vomit!" said Ranga, giggling.

"Believe me, if Ganjoo is not vomiting, then he must be defecating! Bottom line is, the *samosa* is supposed to be returned," Pyare improvised.

"Chhi-chhi! You are gross!" said the boys in chorus.

"What do you say, Jashan? Do you believe my theory, or are you still stuck on your candle dance theory?" Pyare bantered with Jashan.

"You are going to get f@#$%d!" came the anticipated reply from Jashan, and everyone started giggling.

About fifteen minutes, Sandhu came back without Ganjoo, and took Jashan with him. We were expecting Ganjoo to return and unfold the mystery, but it did not happen. We became anxious and a little unsettled.

"What the f@#$%k is this? What did they do with Ganjoo?" said the agitated Bholu, wrinkles of panic showing on his forehead. "What is this? What am I going to do now?"

Bholu did not get any response, for there was nothing we could tell him.

"Ask Pyare, he is the expert," I replied after a long pause.

"Can't say about Ganjoo, but Jashan is sure to do the candle dance!" replied Pyare. Pyare was never serious. Perhaps humor was some sort of defense mechanism for him to deal with undesirable and uncomfortable situations.

So, every ten or fifteen minutes, Sandhu kept coming and taking one of us with him. None of our friends who went with him came back.

Finally, my turn arrived, and as usual, I followed Sandhu submissively. We walked a few meters and joined the rest of the seniors. The place was secluded, surrounded by bushes, with hardly any people around.

"Look, I brought a hero!" said Sandhu.

"Come here, stand right here," another one said.

Within no time, I was surrounded by fourteen or fifteen over-excited boys, like vultures that flocked to the mangled animal carcass.

"Look up! You are going to be free in no time!"

"Start with the *funda list*. Quick!"

I started to speak nervously, "Final year… Jammu and Kashmir… Mr. Kamal Kumar, Computer Science Engineering. Umm… Mr. Sumit Kaul—"

SLAP!

A tight slap hit my cheek. Clearly it was Sandhu, as I noticed his hand swinging. Before I could recover, there came another one, out of the blue and even more forceful.

SLAP! SLAP! SLAP!

Followed by several rapid-fire slaps. After five or six slaps, I lost count. There must have been about fifteen or twenty of them in quick succession.

Who said you can't see stars in the daylight? I could visualize the whole galaxy of stars in front of me. My head swung in almost every direction because of the misdirected slaps. Even a football was not hit so many times, and that was my head, damn it! My head was spinning, my ears were ringing, and I felt a mild concussion.

"Ok, that's enough! He's had enough! We need to get the other guys too."

The boys finally backed off after Ravinder's intervention.

"Ok, fine, we are done."

Vikram, my *baap*, took me aside, removed my necktie, and unbuttoned the top two buttons of my shirt. "Boy, you are free now! No need to look at the third button from now onwards," said Vikram, and he whispered in my ear, "And I did not slap you." He said it as if expressing the helplessness of an accomplice in a wrongdoing that occurred against his will.

"Raise your hands towards the sky and say, 'I am free!'" yelled Samar.

"I am free!" I followed his orders by raising my head and hands.

"Louder!" all of them screamed in a chorus.

"I AM FREE!" I shouted.

"Ok, now run to join your friends and keep saying it!" Susheel pointed towards my friends (those who had gone before me, had disappeared, and were now also free), sitting some distance away.

"I am free! I am free! I am free!" I ran to my friends with the tie in my hand.

The IG session was over, and so was my ragging period. My score, which was hitherto forty, went past sixty after that day's session. It was perhaps the most among my folks, thanks to the maximum contribution by Sandhu.

It took another hour or so for the rest of my friends to go through the ordeal. When they were finished, they addressed our group. "Ok, guys, you are free now. How do you feel?"

None of us was in the mood to reply.

"But mind you, we are still your seniors. If we call you or give you some work to do, you must do it. Understand?" said Sandhu.

We again chose to remain silent. I hated Sandhu for his remarks. I hated him for slapping me. Every time he spoke, I hated him more.

"Ok, you are on your own now!"

And the seniors walked away, visibly proud of their accomplishment of wildly slapping a bunch of helpless and innocent boys, one after the other.

And there we were, first year *Northees,* walking back to the hostel. It felt so good to be left on our own. No more bowing down. No more gazing at the third button. No more walking in a queue.

Pyare sang songs in his local dialect with his flat, completely out of tune voice, without caring for the reactions of those who passed by in the market area.

Sushant burst into laughter at Pyare's singing.

Ganjoo laughed too, in his croaking voice.

Ranga kept joking and making fun of Pyare.

Dispensary and Brigadier looked amused but kept mum.

Virender and Vikas, who walked by my side, kept humming some nice tunes.

Dhanjeet walked behind with his plastered ankle, chuckling at every joke.

Bholu looked relieved but still shook his head now and then, perhaps in anticipation of other bad things to come in the future.

Jashan also smiled occasionally, but his sarcastic countenance seemed to be implying, "Fine, all of you are happy now, but you all are going to get f@#$%d."

It felt great walking carelessly and fearlessly. Free! Liberated! Emancipated!

Back in the hostel, Mohit, another boy from Punjab, became so upset upon seeing his distorted face from slapping at IG Park that, in a fit of anger, he punched the mirror of the bathroom, smashing it into pieces. Along with black eye and swollen face, he now had bloody knuckles too.

Dhanjeet rushed Mohit to the dispensary (the place, not the guy) and got his skin stitched up.

That evening, Samar and Ravinder, who had discovered booze mates in Pyare and Sunny, dropped by and took them to some bar called MANDAP and later, around 11 p.m., dropped them back at the hostel, heavily drunk.

Pyare, who walked with great difficulty, was wobbling from side to side and leaning against the wall in the corridor. He went up to his room and hurled through the window, so much that after a while, he was literally whistling as only air gushed out of his mouth.

Ranga and Dhanjeet helped Pyare. "See, you *seeti*! You cannot afford binge drinking with this kind of skeletal body! Now you are throwing up no more, and only blowing *seeti. Seeti* blowing *seeti*!" joked Dhanjeet. Pyare mumbled something in vexation that again sounded like blowing *seeti* exasperatedly.

Delhi boy Sunny, who was wobbling like jelly, went straight into the common hall of Hall One, where some forty or fifty boys were watching a movie. He turned the TV off and started doing the *Naagin* dance right in front of the television, almost falling from side to side.

I quickly turned the TV back on, held his hand, and took him out of the room as the boys were yelling and shouting at the abrupt interruption in the flow of the gripping movie, briefly subjected to the nuisance of a clumsy, dancing drunkard.

Sunny crawled up the stairs with both his hands and legs like a lizard, sat down after five or six steps, stared at me and asked, "Hey, Aahan, when did you come?"

Sunny's speech was slurred due to intoxication. I helped him with the stairs as he would not care for my reply. He crawled up another step and then stopped and turned to me. "Hey, Aahan, when did you come?"

It took Sushant (who met us in the corridor of the second floor) and me about fifteen minutes to bring him to his room. Dispensary, Sunny's roommate, became worried to see him in that state. I asked him to bring some water, and he hurried out of the room with his empty water bottle.

Sunny would lie down on his bed, close his eyes as if falling asleep, wake up twenty seconds later, roll over suddenly and get up from the other side of the bed, asking me each time, "Hey, Aahan, when did you come?"

He repeated it three more times before he finally slept.

I had been with him when he entered the hostel drunk. I was there when I pulled him out of the TV room amidst the chaos. I was there when I helped him crawl up those stairs. I was there when he wobbled in the corridor. I was still there when he did his rolling over acrobatics on his bed. Would it have mattered if I told Sunny that I was there the whole time? He simply wouldn't stop asking the same question. Five times!

The studious boy Dispensary could not get over the shock of the clumsy antics of the inebriated Sunny, and did not remain his roommate any longer, changing his room the very next day.

CHAPTER TEN

Ragging free; all the *Northees* of Hall One. Ragging free; all the boys of Hall One from the states of Orissa, UP, Maharashtra, Kerala, Tamil Nadu, et cetera. Ragging free; all Indian boys in Hall One.

Hall One was basking under its newfound glory, a new status. No more gloomy and dull atmosphere, no more queueing up for college in the morning, no more dressing up formally, no more third button position in front of seniors, no more getting beaten up, no more locked gates, no more signing registers to leave the hostel, no more dark rooms *sans* electricity, no more enforced bonding with other *Northees*, no more confinement of Room B56.

We discovered new hangout places outside of the hostel. One such place was at the edge of the campus, called the Back-Post.

The Back-Post, a smoker's paradise, would easily qualify for the coolest hangout place for the boys, had there been a poll. There were mud houses at the end of the road, which stretched all the way from Hall One to Hall Five. The underprivileged, less literate, local people lived in those small huts with their limited means, and they served tea, cigarettes, and snacks for their livelihood.

For boys (even the unruliest ones), the Back-Post was the heritage of college, always to be looked after, and so were those locals, always to be respected and protected.

Boys would sit for hours together on wooden planks mounted over the rocks to make benches, and blow rings of smoke called *chhalla. Maggi, top ramen curry, samosa, wada,* and handmade biscuits were among some of the delicacies served at the Back-Post. And the most popular one, the king of all snacks, the showstopper item, was a miniature packet of salted peanuts, which everyone relished with tea and coffee.

The place would come to life every evening with playful bantering, leg-pulling, discussions about girls and sharing stories of the acts of valor of the alumni. Sober boys played Antakshri while those high on alcohol who often visited late in the evening sang songs at the top of their voice. Those chartbusters always included the mention of alcohol like "*Chhalkaaye Jaam*," "*Jahan Chaar Yaar Mil Jayen*," and "*Yeh Jo Mohabbat Hai*."

The Back-Post was also the place for the origin of rumors, the birthplace of the so-called *gulli*. While some *gullis* spread due to lack of awareness, others were the result of the contrivance of some experts, and the imagination of idle minds of those who had mastered the art of rumormongering over a cup of tea.

Though the ragging was officially over, that did not stop the seniors from asking favors and giving assignments. Within a week after the IG session, we were entrusted with a project. The Lohri Project.

Samar, Ravinder, Vikram, and a few other second year seniors paid a visit one evening. All the *Northee* boys gathered in Room B56 of Hall One, the meeting place. Boys occupied the chairs, tables, beds, and any other thing that could help support their buttocks.

"What's up, guys? You seem to be having fun," Samar said with a familiar smile.

"Not really, sir. We still get haunted by nightmares about ragging!" said Sushant with a shy giggle (contrary to his usual burst of laughter).

"Yes, sir! In my dreams too!" Pyare chimed in eagerly.

"Haha… It's ok if we appear in your dreams, but don't take it too far and blame us for your wet dreams!" replied Ravinder.

Everybody in the room laughed. Ravinder was Pyare's *baap*. They were related, according to the college family chart. Both had emaciated frames. Both made crude jokes. Like Pyare, profanity was an essential commodity in Ravinder's jokes, like a condiment adding flavor to delicacies. I did not know Pyare's *dada* and *pardada* that well, but my guess was obscenity ran in the family.

"Ok, let's get to business now! As you know, the Lohri Festival is in just five days and all the *Northees* celebrate it with great enthusiasm! You are the lucky ones who have been chosen to make all the arrangements for the Lohri Festival," said Vikram.

Lucky ones? I thought. *As if they haven't brought enough "luck" to us already!*

"The good thing is, you need not pay for the arrangements, and the even better thing…you will earn money! You must perform in front of seniors to earn cash," said Samar.

"Sir, perform as in…" asked Ranga, trailing off.

"As in Lohri songs, dances, skits…whatever they ask you to do! Remember: No preaching or trying to pass wisdom! There are no saints here, and you won't get a penny if the seniors are bored."

"Every year the most money comes from final year boys, but since the job market has not been good this year, many seniors are still jobless. You will need to put in extra effort to make them loosen their pockets!"

In a nutshell, we were required to perform buffoonery, literally beg for every penny, and then arrange a grand booze event for the seniors in the name of Lohri. And they had said we were ragging free! Well, if this was not ragging, then what was?

The seniors left after giving us all the "necessary instructions."

"What the hell is this whole event management bullshit? Haven't they wasted enough time already?" said an annoyed Dhanjeet, shaking his head.

"Only ten days are left until the semester exams…you all are surely going to fail!" replied Jashan, tapping his fist on his palm, as usual.

"Oh, bhai, don't forget…we have to perform *nautanki* (gimmicks) too," said Ranga.

"Pyare Lal, what are you going to do?" I asked Pyare jokingly.

"Bend over. The only performance left which can satisfy them."

"Haha, you need to prepare a skit, and all of us have to play a role. You bending over will not do!"

"Well, whatever the skit may be, Dhanjeet's role is fixed…he will be the umpire! What else can he do with that fake ankle?"

Dhanjeet (who, by the way, had shown a speedy ankle recovery after the IG session) replied, "Get lost, you *seeti*!"

For the skit, boys chose me as the writer and director, allegedly for my creative vision, and I chose Pyare as my assistant director. I hoped his creative acumen would help me pull off a lewd and vulgar skit.

Another task was to prepare Lohri songs in regional languages. Since popular Lohri poems were known in Punjabi and Himachali languages, our time and energy were saved. The challenge was for the boys from Jammu and Kashmir, Haryana, and Delhi, as they were required to prepare poems in Dogri *(and* Kashmiri*)*, Haryanvi, and English, respectively. (Why English for the Delhi boys? I had no idea.)

Ganjoo and Jashan, the Jammu boys, took charge of writing the poem in the Dogri language, while Faizal, the only boy from Kashmir in the batch, would write in the Kashmiri language. Haryanvi Lohri writing was assigned to Bholu.

Suresh, another boy whose real name was forgotten, like that of Brigadier and Dispensary, was better known as Dilli-Mining for the simple reason that he was from Delhi and in the Mining Engineering branch. Though he was later promoted to the Civil branch, thanks to his good ranking, his fate was sealed with the identity of "Dilli-Mining" for the rest of his college tenure.

Dilli-Mining, who volunteered to write a Lohri poem in English, was another butcher of the English language, but who cared? We were not performing in front of scholars of English literature, anyways.

We spent many hours in preparation that evening and the following day. In the evening, post-dinner, all of us headed to Hall Five to meet final year boy Deepak, as directed by Ravinder. Deepak was in his room on the top floor with the door slightly ajar.

"*Aa Gaye Chandaa Maangne?*" said the jovial Deepak, asking us if we had come for the collection as he received us at the door. "Let me save you some time. Stay here, and I will call all the final year boys from Hall Two and Hall Five." And Deepak left to fetch his friends.

Final year and third year boys occupied independent rooms either in Hall Two or Hall Five. Fifteen minutes later, the room was packed with seniors, and only a few of us managed to stand inside. The rest of us stayed in the corridor.

"Ok, let's hear a Lohri poem! Delhi first! Who is doing it?" said Deepak, visibly excited.

Dilli-Mining came forward.

"Ok, start! And say it loud!" said another boy.

Dilli-Mining, the boy with shining big black eyes, cleared his throat, took a deep breath, and began on top of his voice: "In this life…we were born. Sometimes we don't know why! Baby cry when Daddy says bye! Mummy tells a story, so let us give us Lohri!"

"What the hell is this? We were sometimes born, don't know why…ta-ta, bye-bye! Do you think we are dumb toddlers?" asked Deepak, with an expression that you assume when scolding a child while being amused by their mischief.

"I bet he made up this silly thing just now or on his way to Hall Five and hurled in front of us!" said another.

"How about rhyming like this? 'Sometimes I don't know why, but after hearing me, you all are surely going to die!'"

"And 'Let us give us Lohri'? Did you take English lessons from your *doodhwala* (milkman) or the watchman?"

"No, no, I am sure he took evening classes from the boy who rang the bell in his school!"

And the bantering and laughter went on and on with all the seniors chiming in. By now, all, including Dilli-Mining, were giggling.

"Here, take this! Much more than you deserve for your flop show!" Deepak took out a twenty-five paisa coin from his pocket and handed it to Dilli-Mining.

Another Lohri poem had been prepared in the Haryanvi language, and it had cost Bholu a sleepless night. We had also had to put up with his usual shaking of the head in misery and saying, "What is this? What am I going to do?"

He narrated it to the seniors, and it went something like this: "*Neeche pankha chaale seyy, uppar tau soye seyy! Sote bhookh lagi, khaale tau moongphalli! Moongphali mein dana nai, tau chhat pe jana nai! Lohri de do...Lohri de do!*"

"Hey, that's a copy of a nursery rhyme! *Uppar pankha chalta hai, neeche baby sota hai.*" (Translation: A fan runs above while the baby sleeps underneath.) "How come your *tau* (uncle) is messing with the nursery rhyme?" one of the seniors objected.

"And he modified it! His fan is running below while his *tau* is sleeping above! Where? In the ceiling? This super *tau* has even defied the laws of gravitation!" said another one.

"No, sir. In Haryana, people sleep in the open. I meant, *tau* is sleeping on the roof while a ceiling fan is in the room," Bholu tried to explain the inexplicable.

"Wow! You and your *tau* are two awfully innovative human beings!"

"Is your legend of *tau* over?" asked Deepak.

"Yes, sir," said Bholu timidly.

"Here, take this twenty-five paisa. This is actually for finishing quickly and sparing us from more *tau* torture!" said one guy, amused.

The seniors' motive was to declare every performance a load of rubbish, and they did. Punjab and Himachal Lohri were not much fun for them as they were well-known poems: "*Sunder munderiye ho, tera kon bichara ho...*"

For Jammu boy Ganjoo, they were more amused to hear his croaking voice than his Dogri poem itself. One senior said, "You don't need to say the poem, just scream 'Ae...aee...aeee...aeee.' As loud as you can!"

"AE...AAEE...AAAEEEE...AEEEEEEEE!" Ganjoo screamed, and all were in splits. Deepak even sent Pyare and Sushant to find out how many windowpanes had been broken. Ganjoo was awarded a one-rupee coin just for yelling, the largest earning from all the performances so far.

Since Faizal was the only boy from Kashmir and the only one who could speak the language, Pyare had suggested that he abuse the seniors by using swear words in his Kashmiri Lohri poem. Faizal narrated the poem, and the smart seniors asked whether he had cursed them, to which he denied, but of course, nobody could corroborate that.

We did everything to please them. I performed a mimicry of Bollywood actors, and they seemed to enjoy that. It was well past midnight, and most of the seniors had already left for bed, but all we had gotten were pennies, which didn't even amount to ten rupees. We were worried.

What are we going to do? Are they expecting us to arrange a big event with these farthings?

We stayed up all night in Deepak's room with him and his three friends who had stayed back. I must say, we enjoyed the whole night as they made fun of every performance and shared their experiences with us. At about six in the morning, Deepak took us to the Back-Post, offered tea and *samosa*, which we relished in the morning sunshine, and later slipped an envelope into Ranga's pocket before taking off.

We checked the envelope on our way back to Hall One and found cash worth ten thousand rupees. Apparently, all the seniors had handed their contribution to Deepak well before we arrived last night.

It was such a relief to receive a hefty supplement. Thankfully it was a Sunday, and we had the luxury of sleeping all day with a great sense of achievement.

However the woes were not over yet. We still had the herculean task of collection from pre-final and second year guys. Every evening we would get ready for what Pyare termed *Beizzati ka Durbaar* (the Court of Humiliation). We spent the next three nights going from one room to another, performing skits, Lohri poems, and begging for money.

As expected, most of the seniors remained unimpressed and reluctant to loosen their pockets. One senior even fell asleep in the middle of one of the performances, and we stood for a while, looking at each other, not knowing whether to stay and wake him, or leave. We finally decided to leave his room.

Ranga joked, "Boy, the height of humiliation! Until now, it was in installments, but this one was a lump sum! This is like adding a feather to the cap of humiliation. Ultimate *beizzati*!"

"Yes, the others found faults and made fun of us, but at least they watched! This guy started snoring in the middle of our skit! I now have a newfound respect for all those who mocked, ridiculed, and jeered," said Sushant.

After the collection was made, the next step was a formal invitation to the event. Dhanjeet and Jashan were assigned the task of inviting the seniors and taking their orders of drinks and snacks. An open space opposite Hall Three was chosen for holding the event, and the requisite permission was obtained from the warden.

*

January 13th, 6 p.m.

We, the first year *Northees*, were busy lighting the bonfire in the open area. All arrangements had been made. Two local vendors were busy installing the generator, setting up the microphone, the lighting, and tuning the music system in their tempo car. The drinks and snacks were already delivered to the rooms of the seniors. Our efficient team assigned for each batch—Faizal and Bholu for the second year, Ganjoo and Dispensary for the third year, and Brigadier and Dilli-Mining for the final year—made sure that all the deliveries were done as per the orders and instructions.

"Hey, where are Pyare and Sunny?" I asked Sushant while putting a log into the fire to maintain the flame.

"Boozing! Samar and Ravinder took them to Hall Three," Sushant replied, grabbing some *moongphali* and *revadi* (peanuts and sweet nuts) from the large bags kept near the bonfire.

7:30 p.m.

It was time for the Lohri celebration. We had lined up to welcome the seniors, and the Lohri celebration was in full bloom. The place was rocking with the beats of catchy Hindi and Punjabi numbers, and many of the seniors were already tipsy.

Grabbing the microphone, final year boy Sumit interrupted, "Hey, stop the music! We will do the *butrus'* intro first!"

We established that all the first year boys were supposed to introduce themselves, their name, and their college family tree members.

Second year boy Samar took the mic from Sumit and summoned Ganjoo, "Come, Ganjoo! Hold this mic and cover your eyes with the other hand, ok?"

"Cover his eyes? What for?" I whispered in Ranga's ear. He also had no clue.

Ganjoo followed the orders and began, "My name is Vinay Ganjoo. My branch is—" A small object hit Ganjoo's face, and he stopped.

"Don't look up! Keep your eyes covered and continue!" yelled Samar, who was standing right behind Ganjoo.

Ganjoo went on, "My branch is Computer Science and Engineering. My *pardada's* name is Mr. Kamal Kum—" Ganjoo again felt small objects hitting his face. He peeped through the fingers of his hand that was covering his eyes and realized that the seniors gathered at the other side of the bonfire were throwing nuts right at his face.

"Finish off quickly! Don't stop!"

"…Mr. Kamal Kumar, my *dada's* name is Mr. Sohan Dhar, and my *baap's* name is Mr. Dina Nath Olla." The rest of the intro was finished by Ganjoo in one go amidst the shots of *moongphalis* and *revadis* that zoomed from every corner, striking right at the target, hardly missing.

Next was Jashan, then Faizal, then Bholu, and so on. All of us were subjected to similar treatment during our intro.

That was clearly the price you paid for being a junior in college. Five days of patience and endurance, sleepless nights, sore throats, collection, humiliation, and large-scale event management. The result? *Moongphalis* being thrown at your face.

Humiliation reloaded.

After the intro session, the music started, and the real bash began. It was an exhibition of various dance forms. While Punjabi *bhangra* was the most common dance, certain dance forms were simply triggered by excessive booze, like the *naagin* and *sapera* dance, where one guy would crawl like a snake on the floor while the other one posed like a snake charmer, waving his hands as if playing the flute. Another form was the bird dance, where guys waved their hands just like birds flutter their wings.

The event was not confined to the freaky dancers only, but was a gold mine for talent hunting, as there were stunt masters, too, who performed somersaults and even jumped over the bonfire. A few overenthusiastic lanky Salman Khans removed their sweaty shirts and tossed them up in the air.

While final year boys were more interested in grabbing the mic now and then and to pass wisdom, third year boys—the likes of Raja and Vijay—made sure that every one of us (whether we liked it or not) sipped beer from the bottles which they flaunted openly.

Some seniors shared cigarettes with the few smokers of our batch and felt proud of the new entries in the smokers' clan. Celebrations lasted till the wee hours, leaving everyone exhausted.

CHAPTER ELEVEN

The next day, I woke up late and my head was spinning from last night's booze and crazy dancing. The whole Lohri event management had resulted in burnout. But there was no time to relax. We had another event to manage, a bigger one, a grander one. This time teamwork would not help; each individual had to manage it alone.

The big event was the first semester's exams (popularly known as "end sem"), and there were only four days to go. The tension was brewing as the time seemed to be running like an express train with no stops. Ragging was an excuse for not studying much throughout the semester, but we still had ample time as we had been confined to the hostel most of the time.

What happened when the study material piled up and there were only four days left before exams? The master cut down plan kicked in. This involved cutting down on basic routine work.

First things first, stopping going to college to attend the boring lectures, in order to save time for studies. (Though the lectures were always boring, four days before exams, they seemed utterly unnecessary, too).

Secondly, cutting down on sleep, going from eight to ten hours to half or even a quarter of that.

Next, cutting down on morning ablution time. Certain unavoidable stuff could be done in multitasking mode, like studying and relieving oneself simultaneously. The other less pressing tasks like bathing, shaving, and even brushing could be conveniently avoided. No need to change clothes and hence no washing required, well except for underwear (or maybe not, in some cases).

Quick meal options like noodles and curry, and smoking cigarettes at the Back-Post at odd hours took precedence over mundane regular time-bound meals in the messroom.

Finally, when all the above measures had been exhausted but still proved to be insufficient, we cut down on course material. Since covering the whole syllabus seemed impractical, we took a cue from the previous years' question papers and prepared selective topics that were easier to remember, to have more probability of scoring.

This was the time when the notes and previous years' question papers shared with us by the seniors made life easier. We did not forget that they were the same boys who had left no stone unturned when making our lives hell during the ragging. So, did that make us even?

My *baap*, Vikram Sood, had given me helpful notes, and in his defense, he had not bashed me during the ragging period.

Some nocturnal students committed to acing the exams had only one agenda—to go to bed well after every boy in the hostel. Lights on in even a single room served as inspiration for them to stay awake until they were finally turned off. The hostel easily qualified as the safest place to be during the exams, as the studious boys, like sincere watchmen, kept vigil.

Ranga, like an expert examination coach, explained the topics well and loved to teach his roommates. I think teaching was his way of revising the topics and making his concepts clearer. Another loyal student of Ranga was Sushant, who never missed his coaching sessions, especially during exams.

I was skeptical of Ranga's coaching approach and sometimes wondered if he guided or misguided. He would announce all of a sudden, "Hey, I have referred back to the last five years' papers, and this question comes every alternate year. I bet this question is going to come this year! You are going to regret it if you don't prepare for it!"

Sushant and Ranga's roommates Vikas, Patil, and Biradar, like sincere and faithful students of their expert teacher, would leave aside all the self-study and start preparing for the question with him.

There were boys who had lost faith in self-study altogether by the final night before the exams. Pyare was one of those boys who adopted the shortcut method, *purchi*.

Purchi, the chit, was a small rectangular piece of paper, long in length and short in width, with the answers written in small-sized letters that were just visible to the naked eye. It was used to cheat in exams. You could pass the exam or even score good marks with the help of *purchi*, provided you didn't get caught. If you didn't escape the eagle eyes of the examiner, well, then there was no escape from getting expelled from the examination hall as well. *Purchi* was not for the weak-hearted, as it required risk-taking audacity to cheat and endure the shamelessness and disgrace upon being caught red-handed.

We caught Pyare busy making *purchi* in his room at night before the first exam.

"Boy! These letters are almost microscopic! Can you even read this *micro-purchi* yourself?" Sushant asked.

"Have you guys finished your studies and come to disturb me? Get lost! Let me concentrate!" Pyare exclaimed.

"Oh *bhai*, concentrate! Even the people who study do not use such strong words. And this boy needs concentration to copy from the textbook!" Ranga exclaimed.

"He is just writing these *purchis*, and for that, he wants us to be out of the room. Thank goodness he's not studying, or else he would kick us out of the hostel!" Dhanjeet added.

"These are a lot of *purchis*," I remarked. "You obviously can't keep them in one or two pockets."

"Bhai, then what are underwear and socks for? I have planned out everything!" Pyare insisted.

"Underwear is a good idea; even the examiner can't slip in his hands there!" Ranga said, impressed.

With a triumphant smile, Pyare replied, "Yes, I have one pair of underwear with a pocket, so I am going to wear them!"

"For eight exams?" Sushant exclaimed. "One pair of underwear for eight days? *Chhi-chhi*! Don't even come close to me!"

"No...no! Only during exam time, *bhai*! I will change it once I am back in the hostel."

Dhanjeet spoke up, "How will you remember the pocket with the right *purchi*?"

"That's like asking a gambler if he knows a spade in a pack of cards. Do you guys think I am a layman? I will refer to the index *purchi* for that," Pyare replied, as if it was obvious.

"*Index purchi*?!" we all asked in a chorus.

"Yes, it will tell me the topic I am looking for and the right pocket where the concerned *purchi* is kept. The index *purchi* will let me know the whereabouts of all other *purchis*."

"What if the examiner catches your index *purchi*?" Sushant asked.

"Simple! In that case, he will know the whereabouts of the other *purchis*!"

We all burst out laughing.

*

Examination Day.

The nervous energy could be easily sensed as many boys and girls stood in the corridor outside the examination hall, turning pages haphazardly in their final attempt to revise. People took a sneak-peek at each other's notes and then did a hasty search for the same topic in their own books.

Strangely, you always felt underprepared for the topic that your friends revised at the last minute, and you convinced yourself it was now a sure-shot entry in the exam.

A few boys, Ganjoo being one of them, were busy scribbling the key formulae and equations on the wooden desks allotted to them according to the roll numbers.

People glanced at each other, hardly speaking except for asking the simple question, "How did your preparation go?"

The most common answer? "Not good."

Finally, the examiner arrived, and everyone settled down.

Two words to describe the next three hours: Emotional turmoil.

When the exam was over, I met Pyare in the corridor. He had just come out of the examination hall that was adjacent to mine, and he appeared visibly upset.

"Hey, Pyare! How did it go?"

"Couldn't have gone worse!"

"Why? What happened?"

"That, Professor PK! He caught me!"

"What? How?"

"I don't know! He kept staring at me from the moment I started my paper. I couldn't even take out the index *purchi*!"

"Then?"

"Then I went to the washroom to adjust my *purchis*. I was there, at the washbasin, when he caught me red-handed with all the *purchis*. Imagine, that guy followed me to the washroom! Is there any privacy left in this country?"

"Oops! Then what did he do?"

"Then what? He took all my *purchis* and said, 'Follow me,' and I walked behind him."

"Then?"

"Then at the entrance of examination hall, he said, 'Now don't follow me!'"

"Haha...really?!" I could not control my laughter, visualizing Professor PK's quirks.

"I don't know what he said...something like: 'I bother, you bother, so why bother the botheration?'"

"So, he didn't allow you in?"

"I begged him for almost twenty minutes. He agreed at last, but then only thirty minutes were left."

"Do you think you will pass?"

"I think so. I kind of recalled some of the things while writing *purchi*. I had that whole Lambardar thing written on my *purchi* but forgot it completely."

"What is *Lambardar*?"

"That *Lambardar* principle!"

"You mean D'Alembert's principle? Haha...*Lambardar*! Really?" I couldn't stop laughing at Punjab boy Pyare's *Lambardar* (literal meaning: village head) principle: The Punjabi rendition of the countryside term for the French physicist's name.

"God, I spent the whole night writing those *purchis*. I tell you, there is no respect for hard work in this college."

"Hey! What's up?" Ranga joined us.

"Professor Parimal grabbed his *purchis* in the bathroom."

"What? Really? Thank God he only grabbed his *purchis*!"

We all laughed.

It was a common observation that I often walked out of the examination hall gruntled, believing that the paper went well. Then I met with my friends on my way back to the hostel, discussed the question paper, and verified the answers. By the time I arrived at the hostel, my confidence had taken a hit as I either found out the mistakes in my answers or believed that my friends' answers were better than mine.

Disgruntled, now a good score was neither my focus nor expectation. I added up my marks numerous times, sometimes being unforgiving for mistakes—like a strict professor—and at other times going easy on the errors, emulating a generous professor, to assess my probability of passing the exam.

Seven more sleepless nights and tireless days, and the exams were finally over.

The joy of coming out of the examination hall on the last day of the exam was unprecedented, irrespective of how my exam went. The very thought that I didn't have to burn the midnight oil for the next few months was absolute bliss.

I often wondered what exactly was achieved through those exams. I didn't know about learning, but one thing was for sure, it helped us prepare better for pressure and stress handling. An efficient pressure cooker yielded better results...a nicely cooked meal. So, all the pressure-cookers, efficient or inefficient, were promoted to the second semester. Pyare also managed to clear the exams, despite his *purchi* escapade.

SEMESTER TWO

CHAPTER ONE

The mornings were relaxed, and the evenings became merrier. Mischievous Sushant started what I called the Borrow Club. Every morning, holding his toothbrush, he would walk up to my room on the first floor and ask for toothpaste. Sushant never bought toothpaste.

By sharing every morning, I soon ran out of toothpaste, and the will to buy another one. Now both of us would roam about, from one room to another, from one corridor to another, from one floor to another, to borrow toothpaste.

This practice went on for days and intrigued many others who stopped buying toothpaste too, or at least they said so. Now we had more members of the Borrow Club in our wing and fewer boys who would lend us toothpaste. More borrowers and fewer lenders in one wing allowed us to expand the dealings of the Borrow Club to the other wings of the hostel. Soon, like a business with several branches, the wing-to-wing borrowing became a usual morning practice.

Another co-founder of the Borrow Club was Pyare. He was not interested in petty things like toothpaste or soaps. In fact, what he did would qualify less for borrowing and more for stealing.

He would pay visits to my room in the morning in my absence (most likely in the time when I was trying to borrow toothpaste) and take one of my ironed shirts without bothering to ask me. Sometimes I would find out only when I met him at the college wearing my shirt. And then the lamest excuses came.

"I wear your shirts to make you popular."

"Oh, popular? How does that work?"

"Look, whenever guys compliment me, saying that I look smart, I tell them that's because I am wearing your shirt!"

"So?"

"So, you become popular!"

"Not me, silly; my *shirt* becomes popular! I can do that myself! And you encourage more guys to borrow my shirts! Why would you think I want to be popular for my shirts?"

Borrow Clothes Club picked up fast, and boys borrowed almost everything except for underwear. Boys like Ranga took it to the next level by lending the clothes they had borrowed to someone else. So, Ranga would borrow my jeans, and two days later, I would see Sushant wearing them.

Now, it is time to bring a key topic to the reader's notice: the topic that occupied the boys' interest, and the catalyst of almost all the conversations, debates, and discussions. The topic of girls.

Now that there were no restrictions with visiting the college cafeteria, JAM, the bank, or the college library, the boys got to see and learn about the girls. (I won't use the word interact, especially for *Northee* boys, as that rarely happened.)

Ranga and his roommate Patil, like a dedicated information and broadcasting channel, made a top ten list of girls, the rankings of which would be updated on a weekly basis. The criterion for making it onto that list was the usual: Bold and beautiful. They called their list "the Hotness Quotient," or "HQ" for short.

Patil, like a sincere reporter in a daily newspaper, would collect stories from a wide range of sources—heard or overheard, alleged or corroborated, rumored or witnessed—the likes of who wore what, who talked to whom, who looked hot, and who took a shower and who did not (of course, the shower thing was a mere guess).

Rinki Chandra—the girl I had met during the Premium Club selection process—was famous now, especially among seniors, thanks to her boys' hostel venture with her friend Sonia.

During their first semester, while ragging was still on, Rinki and Sonia had reportedly accepted a dare from a senior boy that they would take a stroll along the main road where the boys' hostels were located. And they did.

The adventure didn't go down well with the senior boys, who perceived it as a challenge to their authority. How could the first year girls dare to visit the boys' hostel region so casually when the first year boys were still locked inside the hostel and walked to college with their heads bent?

The angry and hurt boys blocked their way, and soon Rinki and Sonia found themselves surrounded by some forty or fifty of them.

The warden was informed, and, sharing the misogynistic views of the angry boys, escorted the girls back to the ladies' hostel and warned them against such a dare, citing safety reasons.

Some applauded them for their boldness; others disparaged them for their gumption, and some called them names. Bottom-line, the girls became famous, the talk of the town.

Sushant had a crush on Rinki and made his feelings clear, well, not to Rinki, but to us, his fellow *Northees*. He stated that since he announced it first, only he could lay claim to her, so, nobody else could even befriend her, let alone flirt with her.

He would not befriend her either because that took a lot of courage. He expressed his feelings to everybody else except for her. He believed that if everyone else knew, there was no way she could remain innocent about his feelings.

Another reason for him being so vocal was to indirectly signal to other boys not to try their luck with her, and for *Northees*, he was direct in his appeal.

Sushant, aware of my interaction with Rinki at occasional Premium Club meetings, would often talk to me in reference to her, with a motive of dissuading the possibility of any attempt on my part to hit on her. "Bhai, does Rinki talk about me?"

"Never! I don't think she even knows you."

"She knows me. Reena told me."

Reena was the *Northee* girl of our batch, the only source of internal information, and the only channel of news on the girls and the girls' hostel for the *Northee* boys.

"What did Reena tell you?" I asked.

"That Rinki asked her about me."

"Like what?"

"Like, 'who is Sushant?'"

"Haha! Bhai, when a girl asks who Sushant is, that means she actually doesn't know who Sushant is."

"She knows now! Please don't talk much to Rinki in your meetings. And if she asks you, tell her that Sushant is a very handsome guy."

"Why would I tell a lie to her face?"

"You don't know! I am very good looking! Back in my school days, girls would die for my company."

"Really, Salman Khan? Where are those girls now? Are they all dead?" asked Pyare jokingly.

"Of course they're dead! Don't you see his killer looks?" added Ranga.

"Yeah, yeah... Jealous people. You'll see. You losers will be sipping that stupid *chikoo* shake and scoffing down your noodles in JAM, and I will enter with Rinki. You'll be gawking at us with your eyes and mouth wide open, and I will ignore you," said the overoptimistic daydreamer, *Sheikh Chilli* Sushant.

Another girl who ranked top in the HQ list was Sanaa Rehman.

Ranga told me that she had the best smile, but I was yet to catch a glimpse of her.

One day after attending morning lectures, I went to the bank (located in the college ground) with Ranga. This was in the time when traditional banking requiring a physical presence was the norm, and the new modes of transaction like ATMs and online banking were still to evolve.

We saw Professor PK in the bank. Ranga noticed that he was filling in the pink and blue slips simultaneously. Amused, Ranga poked me with his elbow, bringing my attention to PK's actions.

"Why would he fill both deposit and withdrawal slips?" we asked each other.

He then went to the withdrawal counter, gave the blue slip to the teller, withdrew cash, counted, added more cash from his pocket to the total, re-counted, went to the deposit counter, gave the pink slip to the teller, and deposited all the cash back in the bank. Call it checking the veracity of your passbook or loss of faith in the banking system, but withdrawing your money, counting it, and depositing back was a remarkable way to waste your time.

I had thought he made us laugh every time he spoke, but the man could even crack us up by his mere actions. In PKs case, actions spoke funnier (not louder) than words.

Then I noticed a girl with a passbook in her hand entering the bank through the narrowly opened grill gates.

As she stepped in, her straight combed, dark brown, shoulder-length, silky hair hit her face like restless water waves breaking on the calm and still shore. She had sparkling eyes like dew drops in a green meadow, and shiny red lips like a bed of roses in a sprawling garden. Glittering white pearls rested elegantly around her neck like the morning sunshine. Clad in a blue kurta, the girl was a blend of beauty, elegance, and poise.

Catching sight of my curious eyes, the girl glanced at me for one...no, for two seconds, and then proceeded to the inquiry counter.

Ranga whispered in my ear, "She is Sanaa."

CHAPTER TWO

Valentine's Day was one week away, and the Premium Club had decided to organize the event in the college. It was decided during several meetings that the Premium Club members would team up with local vendors for the arrangement of roses and cards.

Three teams were formed to manage the three-step task: One to manage the orders, a second to coordinate with the rose and card vendors, and a third to manage delivery. Pamphlets with the design and prices of the roses and cards were printed.

My team was responsible for taking the orders from the Hall One boys, writing the sender and recipient details, along with messages, collecting the cash, and handing it to the second team for the arrangement with the vendor. Room B10 on the ground floor, lent to the noble cause by the generous occupants—the boys from Nepal—was chosen as the location for the boys to place their orders and collect their deliveries.

This rosy initiative of the Premium Club triggered an instant excitement among the boys of Hall One, resulting in their frequent visits to Room B10. Boys placed orders for their special ladies, ranging from white roses, yellow roses, and red roses, to bunches of roses, bouquets, and cards. Handmade cards were also accepted.

One of the visitors was Pyare. "Yes, Pyare, what do you want?"

"I want twenty red roses."

"Twenty red roses! Wow. And who is the lucky girl?"

"Twenty roses for twenty girls, *bhai*! Here, I have made a list of them."

"Twenty girls! Are you nuts? And red roses, too? Most of these girls don't even know who you are," I said while taking a cursory glance at his list.

"So what? I know them! Besides, *bhai*, they will find out when they receive the roses."

"And Rinki too? Man...Sushant is going to kill you."

"We are not going to tell him."

"Take my suggestion: Send yellow roses to each of them as a mark of friendship."

"No, no. Once a friend, always a friend. I will send red roses, and whoever responds will be your *bhabhi*!"

"Ok…may God bless them! You need to pay 400 rupees."

"400 bucks? For what?"

"For twenty roses. Each rose costs twenty rupees."

"You guys are charging twenty rupees for a rose? All you have to do is pluck the roses from the garden!"

"Oh yeah? And where is your dad's garden? This money is supposed to be paid to a local vendor to arrange the stuff. Now find someone else to waste your precious time with. I have a lot of work to do."

"Ok then…what about getting a single rose and sending one petal each to my girls."

"*Bhai* Pyare, would you be kind enough to get lost?"

At last, Pyare settled in for three roses for the top three girls on his list and paid the money.

Sushant's excitement had surpassed the normal levels. Not only did he select a bouquet of roses and make a card for Rinki, but he also urged other *Northee* boys, including me, to not send her anything.

While Pyare, with his roses for random girls, was set to shoot cupid's arrows in the dark, and Sushant with his bouquet and card, was ready to convey his love to the girl he had never talked to, Mohit was looking to make friends with two girls in his Mechanical branch. He had planned to send them yellow roses and cards with nice messages, for which he sought my help.

I was shy and an introvert, especially when it came to girls, but my friends perceived me as an outgoing person to whom talking to girls was a cakewalk, thanks to my membership of the Premium Club and symphony band—which I was selected to join based on my singing skills—where boys and girls had an opportunity to interact.

Back home, I'd had a crush on a girl who lived in my neighborhood, but I never mustered the courage to talk to her, let alone ask her out. The best I could do was look at her and then look down as soon as she looked back at me. That was the only flirting I had done (if that even qualified as flirting at all!). I kept looking up and down for years, and she, perhaps tired of looking back at me, looked ahead and moved on.

Why confess my shyness, my inexperience with girls? Why not continue to pretend to be the cool guy that I am in the eyes of my friends? Why not help Mohit write a message, even though I have never written to anyone?

"Ok, do you want to keep it simple and formal?" I asked Mohit.

"No, no…I want to sound funny and cool," came his reply.

"Right. Let's try something casual. In fact, why don't you send a single card to both?"

"A single card? Really?"

"Why not? That's cool, man! You are not proposing or anything…are you?"

"Of course not! Ok, fine. What would you write?"

"Ok, let me think of a cool poem. Let's say… Mmm… Something like…" I evoked my imagination.

The cool poem (well, at least we thought so!) went something like this:

Dear Ria and Neeti,

Every day you come to class, I feel like watching both of you.

Every day you talk to friends, I feel like talking to both of you.

Every day you read books, I feel like reading to both of you.

Every day you write notes, I feel like writing to both of you.

Every day, day-to-day, rainy day or a sunny day.

Love me, love me just for today.

"That's it? You think they'll like it?"

"Of course! What's there not to like?" I assured Mohit.

With a few smileys drawn here and there, his handmade card was done.

Sushant enquired if I had ordered roses for anyone, and I shook my head.

Ranga, being a fantastic mind reader, was quick to suggest Sanaa, but I gave an indifferent shrug, as if that thought hadn't crossed my mind.

I had still not forgotten the glances from Sanaa the other day; that blend of unparalleled charm and unmatched panache that left my mouth dry and my heartbeat abnormal. But it would have been a bold step for a shy boy like me to send flowers to Sanaa, a girl whom I'd had the good fortune of seeing only once.

Premium Club members, the Samaritans of love and friendship, worked tirelessly all day to process and deliver every order placed by the hopefuls—the seekers of friendship and love.

The first batch of deliveries was received at Hall One late in the afternoon, and Mohit was one of the first boys to receive a parcel. It was a letter from Ria and Neeti in reply to Mohit's yellow roses and a card.

Ranga, Sushant, Pyare, Sunny, Dhanjeet, Jashan Jeet, Ganjoo, Dispensary, and I rushed to Mohit's room in sheer excitement. A letter from the ladies' hostel for a boy in our group was a big thing.

Ranga, with Mohit standing next to him, began reading the letter, and the boys were all ears: "*Dear Mohit, you are a well-mannered and suave gentleman of the Mechanical branch. That's what 'both of us' perceived about you until today. The impression that you made on both of us was a mere eyewash. It is a sad realization that you are one shallow and morally bankrupt person who has no respect for women..."*

The voice level and enthusiasm of Ranga dropped suddenly. After a pause, he started to read again, *"'Love me love me just for today'? How can you treat women as an object of desire? You should be ashamed of yourself. You are a shameful blot on the Mechanical branch. In fact, both of us feel that you are a curse on the reputation of this institute and will remain that every day, day-to-day, rainy day and sunny day."*

Ranga stopped reading and glanced at Mohit and then at me. Embarrassed, Mohit's face crimsoned with every passing moment, and so did mine. Everyone gazed at Mohit and then one another, waiting for somebody to break the ice. There was dead silence in the room.

"He is trying to make me laugh," said Pyare, pointing towards Sushant and trying to control his laughter.

"No, no...I didn't do anything!" returned Sushant, unable to control himself any longer. He burst out laughing.

Laughter, yet again, proved to be infectious. Everyone laughed while Mohit settled for an embarrassed smile.

"Love me...hahaha...love me just for today. Hahaha!"

"Blot on Mechanical branch..."

"No, no! A curse...a curse on the institute! Hahaha!"

Friends did not let you get away easily after an episode like this, and I knew they would fan and fuel it for weeks and months to come. The damage was done. A poem that was meant to be funny had made the girls furious. An attempt that was designed to impress had proved to appall them. An effort that was meant to look cool had made the girls lose it.

Being cool is nothing but being yourself. That was my takeaway from that episode. I was sure Mohit's takeaway was not to take my advice on girls anymore (or on anything, for that matter).

Another lucky boy to receive a parcel was Sushant. Again, there was the same level of excitement among all the friends, who now rushed to Sushant's room.

The parcel was from Rinki. It was a heavier one, a gift wrapped in glossy paper. Sushant unwrapped the parcel within no time, and the gift inside was unveiled. It was *brinjal* (eggplant). Yes, a purple-colored, oval-shaped, long-tailed, over-ripe *brinjal*.

"What's this? *Brinjal*? You sent her red roses, right?" asked a confused Dhanjeet.

Sushant nodded in confirmation.

"Wait, wait! There's a letter too. Ranga, please do the honors." Pyare picked up the letter and handed it to Ranga, who had become the official reader of the group.

"Dear Sushant, it would be rude on my part if I didn't send you something in return for your roses. So here it is. Cook this, add some spices, and relish it with your friends. Rinki."

Everyone except Sushant cracked up.

"So, what? She sent a return gift!" said Sushant, attempting damage control.

"Return gift! Really?" asked Sunny, holding the *brinjal* from its tail and swinging it like a pendulum.

"I know you guys are jealous!"

"Jealous? That you got *brinjal*, and we didn't get a potato, cauliflower, or a pumpkin? Haha…that's a score!" returned Dhanjeet.

"Dude, you are on the right track. Send flowers every year, and soon you will find yourself with a vegetable patch," said Pyare.

"You guys don't understand. At least she made some effort to get me a present."

"Yeah, yeah! We understand it takes a lot of effort to go to the mess kitchen and pick up the rotten *brinjal* from the garbage!"

"What next, *brinjal* boy? Rotten eggs?" said Ranga, laughing hard, rolling on the bed.

Sushant tried hard to tone down the intensity of the humiliation caused to him, but in vain. Mohit looked relieved as the attention had been taken away from him and the boy who had literally convulsed with laughter over his plight a few hours back was the prime target now.

Pyare, on the other hand, was relieved that he did not get any rotten vegetables. In fact, he did not get anything in response to his three roses for three girls, and he came up with a justification for that. Pyare concluded that no response from the girls meant an eventual yes, with a delay of six months. He explained that those girls were shy by nature and taking time to open up.

"They are seventy percent convinced now and will take their sweet time to make it a hundred percent, but eventually it will be a yes," he predicted.

"A yes from all three of them?" I asked, amused.

"Yes, but I will take it on a first-come, first-served basis! After all, I have some self-esteem too!" Pyare replied confidently.

Valentine's Day brought a lot of excitement, but the efforts of many boys did not pay off. The boys blamed it on the girls for being lame and less enthusiastic.

In the girls' defense, they were probably confused about the sudden over-enthusiastic outbursts from otherwise composed boys.

Some blamed it on the poor sex ratio in the college, which meant the boys had fewer options compared to the girls. Others said that most of the boys tried their luck with the popular girls of our batch, which were about eight or ten in number. So much attention paid to desirable girls did not bring the desired results as the multitude of options made the girls more indecisive. Many seniors who did not get noticed in their batches also turned to the girls of our batch, thereby enhancing the competition.

SEMESTER THREE

CHAPTER ONE

The second semester passed in a blink of an eye. I wondered if good times were short-lived. I knew good times and bad times shared equal proportion in a lifetime; the only difference is that we keep track of bad times as we badly want them to be over. So, a minute felt like an hour and an hour like a day. For this reason, the first semester had felt like a life sentence in prison, while the second semester was like one short vacation.

Speaking of vacation, I finally got one after an eventful year, and I visited my home. Home, as in "the house of Mommy and Dad." I vividly remembered that was the answer I had written for the definition of "home" in my second (or maybe third) Standard English language test. After all these growing-up years, the innocence of that answer did not lose its relevance, as the home was still the place where my mom and dad lived.

The third semester kicked off with a lot of excitement. The butterflies in our stomachs and the element of curiosity were killing us. We were going to have a fresh batch of newcomers in the college. The excitement was twofold, since we were promoted to the much-awaited league of a senior batch and would be getting our own *butrus*.

It felt like we were in an adoption center waiting eagerly for the custody of our long-lost grown-up kids. We would soon be referred to as "*baap*." I had not known the feeling of being a father, but this was something close to that.

Well, that would be an exaggeration. We were like a bunch of overstimulated kids, waiting eagerly for their presents, who not only cared for what they would get but also what the others were to receive. After all, our reputation was at stake.

Butrus were classified into various categories in college, like smart *butru*, dumb *butru*, *fundu butru*, et cetera. And we, the so-called *baaps*, were hoping that our *butrus* would turn out to be the smartest in the lot. The poor *butrus* were unaware that they had a huge responsibility on their shoulders to make their clan stand out.

We met the *butrus* on admission day, the day when the second year seniors took their *butrus* for lunch in the hostel, showed them around, and gave false assurance to their parents of taking good care of them. This was the day when the seniors spoke to the newcomers casually and formed an opinion about them which would decide the magnitude of torture they would be subjected to over the next six months.

However, the opinion formed by the poor *butrus* about the seniors on this very day was sure to change over the next few days.

We interacted with the juniors on admission day. My *butru*, Sujit Sanyal, was an interesting fellow.

"Do you have a girlfriend?" I asked.

"No, no, sir," Sujit touched his ear and shook his head in denial.

"What did you just do? Why are you touching your ear?" I asked.

"Sir, the girls are like my sisters."

"What? Which girl? Your sister has also joined this college?"

"No, no, sir. I mean all the girls. The female species. I see them as my sisters."

"Female species... Hmm. Joking with seniors on your very first day?" asked Jashan.

"No, no, sir...I swear. I have become a *baba*."

"*Baba*! What do you mean?"

"*Baba*, sir...a saint. I have taken an oath of celibacy. Now my eyes can either see a mother or a sister in the female species."

"Celibacy? Huh. So, you are not going to date or marry because girls are either your mothers or sisters?"

"Yes, sir."

"Since when did your baton stop glowing?" asked Pyare.

"Sir?"

"Erectile dysfunction?" Pyare mumbled.

"What, sir?"

"He said, when and why did you decide to become a *baba*?" I cut in.

"Three years ago. I fell in love with a girl, but she rejected me. I was shattered and almost failed my exams. Then one day, Lord Krishna came into my dreams and said, 'Son, I did not bring you into this world to be a slave of your desires. You must strive for knowledge. Don't waste your time looking for a date when there is so much to update. Cleanse your karma.' And that was it," said the spirited Sujit.

"Cleanse your karma!" Pyare turned to me and joked, "*Bhai*, look what you have got! Whether he does or not, you, my friend, definitely need to cleanse your karma!"

"I see, so you became celibate on the advice of Lord Krishna, who allegedly had 16,000 wives?" said Ranga to Sujit.

"So basically, you intend to avenge your rejection from the whole female species. My God! How could you subject the womankind to such a grave loss?" said Sushant with a mischievous smile.

"And what happened to that girl?" asked Ranga.

"She left the town a few months later."

"She left? You said you asked her out, right? Or did you stalk her?"

"No, no, sir. I never talked to her after she rejected my proposal."

"But she still left the town. I see now. It didn't happen later…you were already a *baba*. The girl was scared that she had pissed off a *baba* who would bring a bad omen. I guess that's why she left town."

"No, no, sir. Nothing like that. Her father got transferred," said Sujit, again shaking his head and shrugging his shoulders.

"Father, too! Did you curse him? *Bhai*, be careful with the *baba*; one curse and we will all be out of college. And they don't transfer here," joked Dhanjeet.

"Don't worry, wait another six months, and all supernatural powers of *baba* will be gone," said an amused Ranga.

The batch of newcomers occupied all the space in our conversations for the next few days. For the first time, the evergreen topic of girls took a back seat, not to take away the credit from the fresher batch girls, though, who found some mention in the discussions. But which *butrus* were smart, which were over-smart, and which ones needed to be brought to book were the key elements of our conversations.

Apparently, we, the new entries in the elite club of seniors, were preparing to pass on to our juniors a similar legacy of hostility that we had received from our seniors one year ago.

For the first few days, it was not easy to get hold of the *butrus* as they were escorted to college in a queue, the gates to Hall One were always closed, and the warden paid frequent visits, but the hunters kept looking for the prey with patience and perseverance.

One evening, Sushant, in sheer excitement, broke the news to Ranga on the phone that he and Dhanjeet had managed to get custody of five *butrus* and were taking them to the playground. Ranga quickly informed the other *Northee* fellows.

I was reluctant to join them, but Ranga insisted, "*Bhai*, c'mon, join us! We will have fun."

Soon we were at the playground. The sheepish young boys with their heads bent in third button position stood there trembling with fear in front of the roaring older boys, who were snorting arrogantly.

"Narrate your *funda* list, quick!" yelled Ganjoo at Haryana-Chemical, his voice shriller than ever.

"Look up, you idiot!" shouted Jashan at Himachal Electrical.

"Bastard! Where's your third button?" screamed Dhanjeet at Punjab-Mechanical.

SLAP!

A tight slap by Sushant caught attention momentarily amidst the yelling, and Delhi-Civil almost tripped over.

SLAP! Another one came from Jashan.

SLAP! SLAP! SLAP! Five or six slaps came in quick succession, with the *butrus* all tumbling over.

SLAP!

Call it adrenaline rush, peer pressure, or simply getting carried away, I smacked the face of Jammu-Computer. My first ever slap hit him so hard that his nose started bleeding.

A freakish feeling of witnessing red droplets oozing out of a nose right in front of my eyes came over me. The uncanny feeling of inflicting pain on someone I hardly knew. A startling mental image appeared in my head of the senior Sandhu, whom I hated, smacking my face, and then my mother's helpless countenance.

All this happened to me in a few seconds, and the next thing I remember was storming out of the playground with my friends yelling my name behind my back. I did not turn around.

Back at the hostel, I laid on my bed in the darkness of my room, for an hour or so, guilt-ridden.

BANG!

The door slammed open, breaking the silence of the dark room, and I saw Sushant and Dhanjeet standing in front of me.

"Are you alright? What are you doing here in the dark?" asked Sushant. Dhanjeet turned on the light.

"I am ok."

"Why did you run away from the ground?" asked Sushant. "We kept calling your name."

"Nothing... The bleeding nose of Jammu-Compu freaked me out. I could not stand it anymore," I replied.

"He is alright, do not worry about him. Pyare took him under the tap. The bleeding stopped quickly," said Dhanjeet.

"Ok, good. So, how was the session?" I enquired.

"Great! Dhanjeet hit four, and I hit nine... The most among everyone," replied a visibly enthusiastic Sushant.

"Great! I guess that is equal to the total score you had last year," I said, and the excitement on Sushant's face dropped, sensing my sarcasm.

Sushant had had the lowest score during our ragging period. He was one of those lucky boys in our batch who got very little smacking from the seniors. We often teased him that he hid behind other boys of the group and gave silly excuses to the seniors to escape beating.

Ironically, the same subdued boy who had kept a low profile in front of seniors back then was aggressive with juniors now and super thrilled with his ragging session.

"I know where you are going with this," said Sushant.

"What? Where?" I asked.

"You don't like ragging. But you can't stop everyone. Remember how we all were treated by our seniors? Did anyone show us pity? Remember Sandhu?"

"*Bhai*, I remember vividly. But did we ever complain to them about their hostile behavior towards us, let alone confront them? If ever you want to avenge the torture you went through, those seniors are the ones."

"But, *bhai*, this is the reality of ragging. Every batch follows it."

"Ok, first, we were tortured by those losers, and now we are following in their footsteps! Who is the bigger loser here?"

"But ragging is necessary, *bhai*. How else do you expect the guys to respect you?" interrupted Dhanjeet.

"Respect? Tell me one senior who smacked your ass who you respect. Do you respect that bastard Sandhu?"

"*Bhai*, you just don't get it! You are getting carried away. Don't be emotional," said Sushant jestingly.

"Yes, Sushant, I got a bit emotional today. I remembered the first day in the hostel when I met you in the telephone room. You were weeping helplessly while talking to your mom. I fear those juniors who got the beating today will be doing the same."

"What nonsense! There is no connection here in what you are saying," said Sushant, a bit unsettled.

"Leave it! He has got it all wrong. Let's get out of here," said Dhanjeet to Sushant, holding his arm.

I chose not to reply, and Sushant and Dhanjeet left the room, leaving the door ajar. According to them, I was not making sense, but all I could hope was that they would come to their senses soon.

Hereafter I never joined my friends in their ragging spree. Their attempts to make me a partner in crime did not see the light of success.

I wondered why they insisted I follow them. Did my support matter so much to them? I didn't think so. If you believed in what you were doing, nobody's opinion mattered. But when you had doubts about your actions, you needed support, followers, accomplices. For my *Northee* friends, more accomplices perhaps meant reassurance that whatever they did was ok and cool.

Why would any right-thinking person want to inflict pain for no reason? Why did we get swayed by emotion and become victims of the so-called mob mentality in college? For days, I struggled with the answers without luck.

CHAPTER TWO

My birthday was just around the corner, and plans were being made.

Sushant, the master planner, loved to organize every event, small or big, whether it was in the hang-out places, or group studying, or partying. His favorite, though, was planning meals. A complete foodie himself, he loved to eat, think, and dream food. At the dinner table of the hostel messroom, he would suggest the menu of the next day's lunch and the ice cream flavor later for dinner. The venue of every dream that he shared with us would be some eatery like the college canteen, cafeteria, the JAM restaurant, or the Back-Post.

Pyare often joked that ninety percent of his brain was occupied by rice, *dals*, *roti*, ice creams, sugarcane juice, *chikoo* shake, and only ten percent space was free for the rest of his thoughts.

Sushant came up with an idea to celebrate my birthday at Spring Lake.

"Spring Lake? What's that?" I asked.

"Don't know. Some countryside lake or river... Oriya folks told me that it's about four or five kilometers from college, and people organize picnics there," replied Sushant.

"So, we will have a picnic at the lake?" said Ranga.

"Yes, you can swim in the river and enjoy the sun. We will bring food and snacks. For snacks, chips, cookies, chocolates, and sandwiches—both veg and chicken—would be enough. Later in the evening, we can sit at MANDAP restaurant and have booze and chicken *tandoori*. We can also try mutton *chaamp* this time. It's very delicious," said Sushant with a spark in his eyes.

"Chicken *tandoori* and mutton *chaamp*? What about vegetarian items?" asked Pyare, amused, poking me stealthily with his elbow.

"Oh, for vegetarian we can have *paneer tikka* and *gobhi masala*. They also make good mushroom-*do-pyaza* and of course our peanut *masala*." Sushant observed the smile on everyone's face and took a pause. "I see what you guys are doing here," said Sushant, realizing that he had gotten carried away with food once again.

Everyone cracked up.

"Yes, yes, peanut *masala*, and what else?" asked Pyare.

"No, I am not talking food anymore," said Sushant.

"I am sure he did not spend much time on Spring Lake and the activities there. All he planned is his lunch, snack time, and dinner," said Pyare.

"Strange he did not include breakfast in his all-day feast plan. Talk about birthdays or any other event, and our buddy comes up with his menu card for the day," cracked up Ranga, and the bantering went on.

Sunday arrived, and so did my birthday. My day started with a wake-up phone call from Dad and Mommy, and the wishes kept pouring in after. I wore my new red shirt, which I had managed to keep away from the eagle eyes of Pyare and Sushant till now. I was aware that once my shirt came into the public eye, I would be deprived of the rare joy of wearing my own brand-new shirt in college.

Around one o'clock, we were all geared up for our Spring Lake outing. Our group of thirteen boys hired two auto-rickshaws from the rickshaw stand near the college gate. Seven of us occupied the first auto, and the other six took the second one.

Yes, I know, ideally, a rickshaw was meant for three passengers, but that's not how it worked in the real world, the world of college. Six or seven boys in an auto were no big deal as one boy could take the front seat alongside the driver, four could occupy the back seat, and the remaining ones could be adjusted on their laps. Even the auto drivers would not object to that number.

However, the challenge would be accommodating ten boys where two took the front seat at both sides of the driver, four took the back seats, two sat on the laps of those four, another one lay over the lap of those two, and the remaining two stood firm-footed with their heads hanging out of the auto.

Boys managed such arrangements at times, despite the objection of the auto-drivers. Believe me, the only people standing in the way of boys' claim to the coveted *Guinness Book of World Records* were those auto drivers.

A useful tip for the ones taking the front seat of an old lever-start auto: Let the driver start the ignition first. If you are already sitting and then open your legs apart to let him jerk up the auto-rickshaw lever to start the ignition, may God save your balls.

Ranga, Sushant, Brigadier, Dispensary, Bholu, Faizal, and I hopped in one auto. Sushant was a bit reluctant to join us as the eatables were loaded in the other auto, and parting with food for the next ten or fifteen minutes was almost cruel in his case. On Ranga's insistence and to avoid food jokes, Sushant decided to board our auto.

The driver was looking for a specific address, but all we knew was Spring Lake, which, according to him, was a large river across the other side of Koel Town. We told him to drop us someplace near the river, and he did and left.

The place was a bare strip of land with the river at one side and a bunch of old, dilapidated houses on the other side. The river was big and appeared to be deep. The place certainly did not look like a picnic spot.

Bholu turned to Sushant, "*Bhai*, where's the picnic spot?"

"This place does not even qualify for a spot, forget picnic spot," said Dispensary.

"And where's the other auto? They were supposed to follow us. Did the driver take them to the other side of town?" Faizal wondered.

"Let's ask those guys. They look like the locals... They must have some idea about the place." Sushant pointed at a group of five men chatting in a corner beside an old auto-rickshaw and two motorbikes. They were the only men we could spot in that area.

"Hello, we are wondering if there is a picnic area around here?" asked Bholu.

"Picnic area? What do you mean?" one of the men in the group enquired.

"Well, is there an area around here where people come and have picnics, eat snacks?" Sushant tried to explain.

"This is a village, have you come—"

"Where have you come from?" another man interrupted before the first one could finish. The man's eyes were red, as if he was heavily stoned.

"NCE. We study there," replied Sushant.

The man's eyes widened, and his face distorted with anger. It looked like Sushant's NCE mention had not gone down well with him.

"NCE? That college! Oh! You nerds thought that you could come to the village and fool around? You guys read those big, thick books, but all your brains have is chaff!" uttered the angry stoned man.

"Hey, watch it, bugger! What did you just say?" Sushant raised his voice, visibly taken aback by the man's sudden snap.

"Cattle fodder! Your brains are full of cattle fodder!" the aggressive stoned man yelled back.

"Shut the f@#k up, you crazy idiot!" Bholu pushed the man towards the auto-rickshaw with his chest, almost stifling him.

Bholu was a big and broad guy. We had known him as a boy who was frustrated with himself, who always cribbed and complained and held his fate responsible for every wrong thing. His strong reaction was unexpected and took all of us by surprise.

BAM!

Just as I grabbed hold of Bholu's arm in an attempt to avoid an altercation and stop him from jostling with the stoned guy, another man landed a punch straight at Bholu's face. It turned out they were not simple villagers, but a bunch of goons. Before this man could strike again, Ranga pulled him back by the collar of his shirt, and *BOOM!* Sushant pounded on him. The yelling and pushing had now turned into a violent scuffle, and it was too late to stop.

I turned around and caught hold of the leg of another guy who was trying to kick me from behind and toppled him over onto the ground.

DHOOM! BAM! BOOM!

Brigadier, Faizal, and Dispensary also pitched in, and what could have been termed a simple inquiry had now turned into an ugly brawl.

Just when we thought we had overpowered those hooligans, I noticed a brick flying through the air out at high speed. It missed Brigadier's head by a few inches.

I turned around to see where the brick had come from and found three men yelling and rushing towards us, two of them holding long sticks and the third one grabbing a brick. I wondered where these men had emerged from. They had probably heard the shouting and come from the nearby houses or village streets to help their fellow goons.

Before anyone of us could figure out what was happening, the man hurled the brick, this time aiming at Faizal. Quick to judge the approaching brick, Faizal bent over backward, barely managing to dodge the brick, and then ran away exasperatedly.

Bewildered by the sudden ferocious attack by the approaching armed men, Ranga, Sushant, Brigadier, and Dispensary shoved and pushed away from the men with whom they were engaged in the scuffle and hastily ran in the direction of Faizal with all their strength.

Perplexed by the turn of events, I lost all the will and courage to fight. Dumbfounded, I could only spot Bholu, who was still busy grappling the stoned man, unaware of the fact that his buddies were running away from the violent attack by men armed with sticks and bricks. I tried to flee by shoving the man fighting me, whose morale had suddenly skyrocketed upon realizing that his accomplices had outnumbered us.

There were four possible routes to escape the madness. First, to jump in the river in the hope of crossing it on foot.

Second, to run towards those shabby houses, the lion's den from where those men armed with sticks had most likely emerged, and where more wrathful men could possibly be found.

Third, run to catch up with my friends, who were being chased by five or six furious men, who looked like raging bulls.

Fourth, to run in the opposite direction, to the concrete road that our auto-rickshaw had taken after dropping us in this so-called picnic spot. That perhaps would have been the safest choice, but it meant being without my friends.

I had no time to evaluate my options. I simply followed my instinct and ran towards the river. As I got closer, I realized my mistake, as it was not shallow enough to wade through, and I could not swim. I was desperate to escape but certainly not foolish enough to drown myself. I quickly changed my mind and ran to join my friends.

"Run, Bholu, run!" I shouted as I ran, trying to get Bholu's attention. He was still fighting, this time with two men, including the stoned guy, and appeared to still be clueless about the situation.

I was not sure if I had succeeded in gaining Bholu's attention or breaking his concentration, for I did not bother to look back.

My hope of uniting with my friends was short-lived. It turned out those hooligans had cut short the chase they gave to my friends and returned, only to find me on their way back. I desperately tried to dodge them, but, alas, it was too late.

The angry, belligerent men pounced on me. One man pulled my hair, almost tearing off a piece of my scalp. The other one punched my face with such force that I felt a cracking pain in my jaw. The third man smacked my shin with the long stick, shuddering me from head to toe.

And the fourth and fifth men! Well, I completely lost track of which body parts they targeted. I had the drubbing of my life. The beating of the bamboo stick left me groaning in excruciating pain. Never in my life had I been clobbered so badly.

I could not remotely relate this to the IG session during the ragging period when a bunch of seniors had thrashed me. There, at least, there were some rules. For instance, if you bled or bruised, they would give you water and money for a bandage. And they served refreshments for the session. But here! It was a wild and freestyle beating.

The irony of my life? It was my birthday. And they were certainly not the birthday bumps I expected, even in my wildest nightmares.

I made a desperate attempt to shove the beasts off my body and run, but they besieged me again within a few meters. One angry man lifted a heavy rock. Petrified, my heart skipped a beat.

How did it feel to be surrounded by five ruthless beasts, with one of them just about two steps away, aiming a big rock straight at your forehead? That moment sent shivers down my spine.

The man with blood-red eyes and a spiteful, distorted face was ready to crack my head open, and his accomplices had encircled me to ensure no escape. It felt like standing at the doorstep of inevitable death in front of *Yamraj* (the Lord of Death), ready to pull me in.

"No! Not the rock! Please!" I literally begged for mercy, folding my hands to spare the precious gift, my most valuable possession...my life.

Then something happened. The man who had aimed the rock at me with a sense of certitude to finish me off dropped the rock on the ground.

Call it a better sense that prevailed or something else, I don't know, and I didn't care either. That very moment I pushed away one of the men and sprinted off with all my might.

The next fifteen seconds were the biggest race of my life, the one that could have even qualified me for the coveted *Guinness Book of World Records*. No one could have run faster, be it Carl Lewis, Usain Bolt, or our very own Milkha Singh. Only a man who visualized a horrifying death could have come anywhere close to me.

I took the concrete road, the fourth route, inadvertently. I had no idea if they had followed me, for I did not look back, but I was positive that nobody could have caught me this time.

I ran and ran and did not stop until I had run out of breath. I found myself in a busy marketplace and turned back to ensure that nobody was following me anymore.

I felt that almost everybody who passed by glanced or took notice of me. Well, not to blame them. With a worn-out unbuttoned red shirt, spoilt jeans, messy hair, a black eye, a blue face, and crimson red ears, I certainly did not look like a dapper young boy.

I started to walk carefully. I had no idea where my friends were and did not have the energy to look for them either. Hurrying back to the college was the only thing on my mind. It was the only safe place, but I didn't know the way.

I saw a man walk out of a nearby shop with a bundle of clothes in his hand. He walked over to a motorbike, kick-starting it. I went up to him and asked, "Hello, do you know where NCE College is?"

"Yes, I know."

"Would you be able to drop me there, please?"

The man took a brief look at me, top to bottom, and said, "Yes, sure! Get on."

"Let me take these!" I took his bundle of clothes and hopped on the bike, a little relieved.

"So, you study at NCE?" he asked as I made myself comfortable on the backseat.

"I do," I replied with a pause. He seemed to me to be a gentleman.

"I have a friend whose daughter studies at NCE too," he said.

"Ah, ok, that's good," I replied. I had no will to engage in a conversation and replied only out of politeness. I realized that the man was going in the same direction from where I had sprinted off, which made me suspicious of him.

"I think this is not the right way to the college," I said, a bit jittery.

"Yes, I know. Let me drop this bundle at a shop, and then I will take you to the college," he replied.

"No, that's ok. You can drop me here. I will find an auto-rickshaw to take me to the college," I insisted.

"No need for a rickshaw. Can you see that shop around the corner? I will deposit the bundle there. It will take only two minutes, don't worry."

The man parked his bike in front of the shop and went inside with the bundle of clothes. I stood there in a bit of a dilemma about whether to wait for him or take off. Though the man looked gentle, and I had no reason not to trust him, I was in that mental state of apprehension, imagining that everybody around was conspiring against me.

"Aahan! Aahan!" someone called my name.

I turned around to see my friends Dispensary and Faizal approaching me. I felt a huge relief.

"Hey, you guys, you're still here! I thought you guys took off! Where are the other guys? What happened? Is everybody all right?" overwhelmed, I asked many questions without waiting for an answer.

"Are *you* alright?" asked Faizal.

"Yes! Where are the other guys?"

"They are coming too. We were looking for you. Those guys said you ran away."

"Those guys? Who?"

Before they could answer, we were interrupted by another voice.

"Hello! Are you coming?"

I turned around to see the gentleman who had come out of the shop and was now waiting for me on his motorbike.

"Hi! I found my friends. You carry on, please. And thanks a lot."

"Ok, fine, no problem!" said the gentleman, and he rode off.

The next moment I saw Ranga, Sushant, Bholu, and Brigadier approaching.

"Hey, guys! I thought you all left! Bholu, are you alright?" My face lightened up as I spoke.

"Yes...kind of," replied Bholu, looking exhausted.

"We've been looking for you! He said that you ran this way," said Sushant.

"Who?"

"Headman."

"Headman? Who do you mean?" I asked.

"The head of the village. The kind of *sarpanch*. He said you took off, but we thought they had captured you," replied Ranga.

"I told him that it's your birthday and asked them to release you," Sushant chimed in.

"I don't understand a thing. Tell me clearly what happened."

"Ok, ok, I will explain everything, but let's call the seniors first," said Ranga.

"Seniors? For what?"

"We need to ask the seniors what to do. We can't let those goons get away so easily," said Bholu.

"But those goons won't wait for us to return."

"Yes, but then the seniors will say that we got thrashed and came back. They will mock us for doing nothing. Let's talk to them," replied Sushant.

"Ok, but who do we call? Samar? Ravinder?"

Ranga called Samar from a nearby PCO in a shop. He explained the whole situation while we waited eagerly.

"Yes, sir... Initially, we beat them, but then three or four more men came with sticks... Yes, not only sticks. Then they started throwing bricks... Yes... Yes, Aahan and Bholu... No, not that bad, hospitalization is not required... Yes, all of us... Right now? I don't know, some shop. Hey, Sushant, what's the name of this shop? Can you read the board?"

"No, no, please... Please don't give my shop address," protested the owner of the shop before Sushant could reply. "I don't know what you boys are up to. I don't want any harm to come to my shop." Apparently, the man had overheard Ranga's telephone conversation and had got worried.

"What happened? I am just giving him the address."

"Tell them this is Koel Town. Please don't name my shop," appealed the shop owner.

"Ok, ok, relax!" said Ranga, and continued on the phone. "Sir, we are in Koel Town right now! What do we do now?"

There was a long pause.

"What's happening?" I enquired to Ranga, who was still holding the receiver.

"Wait, wait. He is talking to somebody," Ranga whispered to me.

"Yes, sir... Ok, ok... No, we are coming... Bye." Ranga put the receiver down, and we—including the shop owner—were all ears.

"What did he say?" asked Bholu.

"He says to come straight to college, and not to talk to anybody. *Bhai*, how much is it?" Ranga asked the shop owner.

"That's all right, no need to pay. But please don't mention my shop to your friends. I don't want any hassle," the shop owner pleaded.

We walked back to the college. On the way, Ranga explained that when the attack from the men with sticks got fierce, they ran away initially but returned soon to look for Bholu and me. They spotted some twenty or twenty-five men, many of them holding sticks. Two men held Bholu in captivity. An elderly man, probably in his early fifties, who looked like their representative, stood about two steps ahead of the others.

Ranga continued, "The headman shouted, 'Hey! Your friend is in our custody, and there is no way for you to escape. Come here. We will not harm you. We want to talk.' Then Sushant said that we would not come close unless all the men dropped their sticks. The headman directed the men to put their sticks down, and everyone followed. And we went up to them."

"Then?" I asked.

Ranga continued, "Then the headman asked, 'Why did you come here?' I told him that we came to celebrate our friend's birthday as our classmates had advised us that Spring Lake was a nice picnic spot, and when we enquired with the men, they had started abusing us."

"And then that stoned guy said, 'No, no! We did not abuse, they did it first, and we taught them a lesson. These kids don't know us.' He was very aggressive," said Sushant.

"Yes," continued Ranga, "but then the headman raised his voice. He said, 'Ok, enough! Drop it now! I don't want any arguments.' And then one man brought a piece of paper and handed it to the headman. He gave it to me and said, 'Write a statement that a compromise has been reached and the case closed. Also, mention that you or any of your college friends won't engage in an altercation with the village people hereafter. If you write that, along with your signature, I will let all of you leave unharmed.'"

"And did you write all that?" I asked.

"Yes, I did. There was no other option to get you and Bholu released, and we were scared. We worried for you as you were nowhere to be seen, and we thought that they had captured you and taken you somewhere else."

"But you know what, Ranga? You probably could have written some fake name in the statement," Faizal pointed out.

"*Bhai*, you are right! But I was caught off guard, and my mind was not working. I put my real name."

"Ok, then what happened?" I asked.

"Then the headman slipped the paper into his pocket, and they released Bholu. We asked your whereabouts, and they told us that you ran away. We were apprehensive, but the headman reassured us. He said, 'Your friend ran in that direction. Follow this path, and you should find him.'

And we followed."

"And he gave us a warning," said Bholu.

"What warning?"

"He said, 'Don't you guys dare come back, or else I will show this paper to your director.'"

"Bullshit! Who does he think he is? Justice Chowdhury carrying some judicial paper? First these goons thrash us and then they intimidate us with that shitty piece of paper?" I was appalled.

By the time we arrived at the college, I was weak and exhausted. The excruciating body pain caused by the merciless battering and breathless galloping that had been forgotten in the heat of the moment was now unbearable. My scalp ached from the hair pulling, and my back and shins hurt badly due to the stick beating. My right hand was swollen, and my fingers moved with great difficulty.

While my friends got busy describing the whole incident to the curious seniors who met us on the way back to the hostel, I went into my room with low spirit and energy, reluctant to talk to anyone. Tired, I lay in bed and closed my eyes.

Dhanjeet came in a few minutes later. "Hey, are you alright?"

"Not really. My body is aching badly. It looks like I have a fever, too. Where were you? You guys were nowhere to be seen," I said.

"Don't know; I think that rickshaw man took us to the other side of the lake. We waited about half an hour for you guys and then turned back," replied Dhanjeet.

"What's happening outside?"

"Boys are going mad. Samar was saying, 'There is a fear of NCE boys among local people. If we don't react today, anyone could beat our boys tomorrow! We will not let that happen!'"

Dhanjeet left, but the boys kept paying brief visits and updating me. Pyare painted quite a picture of the delirium that was unfolding outside. "People are going crazy outside. There are about 150 boys from second and third year gathered outside Hall Three. That Sodhi was saying, 'Burn the city, set all the buses on fire! Somebody bring me the kerosene! Get me a matchbox!' and another guy flashed his cigarette lighter and said, 'How about this?'"

"Really?"

"Yes, you know that funny boy Sinha? He immediately took out a cigarette and asked, 'Can I have a light please?'"

"He's funny!" I said, laughing.

"And that Bunnu, who has a sexy girlfriend, was saying, 'We have the full support of the ladies hall.'"

"The girls' support? How are girls supporting them?"

"Don't know, as per Bunnu, the girls said 'We are with you, go and take revenge,'" replied Pyare.

"Oh, I see. He meant moral support."

The news had spread like wildfire, much faster than expected. Even the girls in the ladies' hostel were made aware of the incident, thanks to the handful of boyfriends—that rare breed—who kept their girls updated with trending topics, even before Twitter came into existence.

They were like those warrior kings of the fifteenth century who received moral support from their queens when heading for war. The only difference, though, was that the girls did not anoint their foreheads with sandalwood paste, nor did they hand them sparkling, razor-sharp swords. They sent them off through telephone calls.

There was anger and outrage towards this incident as the pride and honor of one thousand boys was riven asunder. Emotions were running high and patience running short; everyone was eager to avenge the humiliation caused.

The hostel was almost empty a few minutes later. I met Brigadier in the corridor, who was passing by while carrying a chain with a lock tied to it.

"Hey, what's up? What's this?" I asked.

"Yes, a chain and lock! The boys are going to the Spring Lake area. They said to bring locks, chains, curtain rods...whatever you find in the hostel. I got this from my luggage trunk," replied Brigadier.

"How many boys are going?"

"Should be about two hundred, second year and third year together."

"Two hundred boys going together? Don't you think the police will catch you midway?"

"No, no, boys have split into small groups. They will join together once in the town."

"Ok, stay safe! Don't get carried away," I warned.

"Don't worry! You rest," said Brigadier, before walking out.

I knew that no right-thinking person would approve of this mode of revenge taking, but what the hell! The whole college was standing up for me, and it felt good. Even if I did not agree, there was nothing I could do, as stopping an angry college mob was beyond my control. But I was worried and hoped things would not blow out of proportion.

CHAPTER THREE

I lay in my bed thinking what those two hundred angry boys were doing.

My scalp hurt badly from the hair-pulling. Dad had always encouraged me to keep short hair. In his words, 'You should keep the *fauji* cut,'—the haircut of army men.

I would disagree and point out the benefits of long hair, which could be styled, suited my face shape, protected my head from cold in winter, et cetera. Short hair only had shortcomings, in my view, rather than any benefits. One benefit that I had not realized until now was that short hair could easily escape the clutches of raw, unforgiving hands.

Speaking of hair pulling, Dad had a similar experience when he was a young boy. Back then, my grandfather, who wanted to set up an apple orchard, had bought a piece of farmland in the countryside hills of the state of Himachal. An unknown family inhabiting the area did not go down well with nearby residents—the disagreeable farmers who perceived it to be an intrusion in their territory.

While our under-construction house was located at the top of the hill, there was a small shed in the middle of the farmland. One afternoon when Dad was alone in that shed listening to the radio (the only electronic possession of the family), six or seven men barged in. They beat him, pounded him with their fists, dragged him, and pulled his long, puffy hair.

Fortunately, a gentle lady who had witnessed the madness sent for my grandfather, who was in the under-construction house. He, along with my granny, their other three sons, their daughter, and the dog, rushed to the spot, and those men soon found themselves at the receiving end.

I wondered if that was the reason why my dad always vouched for short hair. Did this suffering of hair-pulling run in the family? Did it mean that my words of wisdom to my future child should also be haircut advice?

My chain of thoughts was soon blurred, as I dozed off.

KNOCK! KNOCK!

"Aahan! Aahan!"

Have you ever had that feeling when you wake up suddenly in a dark room, confused, wondering if it is early morning or late evening? You ask yourself, Who are you? Where are you?

"Who is it?" I asked while struggling to reach out to the light switch, unable to see it in the dark.

"It's me, Patel, the warden. Open the door."

Hearing the warden's name brought me back to my senses quicker and activated my night vision a bit faster than usual. I fumbled about in the dark and opened the door, finding a lean figure with a trademark pair of big spectacles. It was indeed the warden.

"Are you Aahan?" Warden Patel asked in a stern voice.

"Yes, sir."

He slipped his fingers into my hair, gently maneuvering it like an expert barber trying to examine the length.

"What happened, sir? Is everything all right?" I asked.

"So, you were in your room?" he enquired, without answering my question.

"Yes, I was sleeping."

"Ok, stay in your room. Do not go anywhere. Understand?"

"Y—Yes, sir."

The warden left me standing there, confused. It was 7 p.m., and I had slept for two hours. It was drizzling outside, and there was no light in the hostel thanks to the daily power cuts by the local hydro-electric department. I could relate the unannounced visit of the warden to the afternoon's incident, but the way he had enquired about it was strange.

The hostel that had been almost empty two hours ago had suddenly come back to life. I wondered what had happened while I was sleeping.

I met Dispensary in the corridor. "Hey, what's up? What is the warden doing here?" I asked.

"He got the news of the fight. There are three more professors sitting in the warden's room."

"Really? The warden just came here to see me. I don't know why, but he was playing with my hair!"

"Must be checking for dry hair to make sure you were in the hostel. It's raining outside. They have closed the main gate and are stopping every boy who is coming from outside."

Dhanjeet and Pyare joined us.

"Hey! Any news? What's going on?" I asked.

"Warden asked for Ranga and Sushant. I saw them in the warden's room. There are professors in the room, too."

"I don't get it. Who informed them? Tell me the whole story!"

Dhanjeet was about to speak when we saw Ranga and Sushant approaching, crimson-faced from the professors' grilling.

"Hey! What did they say?" asked Pyare.

"*Bhai*, they blasted us! They wanted to know how the fight got started. They know the names of all seven of us," replied Ranga.

"Really? Did you tell them?"

"They called Bholu first. You know Professor PK is also there in the warden's room? He asked Bholu, '*Whhhatt* was the purpose of you fighting the *vhillage* people?' And Bholu said, 'Sir, I don't know anything, I was sleeping in my room.' And you know what PK said? 'So *whhen* they were breaking your nose, you were sleeping? You idiot boy trying to throw powder in our eyes?'" repeated an amused Ranga.

"To this, Warden Patel prompted PK, 'Sir, dust! Dust!'" Sushant chipped in, chuckling.

"And PK said, 'Yes, sir, he is throwing dust powder in our eyes!' And Patel gave up, shaking his head in frustration," said Ranga.

"PK also yelled at Bholu, saying, 'Go back to your sleep, you sleeper!' And then they called for me and Ranga," added Sushant.

"I knew it was futile to lie in front of them. So, we told them the whole story. Sushant told them that those local people abused us first. Patel asked, 'What did they say?'"

"Yes, yes. I told them, 'Sir, M@#$%R F@#$%^R!' and PK asked again 'What...what?' And again, Patel prompted him, 'M@#$%R F@#$%R, sir! M@#$%R F@#$%R!'"

"How did they take it?" I asked.

"They calmed down after we narrated the whole event. In fact, they were even amused! Patel said, 'Everything else is ok, but you should not have written your real name in that headman's letter!' I told him I was nervous."

"Did they inquire about the second time?" asked Dhanjeet.

"No, they didn't ask us, but—"

"I need to know now! What happened the second time?" I asked, interrupting Ranga. My curiosity was at its peak.

Ranga described the sequence of events that had unfolded while I was sleeping in my room.

Apparently, those two hundred boys who had left in small groups gathered in the Koel Town area and rampaged through the town and the Spring Lake area. They vandalized shops, smashed glass panes, broke headlights of the cars, damaged streetlights, and pelted stones at the houses. They abused, threatened, terrorized, and assaulted the local commuters and bystanders.

Those maniacs who had assaulted us at noon were nowhere to be found, and expectedly so. Why would they wait for a mad mob to turn up?

Samar, Pyare, Ravinder, and Sunny stood out amongst others in vandalism as they found a vent to their anger by damaging public property.

The college head boy Naidu—a third year—like an accomplished event manager, supervised the event of fury and destruction. Naidu, upon realizing that emotions were running high and boys were angry and unstoppable, took charge of executing a modest destruction event. He let the boys vent out anger on public property but tried to make sure (well, as much as he could) that they did not go overboard and assault common people. He kept everyone together in one group, and tried to keep the event short, fearing the arrival of local police.

Soon, he guided everyone back to the college. Then he informed the college authorities before they could find out on their own.

That explained the warden's and professors' visit to the hostel.

"The warden is stopping boys at the main gate who came from outside," said Ranga.

"Yeah, Patel caught Kamra at the main gate," continued Pyare. "Don't know from where he was coming, and he had no idea of the whole incident. Patel said, 'Welcome back, you rioter! How many windowpanes did you break?' Kamra had no clue what he was talking about. He said, 'Sir, I am coming from my guitar classes.' Do you know what Patel said? '*Achha*, Brian Adams? Where is your guitar? In your pocket? Did you break someone's head with it or choke them with its strings? Go and stand in that corner.'"

Kamra was one of those detached souls who never kept track of college affairs and lived in solitude. He could be spotted at the darkest hours in the secluded places on campus, wandering with his one and only soulmate, the guitar. Like his eternal love, he could never part with his guitar, the reason behind his low attendance to lectures. Boys regarded that guitar as his girlfriend, as a living member of the Kamra family.

In his room, Kamra would play his guitar, pull its strings, and tune it repeatedly, so much so that boys worried about the health—not Kamra's, but the poor, helpless guitar's.

Pyare and Sushant often bantered with Kamra, enquiring about his guitar's wellbeing. Pyare would joke, "Kamra, how's your guitar doing? I heard it was crying badly last night. Did it sleep well?"

It was funny for boys to see the aloof and reticent Kamra getting pulled up by Warden Patel for no fault of his own.

The professors left after finishing their prima facie investigation.

Rumors were rife that the villagers were planning a retaliation. Jashan, as usual, added fuel to the fire, proclaiming, "Village people have gathered in large numbers and at midnight they will storm into the college and attack us with weapons like bows, arrows, and spears."

Fortunately, that did not happen.

I was a popular boy the next morning, though not the kind of popularity I would have dreamt of. The local newspaper headlines read, "*Goons Celebrate Birthday, Vandalize Town.*" Another one read, "*Birthday Boy and His Drunk Friends Storm the City.*"

The stories in these newspapers were as misleading as the headlines, containing a biased and factually incorrect version, the version most likely gathered from the incensed villagers, conveniently ignoring the other side of the story.

It read: *The birthday boy and his friends who were intoxicated under the influence of alcohol, purposely engaged in a scuffle with innocent men, molested girls, abused and attacked locals, and damaged public property. Later, an angry mob of two hundred college students, led by the birthday boy, went on a rampage and vandalized the village and market area.*

Unable to bear the mental trauma that had stifled me since the previous evening, I visited the college in the hope of attending lectures to take my mind off the constant worry, but all in vain.

It turned out that the incident was the talk of the town, and so was the birthday boy and his involvement, like a protagonist in a drama. I noticed the curiosity, pity, hesitation, and sympathy in the eyes that fixated on me wherever I went.

I could not blame them as the news had spread like wildfire, and if a few ignorant people—the likes of Kamra—were still oblivious to it, my fragile countenance and swollen bandaged hand clearly distinguished me from the healthy and non-swollen features of other humans.

On my way back to the hostel, I overheard conversations in the college cafeteria, the hostel canteen, and at the Back-Post, where people speculated, conjectured, suspected, and predicted the fate of the birthday boy and his accomplices. And it was not always unintentional overhearing; some boys enunciated for the benefit of my hearing. My heart was palpitating, and nerves were getting better of me.

Someone said, "Those seven boys will not be spared. They might be suspended for a few months!"

"Are you kidding me? The authorities are strict; they may be rusticated from the college!" another one proclaimed.

"I think they might get arrested soon. Don't you see those police vans around campus? The police must be looking for them. The birthday boy is already in the news," uttered another boy.

Back in the hostel, I found an envelope under my door. The letter read:

----------------------- NOTICE -------------------------

Issued on 2nd September,

Aahan,
Following the Spring Lake event, please note that you are required to
attend the investigation committee headed by Professor Bhaskarudu.
Please be on time. The details of the place and time are given below.

Place: Room B1, Department of Chemical Eng.
Date: Tuesday, 3rd September
Time: 11 a.m.

Panic-stricken and holding the letter in my hand, I rushed to my friends
to check if they had received a notice too. I found everybody in Ranga's
room with their respective copies. It was sad to be in a sinking boat but I
was relieved to find out that I was not the only one.

Ranga pointed at Bholu's notice, "Hey, how come it is 'face the
committee' for you when it is 'attend the committee' for everyone else?"

Apparently, in Bholu's copy, the word 'face' was handwritten just
above the word 'attend'. It seems the word 'attend' was not legible due to
ink spread, thanks to the bad printing.

"What? Show me!" Bholu looked at the other copies.

"Looks like they replaced 'attend' with 'face' for you," said Ranga,
amused.

"I don't know. I should also be given a chance to attend the committee.
Why should I face the committee? What have I done to deserve this?"
replied Bholu with pensive sadness.

Bholu was soon overwhelmed with melancholy and despondency. The
mere mention of something as trivial as an inadvertently replaced word
was enough to make him nervous.

"Strange! I think they first printed 'attend' but then changed it to 'face'.
Are you their prime target?" Sushant asked Bholu, winking at me. Sushant
never missed any chance to catalyze on Bholu's anxiety.

"I don't know why it happens to me. Every time, I get singled out. I
was as much a part as you guys were!" claimed Bholu.

"I heard senior boys talking outside. They said we will be suspended."
I could have avoided bringing up that conversation at that moment, but I
was tempted by Bholu's reaction.

"It will be only me, not you guys. You guys are only *attending* the
committee. It's me who is supposed to face the anger!"

"But Bholu, all of us need to go to the committee," said Ranga.

"What do you guys have to worry about? You will attend the committee just like you attend a seminar. Then you will come back to the hostel and watch me pack my bag!" Bholu stormed out.

The room burst into laughter.

CHAPTER FOUR

We revisited the sequence of events in our discussion together so that all of us could stick to a common story in front of the inquiry committee.

Dispensary, who was nervous to bear the pressure of the anticipated grilling at the committee, proposed, "Listen, I can't remember that many details. I will simply say, 'Sir, I got scared when those guys attacked us! I ran away and hid behind the bushes. I don't know anything else!'"

"You don't even have to say that much! Just by looking at you, they will guess that you were the first one to run away!" joked Sushant.

"Yes. In fact, tell them that you climbed a banana tree, hid behind the banana leaves, and spent all night there. They will believe you," chuckled Ranga.

"Don't worry! I don't think they will even notice you," said Ranga, "You have been invited for a guest appearance. In fact, they should have put it in your notice, 'Please feel free to attend the committee in case you are interested.'"

The next day, a 10:45 a.m., the seven of us—Ranga, Sushant, Dispensary, Faizal, Bholu, Brigadier, and I—waited in the lobby outside the Room B1 of the Chemical Engineering department.

The plan involved a display of sad and dejected countenance laced with a shabby and dull appearance. Not much preparation was needed for the sad expression, though, as we had already been stressed and exhausted for the last three days.

However, we put some thought into our clothing. My outfit for the occasion was a plain off-white shirt that I did not tuck in, a pair of dull grey pants that I had not worn before, and a pair of old rugged shoes that had never matched with any of my pants.

We were nervous and spoke very little to each other, but Bholu's restlessness was vivid. He had taken his "facing" the committee as opposed to "attending" very seriously, and that made him jittery and fidgety. He walked back and forth with his grim expression and the usual shaking of the head, as if the last ship on planet earth had sailed without him.

Dispensary, on the other hand, had kept silent since that morning, and there was little hope for him to speak up in front of the professors either.

At 11:05 a.m., we saw Professor Bhaskarudu, Prof Narayan, and Warden Patel approaching. We greeted them with a respectful nod of the head.

Bholu's bow was distinct as it was not merely the head, but the upper body also bent forward. Given the condition of Bholu, it would have been no surprise had he kneeled and attempted a kowtow.

"Wait here! We will call you boys one by one," said Professor Bhaskarudu while Warden Patel took a large key chain with a bunch of keys out of his pocket and inserted them one by one randomly in the big, rusty iron lock. He successfully opened the door with the third key, and the professors went in, leaving us waiting nervously outside.

A few minutes later, Warden Patel came to the doorstep and pointed to me with his finger, "Aahan, come!"

I quickly followed his orders and entered the room. It was a small room with shelves against the walls where books were arranged neatly. There was a round table with four chairs, three of them occupied by the professors.

I greeted them again, and Professor Narayan signaled me to take a seat with a gesture of his hand. I quickly grabbed the chair.

Professor Bhaskarudu slid his big glasses to the tip of his nose and looked briefly at me over the top of his glasses, and then slid them back up. His eyes looked big and scary in those thick glasses, as if ready to bulge out at any minute. He then looked at the piece of paper lying on the table, which had our names typed in bold letters, mine at the top.

"Hmm… So you are the birthday boy. Couldn't you find a better location to celebrate your birthday?" asked Bhaskarudu with a sarcastic smile.

I continued to portray the sad figure.

He wrote *birthday boy* on the paper next to my name and then looked at his colleagues with a smile. The professors also acknowledged him with a smile, perhaps a gesture that the inquiry had kicked off in style.

Professor Narayan instructed me to narrate the incident in detail, and I did, deliberately keeping the tone of my voice soft and tired.

As I narrated the story, Bhaskarudu kept scribbling on the paper, taking notes now and then. He summed up the incident in a few lines, something like: *Birthday boy's birthday celebration… The group of seven went in an auto-rickshaw… Fight at Spring Lake with locals… Friends ran away…*

Birthday boy was beaten up and ran… All came back to college.

As he wrote on the paper, I felt like those quivering eyeballs behind the vintage glasses could drop on the table at any point, like two glass marbles.

For every line he wrote, Prof Bhaskarudu kept beaming with pride and his fellow professors nodded in acknowledgment. Though the incident was no longer a mystery in the college, it seemed that our Sherlock Holmes and his entourage thought they had managed to discover unknown facts about the incident.

"Who met you when you returned to college?" asked Professor Narayan.

"Mmm…nobody," I fumbled.

"Nobody?"

"Sir…I was tired and exhausted. I went straight into my room and crashed on the bed," I replied, collecting myself.

"Did you talk to anyone in the hostel?"

"No, sir. As I said, I was so exhausted with pain that I dozed off in my room."

"Did anybody visit your room? Did your friends talk to somebody at college?"

"I really don't know, sir."

Now that was a tricky one. They seemed to be more interested in the raucous created by two hundred boys after the initial fight. Clearly, they were looking for names, probably of the leaders of the group that vandalized the village. They wanted me to spill the beans. I was not prepared to slip out names as it would lead to a trail, but it looked like they would not let it go so easily.

"Now you are hiding the facts. We understand you were a victim of this incident, and your story also seems believable, but how could you have not told anyone in college about it? I cannot believe it," said Professor Bhaskarudu.

"Exactly! You are trying to protect your friends," said Warden Patel.

How do I get away with this? What do I do? What do I say?

I was only partly hearing the professors as my mind was thinking hard, sending signals back and forth to my clueless brain, trying to figure out a believable excuse.

And then I broke down.

Tears rolled down my face, and I was sobbing. I could not completely attribute it to my acting skills and belittle the mental trauma of the incident that I had gone through over the past three days. Tension and stress had been building up for a while, and the breakdown was inevitable. I must admit, though, I did not try to hold back once it started as I felt that the occasion and timing were suitable.

"Calm down. What's the matter, son? You can tell us," said Professor Patel. I sensed a display of compassion in the interrogation for the first time.

"Sir, I don't feel good these days. I am shattered... I can't sleep... I don't feel like eating. My hand is still swollen, I am using my left hand only. My body aches all the time... I haven't seen a doctor. I don't know what to do," I said, clearing my throat and wiping off my tears.

"Relax, don't take on too much stress. Take a deep breath, like this," Bhaskarudu demonstrated by inhaling and exhaling. His eyes widened as he exhaled the air onto my face.

I took a deep breath twice.

"Perfect. You can go now. And send Subhash Ranga in."

I came out of the room. My friends were eagerly waiting for me. I signaled Ranga to go in, but he wanted to know the mood in the room, like when you come out of a viva voce, and your friend who is due to go in next wants last-minute advice from you while the rest flock around you for tips.

"They want the seniors' names who were involved in the second incident."

"So? Did you tell?" asked Ranga.

"No, I burst into tears. They went easy on me and let me go."

"You wept, and they let you go?" asked Bholu.

"Yes."

Ranga entered the room, and we waited for him. About fifteen minutes later, he came out, and as usual, everybody surrounded him. Bholu was next to go. Ranga's grilling went like that of mine. He did not take any names and shed some tears.

"You wept too?" asked Bholu.

"Yes."

"And they let you go?"

"Yes."

Bholu took a deep breath, shook his head several times, gathered courage, and went into the room. We waited for him anxiously.

Within a minute, Bholu came back out.

"So early? What happened?" asked Sushant.

"They kicked me out!"

It turned out Bholu had started sobbing profusely the moment he entered the room. He did not wait to grab a seat. He did not even wait for any questions to be asked before bursting into tears.

The professors, who were taken aback, asked the reason, to which Bholu replied, "Sir...I didn't do anything! *Sob...sob...* I am innocent! I did not talk to anyone in the college! I don't know any other names! I swear to God! Believe me…"

Bholu's takeaway from mine and Ranga's inquiry sessions was that seniors were not to be named, and weeping could help him get away easily. Nobody told him to wait for the questions to be asked first. So, saving everybody's time, he got to the point straight away and left the professors startled.

No wonder this irked the professors and made them very angry.

"What nonsense is this? We did not even ask you a single question, and you are howling your eyes out already!" said the frowning Warden Patel.

"I see now. These guys have planned all this drama. They think they will be spared of tough questions. This is bloody emotional blackmailing! Get out of the room! The meeting is over! No need for anybody else to come and shed those crocodile tears," said an angry Professor Bhaskarudu, showing him the door.

So, it took only a minute for Bholu to ruin our forty-five minutes of effort. The shedding of tears of three boys (including mine—authentic ones) ended up being equated with those of a crocodile.

All of us gazed at Bholu with an expression familiar to him.

"What could I do?" protested Bholu. "These guys also wept. And don't forget that notice; you all were supposed to 'attend the committee' while I had to 'face' it. They would not have let me off easily. Did I do something wrong?"

"You did great. Let's go!" Ranga gave up, shaking his head in dismay. Nobody wanted to waste time in challenging Bholu's wisdom.

We came out of the department, and I sat under the shade of the big banyan tree across the road. Ranga joined me while Bholu, Sushant, Faizal, Brigadier, and Dispensary headed back to the hostel. We did not speak much; there was little to talk about and a lot to worry about. Engrossed in thoughts of the uncertainty of our future, we did not notice any passersby until one of them joined us. It was Mathura.

Mathura—another boy whose real name was perhaps only known to him—was named after the city he was from. His slight oversight, which he perhaps regretted later, was that he would tell stories keenly about his city of Mathura when he joined the college, only to realize later that people had started calling him Mathura, and by then it was too late. The boy could tell a story at the drop of a hat.

He tried to sympathize with us. "I know what you guys are going through. In fact, I can relate very well to your situation. You know, back in Mathura, I experienced a similar situation in my school days! One day I bombed a bus and came back home. A riot-like situation happened in my town. My father was angry with me and did not allow me to go out of the house for three days. Three days! Can you imagine? I was so stressed out.

So, believe me, I can completely understand what you guys are going through!"

Absorbed in my thoughts, I could not pay attention to his story. Realizing that his story did not garner the slightest interest, let alone a response, Mathura took off.

"Did he just say somebody bombed a bus in his town?" I asked Ranga as I started catching up.

"No, he said *he* bombed the bus!"

"Wait a minute! What? Did he bomb a bus?" I asked in sheer disbelief.

"Yes, and then went back home! Just like that! That's what he said," replied Ranga.

"Is he freaking nuts? Did he bomb a bus on his way back from school? Who talks like that?"

"He said he bombed the bus that led to riots! That is utterly preposterous!"

"And where did he get that bomb from? Did Daddy buy it at the vegetable market?"

"I don't know. We still have law and order in our country; you get jailed for bombing a bus!"

"Well, I don't know about the bombing of the bus, but he should definitely be jailed for telling such a ridiculous story. And by the way, where was he coming from? Did he attend a lecture today or some drama class?" I was furious.

We often suspected the veracity of Mathura's boastful stories, but on this occasion, he had cranked it up several notches. I gave him credit for his intervention which, though did not prove to be a stress buster, was a temporary distraction from the worry of the failed inquiry. This was one of those badly timed stories of Mathura's that annoyed us but was sure to go down as a funny moment later along memory lane where the mere mention of his bombings would crack us up.

My classmate Roy took me to the general hospital on his motorbike to get my swollen hand checked. The swelling in my right hand was not subsiding, and I hadn't been able to use it much since the injury. We were made comfortable by two friendly nurses in the hospital.

"Have a seat, please. The doctor should arrive any minute. What happened to your hand?"

"Mmm...I fell in the bathroom."

"Ah, do you study?"

"Yes."

"Where?"

"NCE."

"NCE! Did you say NCE?" the nurse suddenly raised her brows and gave me a frowning stare.

I nodded my head with some hesitation.

"Are you one of those boys who beat the local people?" the nurse asked and then, without waiting for a response, turned to the other nurse, "You know, the second year NCE boys vandalized the city, and a man in my neighborhood was critically injured. He was admitted here, in the ICU, in this hospital. The doctors say anything could happen. The people are very angry!"

"No, no, we don't know them! We are in the final year. We do not talk much to second year boys; we only study!" Roy quickly chimed in.

Then entered the smiling doctor, and our nervousness and the nurse's frowned forehead wrinkles both were put at ease. The doctor took an X-ray of my hand and concluded that I had a hairline fracture in one of my metacarpal bones. He gave me a splint to support my hand and prescribed a few anti-inflammatory pills.

Back in the hostel, I mentioned the angry nurses and the man in ICU.

"What? There is a guy in ICU?" asked Sushant.

"Yes," I replied.

"Is he critical?" asked an anxious Dispensary.

"Yes, that's why he is in the ICU! Intensive Care Unit!"

The boys were tense. Dispensary stood there for a moment and then went straight to his room, slipping into bed.

"What happened to him?" I asked.

"Well, what do you expect from a dispensary when you mention hospitals, doctors, or nurses?" Pyare joked.

Dispensary had been shattered by the incident and ongoing inquiry. He would drown himself in deep melancholy every time someone brought bad news or spoke about it, like the critical condition of the man in the ICU or the magnitude of the likely punishment of the involved. Upon hearing something positive, he would cheer up, but optimism in the hostel was like a rare commodity.

There were two types of people: Those who brought bad news, and others who broke it down with detailed analysis, often exaggerated, to make it worse. So, when Dispensary heard something bad, he would spend hours in the confinement of his bed.

Pyare would often joke around, calling him a corpse. Pyare would stop at Ranga's door to inquire about Dispensary in the adjacent room, "Hey! How is the dead body doing? I hope he is an arrow today?"

"No! He is still a bow," Ranga would reply, peeking into his room.

Dispensary's reclining state, as per Pyare, was either a bow or an arrow. Bow meant in the curled-up position, where Dispensary was laying down on one of his sides with his folded legs close to his chest. That sleeping posture would be the result of bad news. The other position was lying on his back with raised hands and stretched legs, all in one straight line. This arrow position, according to Pyare, indicated the content state of Dispensary, an outcome of positive news. Dispensary could continue in those two trademark positions for hours.

To be honest, all seven of us were equally as distressed as Dispensary was, minus his bow-arrow idiosyncrasy. Our fate was in the hands of the inquiry committee, and one bad decision could lead to our career being in shambles.

Sushant broached an idea of garnering public support. He suggested that we get most of the boys in the hostel to sign a paper in our support and present it to the committee. "We can write that the boys are innocent, and the second year batch is with them. This will make our case stronger," he proclaimed.

Everybody liked the idea. Dhanjeet, Ranga, Mohit, Sushant, and Pyare volunteered to visit each room and gather everyone in the corridor of the third floor that evening. Some fifty people showed up. While Ranga made an emotional plea, Sushant put the paper signed by all *Northees* on display.

"We urge you to support us! Your one signature can help clear our names from the inquiry. Tomorrow, if anyone is in trouble, we promise to reciprocate and stand by you!"

Many signed the paper immediately. While some boys jokingly demanded tea and cigarettes in exchange for their signatures, others were serious enough to question how they would benefit from doing so. Many rounds of apprehension, persuasion, and comprehension took place.

Some wanted to play safe and promised to sign the paper once they saw at least a hundred signatures. Others, who showed support initially, were nowhere to be found later at the time of signature. One boy feared that Professor Bhaskarudu would not be pleased upon seeing his signature. Sushant explained that it was unlikely the professors would notice him, considering there would be many other names on the list, but in vain.

The persuasion effort continued until midnight, and by the next morning, we had managed to hit the 150 mark, which was close to eighty percent of the boys in the hostel.

Inspired by the encouraging results, an over-enthusiastic Sushant and Pyare suggested trying the girls' hostel as well for sympathy signatures. Still, the other wise boys decided to settle with the signatures in hand.

We hoped our plan of garnering the boys' support would help us secure freedom from the inquiry like they often did in politics when the potential candidates gathered public support and used it as a show of strength to secure their candidature.

It was decided that Ranga and Sushant would visit Professor Narayan, the only sympathetic professor on the inquiry committee and present the paper to him.

In the evening, they visited Professor Narayan's residence, and we eagerly waited for their return. They returned an hour later, and about ten of us quickly gathered in Ranga's room.

"So, what happened?"

"We are screwed!" said Ranga, shaking his head.

"Why? Did he meet with you?"

"He did."

"Then what? Did you give him the letter?"

"We did," said Sushant.

"Then what?"

"Wait! Wait! Let me start from the beginning!" Realizing the curiosity that was aroused by the one-word answers and pauses, the master storyteller Ranga began, "We knocked on his door, and Professor Narayan, dressed in a *lungi* and vest, received us. He said, 'Yes, boys? Is everything fine?' And I said, 'Sir, we wanted to talk,' and he let us in. He showed us to his living room and signaled us to take a seat. 'Yes! Tell me now, what is it?' he asked, scratching his hairy chest."

"Like this!" Sushant showed us exactly how, by scratching his own chest, though we had kind of guessed already.

"I told him, that we are all stressed out because of the incident, and we are innocent, to which he replied, 'Yes, the committee is looking into all aspects and will make an appropriate decision.' Then, Sushant took out the letter and Professor asked what it was."

"I said, 'Sir, it's the signatures of all the boys supporting us,' and I gave it to him," added Sushant.

"He glanced at the paper, and his expression changed in a split second. He said, 'What nonsense is this?' and angrily tossed the paper in the air."

"Like this!" It was not difficult to imagine it this time either, but Sushant again demonstrated how the paper was tossed.

"He rose from the chair, and so did both of us. He was furious. He said, 'How dare you show this to me? Are you trying to gang up against the authority? Do you think you are some leaders?' We had clearly rubbed him the wrong way. I was thinking of some quick damage control. That's when Sushant knelt down."

"Yes! Like this!" Sushant gave a demo yet again.

"Without wasting time, I came down on my knees too and begged for pardon. 'Sir, forgive us; we did not mean to upset you! We are sorry!' Professor Narayan tried to shove us away, and that's when it occurred to us that we were holding each end of his *lungi*, and that it exposed his bare legs and…something else."

"What? He was not wearing anything underneath?" asked Dhanjeet.

"Exactly!" said Sushant.

"Oh! Professor Narayan going commando?" joked Pyare.

Everyone in the room burst into laughter, and the jokes followed:

"I see Professor Narayan is a supporter of natural air conditioning!"

"Hahaha… Wardrobe malfunction, one of its kind!"

"What were you two trying to do? Set him free?"

"Set him free? Didn't you hear? The guy is already liberated!"

"I am sure he is a firm believer in the freedom of expression."

"I wonder if he wears anything under his pants when he comes to college!"

"That was such an embarrassing moment," continued Ranga, "Professor literally snatched his *lungi* back, and then he said, 'Ok, ok! I know you are stressed out! Let me see what I can do! Take your seat!' We grabbed our chairs, and he grabbed his *lungi*, tied another knot, and sat on his chair. He told us not to show the paper to anyone. And then his daughter brought tea for us."

"Oh yeah, his daughter. Man…she was hot! And you know what? She smiled at me!" Sushant was quick to add.

"Oh yeah? And did you wink at her?" asked Pyare jokingly.

"I swear! I am not joking."

"Really? Did she smile at him?" Pyare turned to Ranga.

Ranga smiled and shook his head in disagreement.

"Oh, he's jealous. I know you guys can't see me getting settled—"

"Settled? With the professor's daughter?"

"Yes, why not? She was so cute. I am falling for her."

"Falling! That's all you guys did there. Falling for the professor's daughter and almost cause his *lungi* to fall."

"Did you fall for the professor's wife too? Because then everything for him would fall apart."

"Oh, you guys are sick. What do you know about true love?"

"Oh, true love already? I bet you, another five minutes, and he will plan a child with the professor's daughter."

"Plan! I am sure he is already thinking of the kid's name!"

"Promise me one thing, don't name your kid Spring Lake!"

As the days passed by, the shocking news of the Spring Lake incident that had once rattled everyone in the college became a mundane affair. My overnight claim to fame as the birthday boy was no longer the talk of the town.

However, my hairline fractured, splint-supported right hand continued to garner sympathy, especially amongst girls. Sanaa would smile at me whenever I ran into her in the college corridors. Those moments filled my heart with joy, and I thanked God for my misery. Thanks to my fragile and brittle hand, I also got excused by my professors and lab assistants from writing my sessional notebooks.

One fine afternoon, after the day's lecture and a hectic lab session, I returned to the hostel where Pyare met me on the ground floor near the warden's office and drew my attention to the noticeboard. The notice read:

This is to notify all that the below-mentioned boys have been fined on account of the Spring Lake incident. Further, all the boys are warned not to indulge in any form of altercation—verbal or physical—with the local public or anyone inside/outside the college campus; otherwise, strict action will be taken.

This was followed by a table with the names of the seven of us, along with a fine of 500 rupees each. The notice concluded with the warden's signature.

My face lit up with joy as I finished reading the notice, and I hugged Pyare. The inquiry committee proved to be more lenient than we had expected as they let us go with a mere 500 rupee fine each.

This was a relief for all of us, big enough for Dispensary to switch his sorrowful bow position in bed—that had been consistent over the past few weeks—to a relaxed arrow position for several forthcoming months.

This event was sure to go down in the history books, leaving an indelible impression in my mind for years to come.

It was time to move on. The soon-to-be-commenced end of semester exams took away the attention. Staying up late at night studying, thanks to the tea and snack stalls in the hostels, soon took precedence over frequent evening visits to the Back-Post and JAM, coupled with endless gossiping.

After eight tests, eight working days in a row, the examinations were over.

What did I learn from those rapid-fire tests? Well, I learned how to deal with the pressure of performing for a new test almost every day. I trained myself to learn and unlearn by quickly discarding the information of one test as soon as it was over and making way for the next one, like the temporary files or the computer's cache, which you needed to trash regularly to refresh the memory and enable better performance.

I also learned to avoid discussing question papers after the test, as the unpleasant surprises of finding out my errors could spoil my frame of mind for the next test, to be held the very next day.

By the time I finished my last test paper, I did not remember a single topic from the first one. Unless my actions were governed by Bernoulli's principle and my decisions were based on D'Alembert's formula, I would forget the theorems anyway.

If I don't use it, I lose it.

I wished how and where to apply the knowledge was equally important in the curriculum.

The results were out a week later, and I advanced to the next level: Semester four.

SEMESTER FOUR

CHAPTER ONE

The topic of girls now occupied conversation among the boys. It was an evergreen topic of entertainment for *Northees*, who bantered with one another. The typical daily routine unfolded with fun time-fillers, aimless wandering, and frequent library visits.

In the morning, during the time between two lectures when the class waited for the next professor to arrive, the brief period that boys liked to call a time-filler would be a lot of fun.

Ranga and Pyare would bet *sutta* (cigarettes) and noodles for random dares. One such dare was to talk to Veena, the girl who sat at the front row, three rows ahead of them, and Ranga offered a whole week of free *sutta* for this dare. One day during a time-filler, Pyare took up the challenge and went up to her.

"Veena?" asked Pyare nervously.

"Yes! What is it?" said Veena, uncomfortable and clearly anticipating some mischief from Pyare.

"Mmm… Can you give me your eraser?"

"Eraser? What happened to yours?"

"Not working," Pyare fumbled.

"Not working? What do you mean?"

"I mean…I forgot to bring it, so nothing is working for me today."

Veena opened her geometry box, took out her eraser, and was about to give it to Pyare when Ranga shouted from his bench three rows behind, "Hey Pyare! You didn't ask me? See! I have an eraser, come get it!" He tossed the eraser in the air with a big smile on his face.

Veena, upset with the mischief, put her eraser back in the box.

"No, no! Veena has a better eraser! Her eraser smells very good!" Pyare tried to cover up the inevitable humiliation, but in vain.

While the front row girls giggled and backbencher boys burst into laughter, red-faced Pyare returned to his seat, eraserless.

Ranga had, by now, mastered the art of giving his word and not keeping it. Such was his art that Ranga would promise to meet Pyare for a smoke at the Back-Post, Sushant for tea in the cafeteria, and Dhanjeet for snacks at the hostel, and not show up anywhere at the designated time. He would get away with a carefully thought-out excuse, making it believable with his convincing tactics, only to prepare them to be tricked on the next occasion.

Due to his habit of fooling people, he was popularly known as *golibaaz* who gave *goli* (a slang term).

Jashan had a particularly painful recollection of his *goli*. During the summer vacation, Jashan happened to visit Gurgaon, Ranga's hometown, and decided to give him a call. Ranga gave him directions and promised to pick him up from the designated spot ten minutes later. Ranga did not show up, and Jashan, who had patiently waited for two hours, furiously headed back to Jammu.

The excuse, or should I say another *goli*, was that Ranga's motorbike had run out of gas, and he forgot his wallet and mobile at home. So, he had no choice but to drag the bike one kilometer back to his house.

Bunking classes and wandering through departments, the cafeteria, the admin block, the AV (audio-visual) hall on the college campus, looking out for girls, was another hobby that the boys popularly referred to as "birdwatching."

Pyare and Sunny, like purposeless nomads, would often wander about the college, skipping lectures and doing hours of birdwatching, making every girl uncomfortable with their penetrating gazes.

They soon became infamous wanderers to the extent that the girls of our batch would change their path upon seeing them approaching from the opposite direction. In the cases where the main road did not branch off, the girls would either slip into the bushes or simply turn back.

Pyare had an explanation for this, "That's how birdwatching works. Birds don't stay back to talk to you. You just watch, smile, and admire their beauty, and as soon as you move closer to them, they fly away!"

The college library, popularly called *Reference*, was another preferred spot to find girls, mainly seniors from third or final year, who would come to study in the evenings. I often wondered if libraries were the place to read and gain knowledge or, as they were portrayed in the movies, were locations you went to *pretend* to read, but actually to gain new acquaintances.

Our college library was no exception. For some, it meant a place to socialize with the opposite sex; for others, it was just a place of visual delight. And the books within those big racks and lying over the tables? Well, they just adorned the whole setting and made it so romantic.

One fine evening, Ranga, Pyare, and I went to Reference. It would be redundant to mention the purpose of our visit. I wrote our names and the entrance time in the entry register.

The librarian sitting in a corner gave us the usual cold stare, his dislike for us evident in his eyes. For him, we were a bunch of mischievous boys who did not belong there. In his defense, his opinion about us was right.

"What's with that man? He is always miffed with Pyare, as if he eloped with his wife," whispered Ranga.

"Wait a minute, Ranga. Do you believe that any female would elope with Pyare? Even the last woman on planet earth would prefer to run away without him. You know that!"

"Yep, I know that you know that, and I am sure his wife would know that too, but do you think the poor librarian knows that?"

"Hey, leave the poor lady out of it! Think of her suffering at having to put up with that librarian. I feel sorry for her!" said Pyare.

"Look at our Pyare Mohan, he has never seen or met her, but he is getting possessive already!"

"Hey, forget the old wine and focus on the tequila shots," Pyare whispered, pointing towards the senior girls.

The large rectangular tables were spaced close to each other in one long, single row. Four girls who had occupied chairs against one of these long tables sat quietly, engrossed in their books and notes. Our presence went unnoticed as we took the seats at the other side of the table, facing them.

"Look, Sridevi is looking hot," Pyare whispered in my ear.

Sridevi was not the real name of the girl. Since we did not know many senior girls, it was convenient to name them after the actresses they resembled the most, at least in our opinion.

Well, our whispers did not make Sridevi bat an eyelid.

Pyare was not in the mood to give up, so he kept gazing at Sridevi, hoping to get noticed.

"Oh, *bhai*, stop staring at her! You'll scare her away. The librarian is already pissed off with us."

"Wait! Let her look up. I am going to make her blush!"

Our hushing and shushing finally caught the attention of Sridevi, who looked at us from the corner of her eye for a second. A few seconds later, she looked again, this time noticing Pyare, who continued to gaze at her.

And then something unusual happened. Sridevi smiled at Pyare.

Amazed, I looked at Ranga, who was equally surprised. Had Pyare managed to impress the lady?

Overjoyed by the response, Pyare sat back, flexed his chest, folded his arms, and relaxed in the chair, without taking his eyes off Sridevi.

Just then, Sridevi whispered something in the ear of her friend sitting next to her. The friend glanced at Pyare and mumbled something to her other two friends. In the next moment, all four girls set their eyes on Pyare.

The overconfident hunter had now become the prey. It was time for Pyare to get a taste of his own medicine. Visibly embarrassed from the collective gaze of four pairs of eyes, Pyare looked down. But the ladies were in no mood to relent.

I guessed that was the first occasion among his numerous visits to Reference when Pyare had had to look at his notes to avoid penetrating eyes. By this time, Pyare had caught the attention of other boys and girls, who seemed to be amused. About three minutes of nonstop staring finally forced Pyare to stand up and walk out.

It was a tricky situation for me and Ranga.

What should friends do in such a situation? Storm out of Reference as a display of solidarity with our friend, or stay back and let him walk away without sharing his humiliation?

We would have loved to stay back and brush off any connection with Pyare, but a thief's accomplice could not cry innocence, even if they had no role in the theft. Sensing that staying would not bring back any glory, we decided to follow Pyare. Little did we expect that the librarian would stop us at the exit.

"Wait, you two, come here!"

"Yes, sir! What is it?"

"Do I look like a fool to you people?"

"Certainly not, sir! Why would you think that?"

"Did you think you could put fake entries in the register and I would not find out?"

I realized that it was about the full names that I had put in the entry register, but Ranga still had no clue what the librarian was talking about. "Fake entry? What do you mean?" he asked.

"Here! Look at this! Is this a name or some sort of sentence?" The librarian rotated the register to 180 degrees and pointed at the name, which read: *Rangaswami Murthy Vankat Subhash Chandra Bose.*

Clearly, I had not chosen a good day to make fun of Ranga's name.

Ranga gave me a momentary *what the hell?* look and turned to the librarian. "Sir, that's my real name. Nothing fake about this."

"Are you kidding me? Which one are you among those four guys: Rangaswami, Murthy, Venkat, or Subhash Chandra Bose?"

"Sir, that's me. In our region, the full name comprises of the father's name and my native place."

The librarian was not convinced. Considering the image he had of us in his mind, it was hard for him to believe that Ranga wasn't lying.

"Believe me, sir! You can talk to my father if you want."

"I don't know... You guys are always up to some mischief. Next time, just write the maiden name, no need to give your address." The half-convinced and fully-annoyed librarian gave up, and we quickly disappeared.

Back in the hostel, I narrated the whole incident to the rest of the gang with all my imagination and exaggeration put together, and they rolled with laughter. The important lesson of college life was to never spare your friends from the bantering and humiliation because when it was their turn, they wouldn't leave any stone unturned, either.

So Pyare and Ranga were the butt-of-jokes for the day, in fact, two or three days.

"Ranga, what's your address? Ah...I am sorry, that's already in your name!" said Sushant, with his usual noisy, convulsive laughter.

"If you want to send mail to Ranga, just write: *To Rangaswami Murthy Vankat Subhash Chandra Bose*, and the postman will deliver straight to his home...because the address is already present in his name!" said Dhanjeet.

"Hey, why is the postal code missing from your name? Add that too! The postman will not have much difficulty in tracing the address then!" added Jashan.

"Add your contact number too!" said Mohit.

Pyare was the other person on the hot seat because of his encounter with the gazing girls.

"By the way, Pyare, did Sridevi wink or whistle at you?"

"Hey, hey...did she hold your hand?"

"So, when are you filing the molestation case against Sridevi?"

"There were four of them, *bhai*! Our Pyare was gang-raped!"

Pyare tried to tone down the humiliation by giving some lame reasoning. "You guys don't get it. Actually, Sridevi was very excited to get my attention, but those other girls got jealous."

"Jealous! Of what...you scaring Sridevi?" joined Ranga, forgetting his own plight for a moment.

"Why don't you add your town to your name, too?" he said sarcastically. "I was admiring her beauty, and the other girls didn't like it. Insecurity, *bhai*!"

"My God, look at this Casanova!"

"Let me rephrase it: Look at this insult to Casanova!"

We all laughed.

CHAPTER TWO

Semester four was fun not just in the hostel, but also in the college. My lab partners Bhuvi, Biradar, and Patra always looked for fresh ideas and out-of-the-box thinking (well, at least they thought so), to make the time-consuming chemistry lab sessions less boring and more sufferable.

The results of the experiments in the chemistry lab required three concordant readings up to the decimal level of accuracy. This meant you kept on repeating the same experiment until you got three same readings.

"What are we going to achieve by doing the same thing over and over?" Bhuvi asked. "I say we stop as soon as we get two concordant readings. There is a ninety-nine percent chance that the next reading will be the same. Why not just *say* that we got three concordant readings? Add some fake figures and do some rough work to make the table look more authentic, then show it to the lab teacher. So, with minimal compromise on accuracy and quality, we can save maximum time, almost an hour!"

"But that's lying," said Biradar.

"I know; but think of the reward! Saving precious time for gossip! I say the third reading will always be the same after two concordant readings. If you don't trust me, let's try it for a week and see."

Like every unique idea, this one received its share of opposition from the honest guys. But like one bad fish spoils the whole pond, the idea soon piqued everyone's interest and became a widely followed practice, not only among our group, but others too.

Bhuvi's innovative thinking impressed Patra, one of my lab partners, so much that they became good friends.

I had made good friends with Bhuvi, who hailed from the state of Bihar. He was plain-spoken and upfront. Initially, I did not like him as he would not shy away from sharing his opinion about anyone or anything, however brutal in its honesty. Normally people avoided sharing their opinions so openly, especially negative ones, but here was this boy ready to pierce anyone with his brutal remarks, even when not asked for his opinion.

On my first interaction with Bhuvi, he remarked, "You look like a homesick mamma's boy who wants to go home! I am sure you don't like it here."

I disliked him, not for being rude, but for making an accurate judgment of me that I did not want to admit. But I soon made good friends with him. It was good to have somebody around who kept you grounded, though that was not my intention behind making friends with him. Perhaps I became comfortable knowing that I could also be as scathing about him without caring for his feelings.

Our shortcut methods to finish the experiments ahead of time left us with a lot of free time in hand. Lab sessions were normally conducted by lab assistants who introduced the experiment topic in the first five minutes and collected our readings in the last ten minutes. So, the lab assistants would be active for a total of twenty-five to thirty minutes, leaving us on our own for the remaining two hours and thirty minutes, during which time they seemed to not care at all.

In the lab sessions, we often engaged in group conversations, sometimes with the girls. Boys would be interested to know about the gossip in the girls' hostel and shared the same about the boys' hostel.

We bragged about what we could do in college and debated about what the girls could not do. Sneaking out of class from the back door in the presence of a professor was one such daredevilry.

Our classmates, Mini and Tia, often tried to dismiss what we boasted about as a daring adventure. "What's this all fuss about sneaking out of class?" asked Tia in one of the lab sessions.

"Well, it's an art," said Bhuvi.

"What art? You guys just stealthily exit while the professor is busy writing on the board. It's no big deal," said Mini.

"No big deal? Well, it requires a lot of skill to maneuver through the chairs and benches to reach the back door and slip out," said Biradar.

"So, what? That's no big deal. We can also do that!"

"I am one hundred percent sure you two could not do that!" exclaimed Patra.

"Yes, yes," I said, "I bet you can't even sneak out during Professor Pranav's class!"

"Oh yeah? Well, we will do it tomorrow!" said Tia, poking Mini with her elbow.

"Yes! In fact, we will slip out of the front door!" said Mini boastfully, taking it a step further.

"If we do, you've got to treat us!"

"You bet. Chai and *samosa* on me in the cafeteria," I said

challengingly.

"Alright then. See you at the 9 a.m. lecture tomorrow."

"Alright! This should be fun," I said, Bhuvi, Biradar, and Patra agreeing.

Professor Pranav was the calmest and most composed professor known in the college. He was super cool. For a lecture of forty-five minutes' duration, he would arrive five minutes late to the class and finish fifteen minutes early. He did not bother to get to know the students well, neither did he care if they attended his lecture or not. He was popular for giving marks graciously, and seniors said that nobody had ever failed in his subjects.

He would hand a piece of paper to one of the boys in the front row to write roll numbers on, which was then passed around the room. In addition to their own, boys and girls often wrote the roll numbers of their absent friends. So, in a class of about twenty present students, that paper would end up with thirty-five entries or sometimes even forty (the total number in the class).

Professor Pranav never looked at the paper and gave it not even a cursory glance. As soon as he finished his lecture, he would simply fold the paper without looking and leave. What he did with the paper, nobody could tell.

I always greeted him whenever I ran into him around the college, and he would return the salutation every time. He often asked, "Oh, are you one of my students?" He must have been either absent-minded or nonchalant to ask that question every time, as I would hardly attend his lectures.

The challenge was accepted. The news spread like wildfire, especially in the ladies' hostel. Boys of the class were intrigued to witness the girls perform what was considered a brave task only ventured by the boys heretofore.

The next morning, 9:10 a.m., Professor Pranav's class.

When he entered the class, he looked a bit perplexed for a moment and checked the door to make sure he had entered the right room. The class being present in full strength was something that his eyes were not used to witnessing. I was certain he was seeing some of the boys for the first time in his life. He quickly settled down, handed a piece of paper to the front boy, and, as usual, grabbed a marker pen and duster, then turned to the board.

Professor Pranav started his lecture. He was one of those Professors who wrote sentences and equations everywhere on the board, not leaving even an inch of blank space. He often crossed the threshold of the whiteboard to finish long sentences and ended up writing on the wall. Boys would jokingly call it an "overflow" sentence. He would turn around occasionally and explain with hand gestures whenever he felt the need.

Ten minutes had passed, and all eyes were on Mini and Tia, who were sitting together in the front row, close to the front door. As Professor Pranav was about to cross the threshold of the board one more time with his overflow sentence, Mini rose from her chair.

Within a few seconds, Mini marched softly out of the front door.

At the same moment, Professor Pranav stopped just at the borderline of the board and turned around.

With eyes wide open, the boys and girls tried hard to hide their amazement at what they had just witnessed. The professor took a brief look at the boys and girls for a moment and turned back to his whiteboard. Clearly, he had sensed some activity, but had decided to let it go. He did not cross the borderline this time and continued on a fresh line.

Another ten minutes passed. The pressure was mounting on Tia now, as her friend had managed the task successfully, and it was now a matter of prestige for her. It was an uphill task for her now since Professor Pranav had shown signs of suspicion when Mini sneaked out.

There was a slight commotion in the corridor outside the classroom where girls, visibly amused, occasionally came close to the front door and waved at Tia.

I saw Sanaa at the door, smiling and signaling to Tia to come out. The momentary presence of dazzling Sanaa at the door illuminated the otherwise dingy classroom, and I blushed at my imaginary pretense of her showing up only for me.

Sanaa and Mini had recently joined Symphony—the band where I was one of the singers—as presenters, thanks to a brilliant idea from senior members, thus adding glamour to the entertainment (as per Bhuvi's expert comments). To the benefit of the popular band, their inclusion had generated lots of curiosity and interest in the college.

I was happy. Whenever present in my otherwise mundane singing rehearsals, Sanaa would often smile at me, making me blush more and perform better.

Tia was running out of time as fifteen minutes had passed, and Professor Pranav, as was known to everyone, would not spend more than twenty minutes in the class. Unable to bear it anymore, Tia rose from her chair.

Call it a great coincidence or bad luck, but Pranav turned around at that very moment.

Both looked at each other for a few seconds. While Pranav was confused to find her standing abruptly, Tia was frozen. Boys and girls held their breath as if a thriller movie had reached its climax and the suspense was about to unfold.

Before Pranav could ask her anything, Tia picked up her bag and walked out of the door. Yes, she left, just like that, leaving Professor Pranav and the whole class bewildered.

"Did she just leave? Just like that? Without saying a word? What the hell was that?" Professor Pranav, visibly displeased, could not believe his eyes.

There was pin-drop silence in the class.

"What is wrong with this class? I hardly teach for twenty minutes and do not care if you attend my lecture or not! But you guys come to the class and shamelessly leave in my presence! Is this fun for you? You know what? I am done with this class!" the vexed professor tossed the marker in the air and stormed out of the class.

While we all chuckled quietly, some boys peeped out of the door to make sure the professor had actually left. Then, the whole class burst into laughter.

This was an unusual sight for the class. Maybe something that happened only once in ten years, as our seniors, or even their seniors, had not witnessed this.

The super cool professor was incensed, so much so that he stormed out of the class. And it was not some mischievous boy who made the professor known to be as cool as cucumber boil over with anger, but a girl. Tia could now boast of something that no boy had attained yet; she did not sneak out, rather walked out of the door in full sight of the professor.

As agreed, Bhuvi, Biradar, Patra, and I met Tia and Mini in the cafeteria, where they were waiting for us. Both looked composed. In fact, they were proud of the whole sneaking out escapade (well, walking out in the case of Tia). I wondered how they could be so relaxed after what they had done to Professor Pranav.

"Professor Pranav was literally shaking in anger. He left without finishing the lecture," I said, hoping to see some wrinkles of nervousness on Tia's forehead.

"That's fine; he will understand. Don't worry," said Tia, sipping tea and grabbing the *samosa* that I had ordered.

"He will understand? Really? Nobody has ever seen him that angry!" I said.

"Yes, nobody! I would guess not even his wife," said Patra.

"Well, remember we told you in the lab session before that the boys can't brag about everything? There are certain excuses that only girls can make. And we don't even have to give the details," said Mini.

It took me a moment before I realized what Mini meant. However, Bhuvi, Biradar, and Patra still did not seem to get it.

"Don't think too much. We will talk to Professor Pranav, and he will understand."

The next morning, when the professor arrived for the lecture, Tia and Mini were present, sitting at their usual front-row desk. The calm and composed Professor Pranav delivered the shortest lecture in his signature soft voice, not once mentioning the other day, as if nothing had happened. As usual, he left early.

I explained to Bhuvi—who was still clueless about how Tia could get away with leaving so easily—that she apparently gave the "time of the month" emergency as her reason for blatantly storming out of the class. That kind of excuse could give her impunity with any professor, let alone the delicate Pranav.

The outspoken Bhuvi learned an important lesson: To not underestimate women. And so did we. He acknowledged that not only could women do what he thought they could not, but they could do it better and manage to get away with it more easily.

SEMESTER FIVE

Rohit Dharupta

Another fun element was introduced into our lives by the recent advent of mobile phone technology. While the public telephone service (PCO) located at the Back-Post was still a popular choice for making long-distance calls to home, the mobile was now a preferred choice for local calling, thanks to cost efficiency.

Calling girls randomly in the evening was great entertainment for boys. The mischievous *Northee* matchmakers had, by now, associated at least one girl's name with each boy, popularly referred to as their "tags."

An uncommon occurrence in the college and a rare occurrence amongst *Northees*, where mutual interest existed between a boy and a girl, was termed "two-sided tags."

A common occurrence in college—a rather widespread occurrence among *Northees*—where only the boy was interested, was a "one-sided tag."

Then there was another one, a "none-sided tag," where there was no interest from either side, only the tag, the concoction of mischievous minds who tagged their friends for the sole purpose of bantering.

Bholu and Jashan were given none-sided tags of girls who, as per the boys, possessed striking similarity to them. The girl tagged to Jashan always looked horror-struck and was critical and cynical of just about everything, whereas the one tagged to Bholu looked equally lost and frustrated, like him. Jashan did not show any interest in his tag, and Bholu had not even seen his girl. As for the girls, well, they perhaps did not know that the two boys existed.

As for one-sided tags, Sushant had a self-proclaimed fancy for Rinki, and for Mohit, it was Riya, despite the Valentine's Day message fail. For Ranga, it was Anu, a girl from the Mechanical branch.

And for Pyare, well, it did not matter... Any girl would do for Pyare. In fact, Pyare changed his tags himself every other day. Needless to say, those girls who he fancied for were not aware, let alone interested.

Pyare was adroit at managing to obtain the mobile numbers of girls without their knowledge. He would gather everyone in a room, dial the number of a girl, put it on speaker mode, impersonate his friends, and talk to their so-called tags.

"Hello, can I speak to Anu?"

"Yes, Anu speaking. May I know who's this?"

"Rangaswami Murthy Vankat Subhash Chandra Bose."

"What? No, no. I am asking who *this* is."

"Rangaswami Murthy Vankat Subhash Chandra Bose."

"Why don't you tell me your name?"

"I just did. I am Ranga."

"Ranga! Where did you get my number from?"

"It's there in the mobile directory."

"What? There is no such directory."

"It is there. I am holding it right now."

"Tell me, what is it? Why did you call me?"

"Ummm… It's very hot in the hostel."

"What? Well, why don't you switch on the fan?"

"But there is a power cut. No electricity."

"So? What can I do? Why are you calling me?"

"I need your help! Something is biting me."

"What? What is biting you?"

"I can't see in the dark. It's buzzing around my ear like *bzzzz*."

"Are you talking about a mosquito?"

"Oh yeah, it must be a mosquito. You are so smart."

"What nonsense is this? Why did you call me?"

"It's dark in here!"

"So?"

"So…I am scared to death."

"Well, you know what? *Just die!*"

As if they could not hold it anymore, all the girls burst into laughter before Anu disconnected. Yes, the girls—plural. It turned out that Pyare was not the only one who had put the mobile on speaker mode for his friends' benefit. Anu did it too. And the boys had a hearty laugh too.

Sanaa was my tag, any association to whom, however casual, I would not mind, for she was one of the most desirable girls. I rather took it as a badge of honor and enjoyed the information our newsmakers brought about her and rejoiced and even blushed at the bantering that those matchmakers often showered upon me.

Ranga mentioned to me one evening that he had overheard Sanaa's friends teasing her by calling "Sanaa Sharma" outside JAM.

"*Bhai*, they said Sanaa Sharma! Imagine! Sharma is your family name!"

"I know you're a liar!" I blushed.

"Swear on my mother, *bhai*! Pyare was there too, tell him!" Ranga turned to Pyare.

"Yes, and she blushed just like you are now! *Bhai*, she is family now!" returned Pyare.

Everything that *golibaaz* Ranga said to me was so charming that I believed him, notwithstanding his reputation of misleading people.

Why would Ranga lie to me about Sanaa? I thought. *Sanaa has always smiled at me. She likes me. Why else would she join the Symphony band as a presenter, where I am one of the lead singers?*

Ok, Mini is the other presenter, but she might have joined the band for its popularity or for keeping Sanaa's company. But Sanaa must have joined for me only.

Backstage at my last performance, which didn't go well—Bhuvi had declared it as the worst performance by any singer, ever—Sanaa had even complimented me after. She had said in her lovely soft voice, "You sang well. Perhaps the music did not complement your voice."

She must be expecting me to make the next move. But what is the next move? What should I do?

This pressing question troubled me for a few days until I resolved to tell Sanaa that I liked her. It was not as simple a task as it sounded. I had hardly spoken to her before. Sanaa was no ordinary girl, for her presence would leave me speechless and make me go weak at my knees.

I thought, I planned, I rehearsed the words I would say, and visualized her positive reaction each time over the next several days and nights.

The preparation for the upcoming charitable event where Symphony would be performing was ongoing. Sanaa and Mini, who would be hosting the event, visited the Student Activity Center (SAC) every evening and observed the rehearsals.

My focus on rehearsing my song was so little that it felt unimportant, for there was something that I had been rehearsing for a few days that needed to be said. Trying to seize one of those rare opportunities when Sanaa was sitting alone in the corner on a stool, I approached her.

"Hi, Sanaa! All good?"

Sanaa smiled, the most beautiful smile I had seen, and nodded her head in acknowledgment. It was the most elegant nod I had ever witnessed.

"Are you enjoying the rehearsals?" I asked. Underneath the effortful portrayal of my calm exterior was my delicate heart, beating fast.

"Yes, I am," said Sanaa. Her lips quivered, whether in excitement or nervousness, I could not tell.

"The songs are going well?"

"Indeed, they are."

"So, how are things?"

"Things are good, as usual."

Firstly, I had never been good at initiating a conversation. On top of that, the short and sharp replies from Sanaa were turning my effort into a question-answer session rather than a conversation.

"It is warm in here. Isn't it?"

"Feels alright to me."

My confidence was now taking a hit. I was terribly short of words. To avoid the awkwardness of a long pause, I strained to recollect one of those jokes I had cracked over several preparatory nights that made Sanaa laugh heartily in my imagination. No jokes made sense to me in this situation.

"Let's go to the cafeteria and have some tea?" I asked abruptly.

"Sorry, I don't drink tea," Sanaa replied with the same coldness.

That reply from Sanaa felt to me as if I had lost my chance. My ears heard, "*Sorry, I don't drink tea,*" and my heart interpreted, "*Sorry, I don't want to go with you.*" My morale dropped like that of a soldier on the battlefield who realized that his side was losing. I felt partly rejected and completely dejected.

"You can have something else! Coffee or a cold drink, maybe?" I returned in a desperate attempt.

Sanaa looked in my eyes for two or three seconds, observed a twitch in my face, smiled at me, and rose from her stool. She said, "Ok, if you insist…"

"Hey! What are you guys up to?" It was Mini, who approached us casually, just as Sanaa and I were about to leave.

"Hey! Nothing. I was wondering if we could… I mean…the three of us could go to the cafeteria?" I said hesitantly. Now that she was standing next to us, looking enquiringly, I had no courage to exclude Mini, whom I spoke to often in the lab sessions.

"I think we better be heading back to the hostel. It's getting late. What do you say, Mini?"

Mini nodded her assent, and they left. Sanaa did not smile this time.

I had another sleepless night, with countless thoughts of how I could have dealt with the situation differently. But my imagination was the only place where everything fell into place, and I was victorious each time.

The next day, while in the bank with Bhuvi, I ran into Rinki Chandra.

"Hey, what's up, Tea Boy? I hear you asked Sanaa for tea?"

"What? How do you know that?" I was taken aback by her bantering.

"Everybody in the hostel knows, my friend. You asked, and she refused."

"She did not refuse. I just asked casually. Why do you think that's funny?"

"I do not; it's serious. So, what next, asking her out for lunch?"

"I will ask you for lunch if that's what you want."

"No, no. I don't eat lunch."

I had before wondered why Rinki always took a tone of sarcasm with me. But on this occasion, her every word punctured my ego. I was angry with Sanaa.

How could she tell everyone?

I had nurtured an image of a calm and nonchalant boy since the beginning and had even guarded it carefully at the time of the nerve-wracking incident at Spring Lake.

How could she tell everyone that she refused my tea offer and make me a laughingstock?

On our way back to the hostel, Bhuvi, having heard my conversation with Rinki, who had perhaps enunciated for his benefit too, asked me, "Hey, what was that asking for tea thing about? Are you planning to ask Sanaa out?"

"No, that was just casual asking! Mini was there too. I am not planning anything!"

"Well, you better not be."

"Why so?"

"Sanaa is engaged."

"No, she's not!"

"She is. Hirwaa told me."

"Hirwaa who?"

"Hiralal from Patna. He is also in the Electrical branch. He says Sanaa will move to Dubai with her fiancé once college is over."

"That's ridiculous. How does Hirwaa know? Did she tell him?"

"No, but everyone in the Electrical branch knows!"

"Really? But how can she be engaged? She is in college!"

"I don't know! But why do you care so much?"

"No reason. Just reacting to news that I didn't know."

Rohit Dharupta

SEMESTER SIX

CHAPTER ONE

The sixth semester was different, or perhaps the same as before to everyone else, only it felt different to me. For some reason, I talked less, I joked less, I ate less, and I laughed less.

The one thing I would do in abundance was thinking; thinking about Sanaa Rehman, for I had no control over my mind. I was not angry anymore. I had no plans to ask her for another tea either. Whenever I would run into Sanaa, she smiled the way she always did, and I reciprocated the way I never did before, for I had no faith in love and no belief in destiny anymore.

We had four lectures in the morning, each an hour long, and I was usually disinterested in attending. I would have preferred to skip the lectures and go to the cafeteria for a smoke and *samosas*.

I soon got the reputation of not attending all four lectures in a row, as I managed to skip one or the other. You do not realize when your reputation becomes a responsibility. If Bhuvi noticed me attending three lectures continuously, he would remind me, "Hey, this is your third lecture. I thought you were setting a record for this semester?" This reminder would make me bunk off of the fourth lecture, thereby saving my record of absence.

Professors at our college could be broadly classified into three categories, strict, moderate, and lenient.

The strict professor would take attendance himself and ensure that the right person responded to the roll call by looking at every face. On the other hand, the moderate professor would not take his eyes off the attendance register while making a roll call, and occasionally ignore the proxy calls made by students on others' behalf. The lenient professor, the most loved one—the likes of Professor Pranav—would simply hand a piece of paper to one of the students sitting in front to write their roll number and then pass it on to others to do the same.

My bunking-off probability was carefully aligned with the scale of strictness to leniency of those professors. The stricter the professor, the lesser my probability of bunking off, and vice versa.

I was not the only one. My lab partners Bhuvi, Biradar, and Patra also liked to skip lectures.

It appeared that professors also classified students into categories. Bhuvi, in one of those lab sessions, quoting his friend Hirwaa as usual, mentioned this theory of a senior professor of the Electrical department about the types of students and their prospects. According to the professor, there were three types of Engineering students:

First, the ones that would never attend lectures. They were warned of the consequences and a note was sent to them or their parents, but all in vain. They would take five or even six years to complete their degree. Such people would either become lost in the wilderness or do something incredible for generations to remember.

Second, the regular and sincere ones. Rainy day, sunny day, come what may, these people would attend every lecture. They would be disappointed, not delighted, if the professor skipped a lecture. They would always get good jobs and never struggle financially.

Third, the ones who missed one or two lectures occasionally. If the professor came to know them and pointed it out, they would become regulars temporarily, say for two weeks, and after that, they again went back to missing lectures once or twice a week, until the professor reminded them again. These people were the future leaders, the COOs and CEOs.

It was a strange theory, and many dismissed it as they felt that the professor was endorsing bunking-off. Some believed it was a whimsical account that the professor had made up for fun.

I supported saying that the professor, with his body of experience, would not make up something for amusement, and Biradar and Patra seconded. Moreover, we fell into the third category, according to his hypothesis, and he had predicted good prospects for this category, which was enough reason for us to believe him.

Bantering and joking never stopped in the hostel. Some people derived entertainment from talking gibberish, just to tease and bore others. There was a term for them—*chaatu*.

Manik was unarguably the most *chaatu* boy in the college. If you were anywhere in the field of vision of this boy, whether you initiated any conversation or not, he would bore you to death.

Sushant was one of his targets. For instance, he asked him, "Manik, how are you?"

"I am alive, my dear friend Sushant. How are you?"

"I am fine."

"Wow, I am just alive, but you are alive and fine, too. You are such a lucky boy; how do you keep so well? Tell me the secret."

"No, no, I am just saying, I am fine. I am good."

"Oh, you are Good? But I thought you are Sushant. If you are Good, then who is Sushant? And who the hell is Fine?"

"Manik, please…I am not ready for this today."

"Oh, you are not ready for this? Then what are you ready for? A party? You never invite me to the parties! Why do you do that? You don't think I am your friend?"

"Oh, God! Why me?"

"Oh! Are you talking to God? Say my hello to God! Ask him what his family name is. Is it God Zilla? Haha! See what a good joke I made?"

And Manik would go on like this for an hour. So, you would be left with two options: Either sit back and hold your forehead helplessly or run for your life. The latter option was the one followed by everyone.

The semester exams went as usual, and we packed our bags to head home for summer vacation. We bid farewell to our seniors Samar, Ravinder, Vikram, Susheel, and others, the good guys who had become good friends, as their tenure at the college had come to an end, and they would be rejoicing in their few final days.

Pyare had one exam left for the sixth semester, which was scheduled for a date three days before the start of registration for the seventh semester. Sushant, Ranga, and I agreed to cut short our vacation by one week and come to college to help Pyare with his exam.

Pyare was confident that Sushant and I would show up at the Hazrat Nizamuddin station, New Delhi, at the appointed date and time to board the train, but feared that *golibaaz* Ranga, living up to his reputation, might ditch at the last moment. For this reason, he booked Ranga's tickets himself and called him several times to ensure that he was on board with us. To his great relief, Ranga showed up at the station, and Pyare perhaps felt that half the battle was won.

One of our favorite pastimes on the moving train would be to walk from one compartment to another looking for attractive girls. And if we managed to see one, what was to be done next, nobody could tell. During one of our leisurely strolls, we saw Sandhu.

"Hey Sandhu!" said Sushant.

"Hey, you guys! Why are you on this train? I thought your registration started next week," said Sandhu, who looked more surprised than us, and rather unsettled.

"Yes, we are going early to have some fun. How come you are traveling to college? I thought you had finished your degree," replied Pyare.

"Yes, I did. I am going to collect my provisional degree. It is required for my new job," said Sandhu, collecting himself.

"I see. Where are you staying? Hall Five?"

"No, not in the hostel. I will be staying in a hotel," returned Sandhu, fumbling.

"Ok, well, see you then."

Running into Sandhu brought back unpleasant memories of the ragging period. The mental trauma and the physical pain that this monster senior had thrust upon my friends and me was unforgettable. He would use the stones of his rings to inflict maximum pain while smacking us hard like some sick maniac who derived sadistic pleasure out of this.

He had never repented or expressed any remorse for his actions, even after the ragging period. I had not spoken to him since and felt like punching his face whenever I saw him.

Back in my coach, I was immersed in my train of thoughts of the time when I had visited home after completing the second semester. It was then that I had opened up to Mommy and Dad about the ragging atrocities of the first semester, which I had downplayed in our previous phone conversations. They were appalled to hear the mental and physical pain and agony inflicted on me by the seniors.

"Why didn't you tell us all this before?" Mommy asked.

"I did not want to upset you."

"But we could have done something to stop those boys. Especially that Sandhu," Dad said.

"Your interference would only worsen the situation. One boy's parents complained, and the warden suspended two seniors for a few days. But then that boy was given an All India Permit by seniors."

"An All-India Permit?" Dad asked, confused.

"Yes, normally, your state or association seniors can slap you, but there is a common understanding that other state seniors will not get physical with you. But those who get an All-India Permit can be beaten up by any senior, irrespective of the state. The boy had to move out of the hostel and become a day scholar."

"Ok, but now that ragging is over, he can join the hostel again. Correct?" Dad asked.

"I don't think so. If he joins now, he will be beaten up by the boys of his batch as they feel that he ran away from the sufferings that we all had endured, and hence does not deserve to be in the hostel."

Mommy looked horrified. "Oh my God, this is so disturbing."

"Yes, it is. But don't worry, next month our junior batch will join. So now it's our turn."

"Your turn?" Dad asked. "What do you mean by your turn? Don't tell me that you will also torment some innocent boys kneeling in front of you like those cowards did to you!"

"Dad, I am not saying we will cause extreme pain. But you need to be a bit rough with them at times. How else can you expect them to be disciplined and respectful?"

"Rough? Did I ever get rough with you? I am your father. Who gives you the right to be rough with them when you are not even their stepfather? Do you think people respect you for being hostile towards them? *Beta*, they are not some criminals who need to be straightened out in prison. They are innocent, talented kids, the future of our nation. Help them and give the right guidance. Had any batch decided that they would not subject their juniors to the same level of treatment that they received from seniors, the ragging would have been extinct long back."

"Promise me you won't hurt anyone," Mommy had begged. "If ever such thoughts come to your mind, think that you are hurting somebody's mother. Think that you are hurting me!"

Despite that promise to my mother, I had slapped a junior once in the heat of the moment and felt horrible, even after apologizing to him later. People like Sandhu not only caused physical torture but were also responsible for brainwashing their juniors to follow suit.

"Let's go and beat the shit out of him," suggested Sushant.

"On the train? You know, there are railway police? They will throw us out," replied Ranga.

"Ok, I have an idea. I will lure him for a smoke and bring him close to the door at midnight. And Sushant, you push him out," proposed Pyare.

"Are you mad? We are not criminals," returned Ranga.

"Ok then, let's choke him with the blanket early in the morning, 3 a.m.," said Pyare.

"No!"

"Ok, ok, I've got another idea…"

CHAPTER TWO

We arrived at the college late in the afternoon. Not many people were to be seen either on campus or in the hotels, as the regular session had not yet started. Even the messroom of our hall was closed, and we had to go to Hall Six for our meals. Hall Six, usually occupied by students who pursued their masters degrees, was located opposite our hostels at the other end of the college. Our only contact with that hostel was through the occasional visits for meals, as that messroom was known for delicious food.

In the evening, the little time spared from bantering, joking, and laughter was utilized to plan for Pyare's exam two days later. Ranga, exhibiting his organizational skills, proposed a unique plan and called it "Project Paper Out."

The plan required the question paper out of the examination hall, brought to the hostel, solved in the hostel, and then brought back into the examination hall. The plan was bold, and the most crucial thing to execute was the time to be stipulated for each action.

After relishing a delicious dinner in Hall Six, we were back in Hall Five, sitting casually in Pyare's room, when Sushant, who was left behind, came running, "Hey! You won't believe what I saw!"

"What?"

"I just saw Sandhu in Hall Six!" returned the excited Sushant.

"Sandhu? But didn't he say he was staying in a hotel?" asked Ranga

"He did. The bastard lied to us."

"Did he see you?"

"No. He is staying in Room 35. That M. Tech boy Prasad told me!"

"God is great! We cannot miss this chance. We must take revenge," said Ranga, visibly thrilled.

"Yes. Yes, we must," said Pyare.

"And Aahan, you should be the first one to slap him! He made your life miserable," said Ranga to me.

"Yes. You must. He deserves this!"

An hour later, Ranga, Sushant, Pyare, and I started for Hall Six. The dinner time was long over, and by now, most of the people had retired to their rooms. Pyare gently knocked on the door of Room 35.

"Who is it?"

"From the messroom. We've got this thing. Is this yours?" returned Pyare in a heavy accent.

The door opened slightly at first, and the four of us barged in, banging the door wide open. Sandhu stood in front of us, frozen.

"Hey! Hey, you guys. You are not from messroom! I mean, you said... I mean, was it you?" said Sandhu, fumbling and swallowing his saliva.

"Yes, you bastard. It's us! You thought you could hide, and we will not find out?" said the angry Sushant at the top of his voice.

"What—What did I do?"

"Hard-Hitter Sandhu! The Terror Sandhu! Now show us how hard you can hit!" said Ranga.

"Aahan, smack his face! Crack his head open!" encouraged Sushant.

"Yes, yes! Hit him!" roared Pyare.

"Hit him, Aahan!"

Sandhu was trembling with fear, begging for forgiveness, his hands close to his face, anticipating.

"On your knees! Quick!" I instructed, and Sandhu immediately followed.

"Look at your third button!" I yelled again.

Sandhu, wearing a night suit with no third button, bowed immediately, as if staring deep into his chest.

"I will not hit him." I said, turning to Ranga. "I just wanted him to know how big of a coward he is."

Ranga advanced to hit Sandhu, but I stopped him and pushed him and Sushant out of the room.

SLAP!

As I turned around, I saw Sandhu lying on the floor. Apparently, Pyare had hit Sandhu while I was shielding him from Ranga and Sushant.

I looked at Pyare.

"Sorry! Only once! That's it. This coward once said that I looked like a lizard!" said Pyare.

We went back to the hostel and did not see Sandhu again. When I saw him bowing down, afraid, helpless, and humiliated, a similar state than I had been subjected to a few years back, my anger went away, and I felt good about not hitting him.

The arrangements for Project Paper Out were made, and our roles were decided. Pyare, of course, would write his paper, but he also had few other tasks to do. The plan was to be executed in three hours, within the duration of the test.

Pyare was highly relieved in the examination hall when he saw that the invigilator was Professor Pranav, the most lenient professor in the college.

Living up to his reputation, Professor Pranav distributed the question papers ten minutes before the planned time, took his chair, and casually opened his book for reading.

The first step of the plan was to get the question paper out of the examination hall within the first fifteen minutes of the exam. Within five minutes, Pyare asked for a toilet break, and Pranav permitted it. Pyare came out in the second-floor corridor, looked around to make sure nobody was looking, and when all was clear, he carefully dropped a matchbox out into the building compound.

The ball was now in our court. Sushant and I casually strolled into the alley of the ground floor to look for the matchbox. I spotted the matchbox and performed a careful maneuver of dropping my pen and picking both up.

Without wasting any time, Sushant started the Yezdi motorcycle, the 1990 Model that Ranga had purchased from Samar for an affordable price, thereby keeping up with the old tradition of the Yezdi passing on from one batch to another. The Yezdi was known to produce its trademark loud sound so much that Pyare, sitting in the examination hall, knew that his paper was on its way to the hostel.

The first two tasks were managed within fifteen minutes, much earlier than the stipulated thirty. Back in the hostel, Ranga was ready in Pyare's room with his books, old question papers, and notes. The matchbox was opened, and the question paper which Pyare had carefully folded and rolled in it was taken out.

Ranga found the answers, and Sushant and I wrote the *micro-purchis*. The teamwork paid off, and we were finished writing in one hour.

Pyare, who was eagerly waiting in the hall with an old, similar question paper on the table kept beside his answer sheet, lest the Professor should get suspicious, was elated to hear the high-pitched *vroom* of the Yezdi. Another toilet break and the *micro-purchis* were handed to Pyare with an hour and a half to spare.

We were delighted with the plan's progress so far and hoped that Pyare would manage to write all the answers in the last leg to execute the plan successfully.

Soon the exam was over, and Pyare came out of the hall to see us waiting eagerly for the good news.

"How was it?" asked Ranga.

"Bad," said Pyare, shaking his head in disappointment.

"Bad? Did you write the answers?"

"I could not."

"What? Why? Did Pranav catch you?"

"No. That PK ruined it."

"PK? Professor PK? But your invigilator was Pranav, no?"

Pyare explained that after half-time passed, Professor Pranav, for some reason, switched halls with Professor PK. Professor PK, who had caught Pyare before, recognized him and kept observing him throughout, making it impossible for Pyare to take out any *purchis*.

"Damn it! At one point he sat on the table near me and kept staring and grinning at my face! I felt so insulted. I tell you; people don't trust each other anymore!" said Pyare.

"So, did you submit a blank answer sheet?"

"No, I was able to attempt three questions which I had read during the holidays."

Ranga, after analyzing the weight those three questions carried and the answers that Pyare wrote, predicted that he could pass, provided the professor was lenient in marking.

SEMESTER SEVEN

The seventh semester had started. The biggest job expo for us final year students was around the corner. Why had we joined an engineering college, or any college for that matter? To learn, to gain knowledge.

As per Bhuvi, who often liked to share his wisdom irrespective of whether you liked it or not, "You can buy numerous books and read them at home and learn. Forget books; nowadays, the internet can give you all the knowledge that you wish to seek. I studied hard to join this college to get a job that would pay me and let me buy stuff without having to depend on my father anymore."

A list of companies that would be visiting our campus soon was displayed in the college building. It was a trending topic of discussion for us final year students. The boys would discuss the topic at length and invent theories about the qualities that those companies looked for.

There was this theory that, historically, the highest-paying jobs were bagged by the class toppers, the branch toppers, and all-branch toppers, who basked in the glory of their eighty-five or ninety percent semester aggregate marks.

But last year, the trend had changed. The companies preferred those who had average academic scores supported by a track of extracurricular activities over the toppers, the so-called high-scoring machines.

Bhuvi put it this way, "Last year the smart ones with good personalities got selected before those *fundu* people."

In the case of girls, the so-called theory concoctors would resort to the usual rhetoric. They would attribute the female selection to their pretty faces and soft voices, thereby conveniently ignoring their academic acumen. Some would generalize by claiming that those corporate companies hired girls mainly to address gender diversity, while others blamed the recruiters for bias.

"Nowadays, they have those young recruiters who visit colleges just to find a suitable match for themselves. The recruitment process for these guys is nothing more than a matrimonial hunt." Then they would cite examples in support of their belief.

For instance, Pyare explained, "*Bhai*, one guy overheard a recruiter of a company in the corridor of the college building asking that M. Tech girl Heena why she did not appear in the test. When she told him that she already had a job offer, he tried to persuade her by claiming that his company offered better packages and perks. He was smitten by Heena's hotness. The guy lost an opportunity of matchmaking thanks to the rule that you cannot apply for another company when you already have an offer!"

Sushant joined Pyare and pointed out, "Have you ever seen or heard of a hot girl that has passed college without a job offer? Never! Only those fools who kept chasing them for four years ended up without a job!"

"*Bhai*, believe it or not, these hot girls are the *apsaras* from another world, like *manekas* who are there to corrupt the minds of all the *vishvamitras*, ranging from boys, professors, lab assistants, recruiters, and even directors. They are like those seductresses who use their irresistible charm to get their way," added the sexpert Pyare who, by the way, had hardly ever spoken to a girl, let alone the hot girls that he mentioned.

The boys would not buy the logic that girls got jobs because they worked hard and outscored many boys in academics, as that would have been a dull and mundane theory. Simple logic did not attract attention, just like water, which does not become interesting unless you prefix it with an adjective like mineral water or distilled water.

However, the explanation for boys scoring less than girls was also presented by those theory makers. As Patra had described, "You see, boys can easily manage to multitask as opposed to girls, who like to focus on one thing at a time. Keeping up with studies along with other important activities like smoking, boozing, chasing girls, and playing table tennis is an art that only boys can pull off."

I was a good contender to bag a job based on the theory of "boys with an average aggregate but a track record of extracurricular activities." In fact, I sometimes wondered if studying was my part-time activity, as I could boast about my active participation in events ranging from performing on the stage, to my membership in Symphony, and recreational clubs like the Premium Club.

Bhuvi predicted that I had a good chance of bagging a job. According to him, "The recruiters prefer somebody smart like you who has a good resume of other activities because it is understood that you possess an appropriate caliber, given that you are studying in a reputed college like NCE."

Now, who didn't want a job? It is human nature that you tend to believe every theory or logic in your favor, and I was no exception. I was glad; people believed that I had good job prospects, despite my average aggregate score. In fact, a boy asked me whether I had decided which company to apply for, as if I would grant those companies an opportunity to pick me and not the other way around. This made me feel very good. Seldom did I think that my lack of preparation could overshadow my supposed smartness.

The stage was set for the biggest event of the college. The recruiters for the first company had arrived, as per the schedule. The recruitment process would be done in three steps: The recruiters' brief about the company, conducting a written test, and interviews for the shortlisted candidates.

So, insight into the company's glorious history and global reach was given through PowerPoint presentation, and we were present in the lecture gallery, all dapper in formal outfits. Finding a sky-blue shirt, a pair of grey trousers, and a purple tie for the occasion was easy, as the clothes had been lying neatly folded in my trunk since our first year ragging period.

I had never even bothered to look at the outfit for the last three years. I had abandoned formal wear, as it reminded me of the mental and physical torture of ragging. I always found comfort in casual shirts and a pair of jeans. Formal wear mostly adorned my storage box and found relevance only on special occasions, such as a job interview.

Like several boys and girls, I managed to pass the written test. I was not happy about my performance, though, and felt as if I had gotten lucky with the multiple-choice questions and no negative marking. But then I reassured myself, thinking that I was being modest and taking my caliber for granted.

Like a player who qualified for the semi-final round of a game and was inching closer to the big win, my hope of bagging the job took a giant leap after I cleared the first hurdle.

Time for my first job interview. I had never had an interview before. The only thing that came even remotely close to an interview—let alone a job interview—was the viva voce conducted by professors for the practical exams each semester.

There were some sixty candidates who qualified for the interview round. Each of the three recruiters occupied a cabin in the academics building and invited the candidates in.

I entered one of the cabins on my turn, and my interviewer made me comfortable. He took a cursory glance at my resume and asked for a brief introduction, and I was well prepared for that. In fact, if you had asked me what I had prepared most for, it was that. I thought that I could set the tone of the interview right away by impressing the recruiter with my long list of extracurricular activities.

I gave an apt introduction, emphasizing my activities, but he soon cut me short and asked the difference between a C and C++. I was able to distinguish comfortably, and mindfully stayed away from the joke we often made back in the hostel that C did not have two plus signs like C++.

He then asked me to write a program on a leap year. I knew that a leap year was a factor of four, so I could at least start the program. I knew another condition—that it should not be the century years, like those divisible by a hundred—so I was able to write a bit more. I also knew that was not all, so I pondered thoughtfully.

The recruiter did not give a hint, nor did he give me adequate time to think, and moved swiftly on to ask a few more questions.

Damn it, leap years; I never thought they were important.

The only significance I had attached to leap years was making fun of a classmate back in my school days whose birthday came once in four years, thanks to the leap year.

I was not sure if the interview was going well or not as the man's plain face and body language did not reveal anything. He neither acknowledged my answers nor showed any sign of disagreement.

"Alright. Is there anything that you would like to ask me?" the recruiter asked.

"Yes, sir! Sir, how did I perform? Do you think I will be selected?" I quickly asked.

The man took a brief pause and said, visibly uncomfortable, "See, my friend, that's not how it works in a job interview. You have the interview, then wait outside with your friends, and then the results are declared, and that's when you get to know whether you are selected or not. Okay? You may go now. Thanks a lot!"

And that's how he ended the interview. So, his body language did give away something, and I was afraid that it was not a positive signal.

As he told me to, I waited outside. When all the interviews were finished, the results were declared, and my name was not there.

After, Bhuvi told me that asking a question about your selection was a strict no in an interview.

Damn it! I thought. *I could have asked him about the company headquarters, or the total campus area, or the global reach that he and his colleagues had proudly mentioned during the presentation. Or simply asked nothing for that matter. If I could go back in time, I would erase that question from the interview. I wish I had a time machine.*

Throughout the interview, I never felt that I had impressed him, and even if there had been the slightest chance of my selection, the question that I had asked in the end probably proved to be a nail in the coffin. So, I concluded that the reason for my rejection was my question, that had put him off. Though based on the kind of guy he seemed to be, even his own questions could put him off.

The first company gave the theory-makers a lot to contemplate. There were toppers as well as average academic scorers in the selected lot. The boys and girls, ranging all the way from Computer Science to the Electronics branch to the Civil and Mining branch, were selected for the software company like a political alliance, where different groups or parties found representation.

The big news was that Sanaa and Rinki had been selected. So, which theory had worked this time? Was it Pyare's "Hot girls always get lucky," or Bhuvi's, "Smart guys with extracurricular activities get picked," (of course, with an exception in my case)? Or was it the least discussed theory that "those who work hard and perform well in the interview get picked"?

Ever wondered what the easiest thing to find is? An excuse. An excuse why you did not make it while others did. All these theories were nothing but an excuse. I didn't think any of it mattered. Theories were based on trends, and trends changed with results. It became clear to me that the only thing that mattered was the result; the result that was acknowledged and accepted by everyone.

I decided to look at the bright side; being a part of the celebration of my victorious friends, partying together, eating delicious food, getting drunk, and looking forward to my chance with the other companies that would visit soon. With the list of companies set to visit our college, it was believed that almost every eligible candidate would bag a job. Well, that was the theory.

Another company visited within a week. I wore the same formal outfit and hoped to get lucky this time. As usual, the company held a presentation, followed by a written test. I failed the written test and did not make it to an interview. My performance standard dropped this time as opposed to the last time, where I at least made it to the interview rounds. Another big blow.

A few more friends and classmates bagged the job. I tried to put up a smiling face and keep my sadness under the wraps.

"*Keep smiling, it makes people wonder what you're up to.*" I liked that quote and tried to follow its philosophy. I believed that smiling would not only keep me in a positive frame of mind, but also amaze the people around who expected the obvious, a befitting countenance, a sad one in this case. Smiling after losing another job opportunity would clearly not be a natural expression.

I looked at the bright side this time as well. I celebrated the success of my friends, ate, and got drunk.

Two days later, another company visited. Would it be third time lucky? I did not wear the same outfit this time. I suspected the outfit to be jinxed, as I had also worn it during my ragging period and had taken a lot of beating then, and now rejection from two companies. I borrowed Ganjoo's shirt, who had bagged the job at the very first shot, so I thought it would bring sure-shot luck.

Another attempt to bring good luck was to invoke the graciousness of the almighty God by repeated mantras that my mommy used to recite back home during the prayers of her weekly observed fasts.

I did not make it to the interview stage and lost another opportunity. God and mantras had not helped, and neither had my friend's lucky shirt. The fortune did not smile on me this time, and the smile on my face was slowly diminishing.

My favorite quote, *"Keep smiling, it makes people wonder what you're up to"* was losing its effect on me. My expression was becoming more obvious now. Forget the people, now I had started to wonder what I was up to. I still joined my friends' celebrations, ate, and got drunk, but it was getting harder now to look at the bright side.

Ever wondered what the easiest thing to lose is? It's hope.

I was comfortable sharing my pain during booze parties with my friend Ranga, since job opportunities were evading him too. So, we would find a corner or a staircase to bond over drinks. You tend to find solace in the company of people who share a similar state as you do, and in our case, it was joblessness, the count of unlucky people that was squeezing rapidly. Whenever someone got a job and lost their jobless state, we would cease to empathize with the jobless and start to sympathize, thus inadvertently growing apart from the jobless community.

Ranga did not seem to care much about getting a job. He had a very cool attitude and would often say jokingly, *"Milega, milega, sabko milega."* He put it this way: "All of us will sail through eventually. Enjoy the party. Have fun; this time with friends will not come again!"

I wondered how he could be so composed. Did it not bother him, or was I the one losing hope too soon? Or did he also believe in the same quote: *"Keep smiling, it makes people wonder what you're up to"*?

I did not think so. The overwhelming emotions associated with bagging or not bagging the first job of your life could not be faked. Ranga, I thought, was either utterly nonchalant or profusely optimistic.

In college, I would often run into Rinki Chandra, who was basking in the glory of her success with the very first company. She and her friend Sonia often bunked off lectures, the art that I had, of course, championed for a long time.

We would talk in the cafeteria or college canteen, and Rinki was positive about my chances of bagging the job. She often said, "A smart and talented boy like you should not worry. Most companies look for the qualities that you possess. It is just a matter of time."

I yearned for support, and that coming from Rinki—a girl—was so uplifting.

A company visited, and another one, and then more. Days turned into weeks and weeks into a month, two, then three months. During one of those written tests, where the company looked for assistance with invigilation, Rinki volunteered and tried to help me pick the answers among multiple-choice questions by glancing around the class and looking at what most people had written. I was gratified with her effort, but it was all in vain.

Rinki was a fresh breath of air in my otherwise mundane, dull, jobless life. Her careless yet cheerful attitude towards life and playful yet supportive attitude towards me was something I had not discovered before. I longed for her company and visited college more often than before, hoping to run into her, to talk to her, to laugh with her, and to temporarily forget all my worries.

Around ten companies had visited, and I had not even bagged an interview since the first one. I was disappointed to say the least. Now the companies visited once a week or every two weeks.

I poured my heart out to Dad in our telephone conversations.

"Son, have you seen those divers standing at the edge of the diving board in the Olympic Games?" he asked.

"Yes." And I knew dad would sprinkle in a metaphor or two.

"Think of that girl. She is ready to jump, and it looks as if she is getting pulled down by the board, but it swings her back. After swinging twice or thrice, she finally attains an adequate height to take the plunge.

"Our life is like that springboard. Whenever you face problems and feel that difficulties are pulling you down, have patience, and don't lose heart. It is an indication that something good is in store for you. Like a spring diving board, life is going to swing you back to achieve greater heights."

Bhuvi informed me at the Back-Post one afternoon that a global telecom company was visiting in three days' time. Lately, in the shell of my deep melancholy, I had almost lost track of the companies that were to visit.

"Read that last chapter on modulation and multiplexing. It's there in the communication theory book. Memorize that AM, FM, TDM, FDM stuff."

"I don't know about this one. I have this unlucky phase going on," I returned in my usual low spirits.

"Hey, don't waste your time sulking. Sulking can wait. You can continue to do so if you are rejected in this one too."

I took note of Bhuvi's jibe and read the chapter. On the day of the company's visit, I was in unexpectedly high spirits. I paid attention to the three wise-looking men and their PowerPoint presentations.

One of them, who spoke the most, mentioned the wide variety of voice and data services offered to customers and displayed images of a vast sub-sea cable network that the company owned. I thought he was perhaps the technical lead. The other one, who spoke mainly about the ethics, vision, and mission of the company, was perhaps from the human resources division. And the third one, who was younger than the other two and hardly spoke but looked carefully at everyone, was perhaps the observer.

I was active in the group discussion they conducted regarding the role of communication in everyday life and was the first to volunteer for the interview when they asked.

After a brief introduction session, the technical lead asked, "Do you know anything about telecommunications that we can ask you about?"

"Sir, I know a bit about switching."

"Oh, do you know the types of switching?"

"Sir, circuit and packet switching."

"Hmm. Do they teach that topic here?" he asked, looking pleasantly surprised.

"Not in detail, sir, but I have a keen interest in modulation and multiplexing techniques," I returned, hinting to him to ask about those topics, for there was nothing else I had done over the last three days but memorize them.

He asked me about analog and digital modulation techniques, to which I answered confidently, and he smiled.

The other man asked where I saw myself in five years, and I replied, "In a telecom company such as this, helping people to connect."

He smiled too.

The third one, who smiled occasionally, continued to observe. The three men exuded positivity, something that was missing in my first interview. When they gave me an opportunity to ask a question, they were gracious enough to explain the criteria for the selection of a cable landing station. (Not the criteria for job selection, for I was careful not to ask any such question this time).

That afternoon, back in the hostel, Bhuvi broke the news, yelling, "You have been selected! No more sulking now! Go to college, they are looking for you with an offer letter."

SEMESTER EIGHT

CHAPTER ONE

Dad's metaphorical illustration of a diving board that brings you down initially only to bounce back significantly proved to be right. I could feel the joy in Dad's sense of pride and Mommy's gratitude to the Almighty when I read my appointment letter to them during our telephone conversation.

Then followed a grand party to celebrate and reciprocate for the job parties that I had been invited to (and they were many), thanks to Dad's generous contribution to my account.

Rinki was the new tag that my friends would tease me with, at times even when she was around, making her uncomfortable, but I did not care for the bantering anymore. Sushant did not like my association with Rinki, but my friendship with him would not change. I was happy.

One afternoon—one of those lazy but bright ones—I found Rinki in the library.

"Hey, Rinki! What's up?"

"Hi. Nothing, studying."

"Oh, that's a heavy book; a lot to study. Don't you have notes?"

"I do."

"I called you yesterday. You did not reply?"

"Yes, I was busy," Rinki replied coldly. Her grim expression was contradictory to her usual bubbly self.

"You could have called back later. I left a message too."

"Aahan, why are you here?" asked Rinki with the same coldness.

"Why am I here? What do you mean? To study in the library," I said, a bit unsettled.

"Did you come here to study or to see me?"

"What? I don't understand! Why are you asking me this?"

"I am asking because you are my friend. I am worried that you are getting emotional. You are being *senti*. All I see in you is a good friend and I do not feel otherwise. You must understand this," said Rinki, very softly but firmly.

"What? What do you mean?"

"I mean what I just said."

A silence followed as if the whole library had come to a halt, a silence that felt loud and unbearable. I was perplexed, unable to comprehend the inscrutable countenance and penetrating words of Rinki. My face was twitching, and my eyes felt a burning sensation. My mind was blank. I could not speak. I had nothing to ask or to say.

"Say something, Aahan. Are you going to break our friendship now?"

I shook my head, but she knew I did not mean it. I rose from the chair next to her and walked out of the library.

Back in my room, I tried hard to process what had happened.

What did I do? How could she be so rude? She says that I am being senti! But when did I ask her out on a date? When did I say I liked her?

When Sanaa refused tea, I felt half rejected, but today Rinki rejected me completely. Am I the only person who gets rejected without even getting a chance to ask someone out? Why does this happen to me?

I could barely sleep that night, and I woke up early in the morning, devastated. I'd had a painful realization that Rinki's fear was not mere unsubstantiated conjecture. I was really falling for her, I felt for her, and I had assumed, subconsciously, that she had felt it too.

Her welcome support at a time when I was sad and vulnerable had developed into an attraction for her that I had not realized. And it hurt. I did not know what to do now.

God is funny; he always maintains scarcity in life by giving something that you don't have but then taking away something else you had. I wanted a job so bad, and I had a friend (perhaps more, to me) by my side, and now I had a job but had lost the friend.

I spent most of the day in my room thinking about what had happened and what to do.

Past midnight, around 1 a.m., I saw Ranga in the corridor of the second floor, walking slowly, almost wobbling at times. His unsteady walk and not so sober appearance made me jittery, and I walked up to him.

He was tipsy (well, that explained the wobbling), and I noticed redness in his eyes. The first three buttons of his pale yellow shirt were undone. Needless to say, the *golibaaz*, the otherwise upbeat Ranga, was a mess.

"Hey, what's up? Are you ok?"

"Hey, my friend, my bro. I am fine. What can happen to me?" asked Ranga with visibly slurred speech, due to the alcohol.

"How many drinks?"

"A little. Just a quarter of a bottle. I need more!"

"Come! Let's go to the room."

"What room?"

"Your room!"

"My room? Nothing is here that belongs to me, *bhai*. I got nothing." Ranga cleared his throat.

"What do you mean? Is everything ok?"

"Everything is ok, *bhai*. See, I don't have a job! Everything is ok... All of you will join companies, and I'd be sitting at home. Everything is ok, *bhai*! What can go wrong with me when I don't have anything?" said Ranga. Tears start to well up in his eyes.

"Companies are visiting, *bhai*! You will find a job soon."

"Where? There was only one company this month."

"We still have a few months left in college. Don't lose heart."

"Don't lose heart? Well, I lost everything! I don't have a job! And not only that, *bhai*... I don't even have a girl! Look at me. I got nothing!" And Ranga broke down in tears.

"Control yourself, Ranga!" I tried to comfort him, but he seemed to be inconsolable.

"What control, *bhai*? Do you know Anu? She has no interest in me. You see this?" he pointed to a torn piece of paper lying on the floor, "This is my life! My life is a worthless piece of paper! In fact, it is a worthless piece of shit!"

I was perplexed. Here he was, my friend Ranga, in my arms, weeping profusely over the assumed mediocrity and worthlessness of his life. And here I was, caught unaware and unprepared for his sudden emotional outburst, struggling to handle the situation but trying to put up a brave front.

"No, no! Not here... Boys are still awake! Come! Let's go to your room." And I dragged Ranga, who was initially reluctant to move but soon walked with me to his room.

I offered him water in his room and sat beside him for a few minutes without saying a word. Ranga soon regained composure and told me he wanted to sleep. I left Ranga's room, making sure that he was fine, and headed straight to my room on the first floor, amidst the sound of chirruping crickets from the hostel lawn in the dead of night.

"Duniya mein kitna Gham hai, mera gham kitna kam hai,
Logon ka gham dekha to, mein apna gham bhool gaya."
(*There is so much sorrow in the world, and mine became lesser,*
When I realized the sorrow of people around, I forgot mine.)

I realized that the audio CD of the classics of superstar Rajesh Khanna was still playing on my PC. I had heard this song many times before, but it had never felt so meaningful and relevant, and never had I realized the impact that mere words of a song could have.

I didn't know if it was just a coincidence or God's way of telling me that I was not the only one in distress. I played the song about four or five times.

I remembered a story of a poor boy that my grandfather often told me in my childhood. The story went somewhat like this:

The boy with messy, undone hair wearing shabby old clothes walked down the street, barefoot. "God, why did you bring me to life? Look at my plight. I don't even have a pair of shoes! What can be worse than this?" he mumbled.

Just then, he noticed a man walking with great difficulty at the corner of the street with the support of crutches. The man had no legs.

The boy, who suddenly felt ashamed and guilt-ridden, mumbled, "Oh, God, I am sorry that I complained about my misery. I thought I was the most unfortunate one. I don't have shoes to wear on my feet. But alas! Look at this man! Forget about shoes, he does not even have feet!"

Amazingly, what occurred to me as just another of Grandpa's stories from my childhood was meaningful and comforting in light of Ranga's misery over mine.

I had always known Ranga as a strong and tough guy who always laughed off his problems, had fun with everyone, enthusiastically joined in the celebrations of his friends' accomplishments, and never discussed his shortcomings.

It had never occurred to me that there could have been a tsunami of emotions brewing up deep inside that calm and quiet exterior, to the extent that it caused a breakdown.

Today I had witnessed his vulnerable side, a side that he had guarded carefully from everyone. Perhaps I was not ready to see that image of his nonchalance shattering into pieces. I did not want anyone else to witness this side of Ranga, and that probably explained my instinctive reaction to quickly take him to his room.

"Don't lose heart? Well, I lost everything! I don't have a job! And not only that, bhai... I don't even have a girl! Look at me. I got nothing!" Ranga's words were still ringing in my head.

On any other occasion, if somebody had burst into tears in my arms, saying they didn't have a girl, I would have burst into laughter and made jokes about it. But this was the irony of college life. At some point, the purpose of college life for every boy meant a job and a girl. If you got both, you were one hundred percent successful. If you got one, fifty percent, and if you got none, you would perceive yourself as a hundred percent loser.

A few days passed, a reputed company visited, Ranga bagged the job, and, like me and like many others, became fifty percent successful.

CHAPTER TWO

According to Bhuvi, in the final few days of college, many boys, except for those few who got lucky with girls, went through the fourth phase of transition. Bhuvi, quoting his friend Hirwaa—the theory concoctor—joyously explained the transition phases that boys went through.

Phase One: Attitude.

Observed in the first year of college, boys thought they were smart and desirable. The simple girls of the college were not worthy of their irresistible charm. Somewhere, outside the college, some beauty queen with dreamy eyes and flowery fragrance would be waiting with a garland for them.

Phase Two: Reality Check.

This phase was mainly observed in the second year of college. Boys felt the girls in the college were not bad. Some of them qualified for a casual fling.

Phase Three: Desire.

Normally observed in the third year, boys in this phase felt they needed a girlfriend, as some of their friends had got lucky. They battled with pressing desire, thinking, *I need a girlfriend too. I have liked this girl since I joined, but is it too late now? Should I look for junior girls? They are all so fresh and lovely.*

Phase Four: Desperation.

The final phase, generally observed in the final year of college, brought frustration. *I am broken and rejected. I like all these girls. Classmates, juniors, professors' daughters, the mess contractor's daughter. Any girl will do.*

The evenings were spent either at the Back-Post over tea, at JAM over noodles, at MANDAP over booze, or at the hostel room over smoke, where boys would gather, chat, and gossip for hours.

During those unending chats, boys would discuss bizarre ideas and dares, such as climbing the boundary wall of the ladies' hostel and sneaking into the corridors, taking the girls by surprise and them shaking with fear in the middle of the night.

We heard stories of such precedents set by the seniors. While few had achieved the feat of conquering the great wall of the ladies' hostel, others had fallen off the wall and broke their legs, or some of them were caught by the watchman, the sole protector of the mighty castle.

The final semester ended with the most casual five days of exams where boys did not study as much, knowing that the marking would be lenient, as always happened in the last semester.

Ranga came to my room in the afternoon, two days after the final year exams were over.

"Hey, get ready! We are going to LH."

"What for?"

"Anu is leaving today. Rinki also. I guess a few more girls."

"Leaving for home? Why? Aren't they staying for the farewell?"

"No. They have a train to catch this evening. Let's go."

"I don't know, man. I just don't feel like going. I am not good at seeing people off."

"C'mon! I'm not sure if we will see them again! Won't you say goodbye to Rinki?"

Ranga insisted, and I acceded. I wondered what he would say to Anu, who had hardly ever spoken to him, and what could I say to Rinki after our last, rather awkward meeting.

I saw Rinki and Sonia at the ladies' hostel main gate, ready with their luggage and the backpacks. As we approached close to them, Ranga applied the brakes to his Yezdi only to slow it down without stopping completely. (A complete halt meant kickstarting the vintage Yezdi again, a one-minute task with a minimum of five to seven kicks.)

I jumped off the slow-moving motorcycle while Ranga waved at the girls, accelerated, causing the trademark Yezdi *vroom* noise, and cruised past us into the hostel.

"Hi! You are leaving?"

"Yes! Waiting for the auto-rickshaw," replied Sonia.

"I thought you would be going after the farewell."

"We were going to, but we booked the tickets a long time ago. It's tough to change them at the last moment," returned Sonia.

Rinki was quiet. She had a mystified smile, as if unsure what to say to me and what to expect from my presence. The auto-rickshaw arrived, and I helped Rinki and Sonia with their luggage. Sonia hopped in first, and Rinki, who was about to follow, turned back to me and said, "Okay, then!"

"Rinki! I just wanted to tell you that I had a great time with you, some of the nicest memories. I wish you all the good luck. Goodbye!"

I held out my hand to Rinki, who looked amazed momentarily. Then she smiled, shook my hand happily, hopped in the rickshaw, and waved at me.

It felt nice. It felt good. I had battled with the question for days, whether I really loved her or if it was just a temporary infatuation that soared exponentially after she snubbed me.

The mental agony I had felt when Rinki said I was being *senti* had subsided after the initial few days. The anxiety of losing something I thought I had, had also lowered with time. But the abrupt ending of that awkward conversation had left a void that I did not know how to fill.

Though brief, today's conversation had no awkwardness, and the void was finally filled. Today, I felt that there was nothing I had that I lost. I felt liberated. Thanks to Ranga, I realized all I needed was to say goodbye.

Maybe I should say goodbye to Sanaa too, I thought. *Maybe that's what you need to say to every girl you can't get, who makes your life miserable.*

Another day passed.

That afternoon, Sushant, clad in a white shirt, blue coat, and black shoes, but with no pants, came to my room after visiting three other rooms, looking for a matching necktie. Over the last four years, not a single day had passed when he had not borrowed something. Everything except for underwear.

I showed him one that he seemed to like and asked, "What about matching pants?"

"Ranga's grey pants are good, but he got suspicious in the morning and has been wearing them since then," returned Sushant.

"What will you do then?"

"I will ask him, but I know he won't give them to me. I guess I need to look elsewhere."

"Don't look at me. I have only one pair of formal pants, and I will be wearing them. Try Pyare."

"Pyare? No way, that *seeti* is so skinny. His pants are too tight to fit me."

"How about Dhanjeet?"

"Haha…Dhanjeet! Really? That big guy's trousers can fit you and me together. The whole soap cake gets used up when he washes those large pants," said Sushant with his usual convulsive laughter.

"Go check with Ganjoo then."

Sushant took my tie and left for a trousers hunt. I met Ranga in the corridor, and he was wearing grey trousers only.

"Not ready yet?"

"Nah, I am looking for a plain shirt that matches these pants. Do you have one?" asked Ranga.

"Hey, you naked rascals, why are not ready yet?" yelled Pyare from the other end of the top floor corridor, dressed in a formal, plain, sky-blue shirt, a black blazer, and dark brown trousers.

"Oh, look! Our cheap groom is ready. We will find you a bride today!" yelled Ranga.

"Who said bride? Get me one too!" shouted Sunny from the ground floor near his room, clad in an off-white shirt and blue trousers.

"No matter how nice you all dress up, I tell you, all of you are going to get f@#$%d!" yelled Jashan, in a jovial mood for a change, as he came out of his room upon hearing the shouting.

I knew Sushant's trouser hunting was over when I heard his roaring laughter and the angry, loud, croaking voice of Ganjoo. The atmosphere in the hostel was lively as the boys dressed gaily for the farewell which was to commence that evening.

6 p.m., Student Activity Center.

Keeping consistent with the typical characteristics of men and women, most boys had arrived before the time, and the girls were yet to show up. The final year boys looked dapper like never before in their coats, blazers, shirts, trousers, and shoes.

The final year girls arrived soon after in small groups, one after the other, as if they all had left together from the hostel and had been scattered on the way.

Ria looked gorgeous in her green suit with a white *chunri*. Neeti dazzled in a pink *sari* with silver lining and trim. Tia was stunning in an embroidered short blue *kurta* and white *salwar*, and Mini looked beautiful in a yellow *sari* and glittering pearl necklace. No wonder why the girls took long, as they clearly outshone the boys, thanks to their beautiful and colorful dresses, artful make-up, and sparkling embellishments.

The boys who had laughed, shouted, and swore out loud before were now most courteous and polite in the ladies' presence, not only to them, but also to each other. In contrast to their usual characteristics, Pyare cracked refined jokes, Sushant laughed gently, and Ganjoo spoke softly.

My eyes were searching for Sanaa.

I dreamed she would emerge in a black *sari* with golden trim and a beautiful crystal necklace resting on her fine neck. The next moment, I imagined her walking in a red *kurta* and green *salwar* with her shiny dark brown, shoulder-length hair curled. I visualized her eyes sparkling under the fine outline of pitch-black *kajal*, and her soft lips quivering like red rose petals.

But this was all in the imagination, as Sanaa was nowhere to be seen.

The atmosphere at SAC had come to life. Boys and girls interacted, exchanged compliments, talked politely, and bantered casually. I spoke curiously to the girls I had not interacted with before and casually to the others I knew.

Mini, like a chatterbox, told me about how girls were excited about the farewell, what preparations they had made, when everybody was going home, and who had left already. She spoke about Anu, Sonia, and Rinki and then posed a curious question to me, as if it was a premeditated one, "What happened with you and Rinki?"

"What do you mean?" I said, hesitating, unprepared to field that question.

"Like the two of you. Getting close."

"No! Nothing much! We were good friends. I came to LH yesterday to see her off," I replied without sharing any details.

"Only friends? There was a lot of noise about the two of you."

"Really? Do girls talk about that stuff? Do they tease a lot?" I returned, trying to evade the question.

"Talking and teasing? That's the thing girls like to do the most!" Mini exclaimed with a wink.

"Wow!"

"For Rinki, it went too far."

"What do you mean?"

"Some girls carved your name at the entrance of her room, like a nameplate on the door. It said, '*Aahan Sharma's room.*' That was a mean thing to do."

"Yes, it was." I nodded in agreement, though I felt good that my name was worthy of being carved in the ladies' hostel, something that I had not heard about before.

I could not help but think, *That's what boys love to do all the time. Carve names. Look at the gates, doors, windows, walls, toilet walls, chairs, tables in the hostel, even the banyan tree in the courtyard... All are engraved with names and signs of hearts, arrows, plus, minus, and equal to.* Then I checked myself for being selfish and not feeling bad for Rinki getting affected by all the teasing.

Mini, when asked, told me that Sanaa would be joining the party shortly as she started from home. Being a day-scholar, Sanaa did not stay in the hostel.

I pictured greeting Sanaa, her beaming at me with that infectious smile. I imagined asking her how she was, and her saying she was fine, but would be better if I was here for her.

Next, I imagined Bhuvi quoting Hirwaa, saying that Sanaa had a fiancé, and then I thought of the time when I asked Sanaa for tea.

I visualized looking into Sanaa's deep eyes and feeling that irresistible urge for a girl who I could not have.

Then I imagined saying goodbye to Sanaa and seeing tears in her eyes. I felt a strange juxtaposition of the simplicity of the warm farewell evening and the complexity of my train of thoughts.

Sanaa did not show up. Biradar and Patra initiated a game of *Antakshari.* Boys and girls joined, formed two teams, and sang songs alternately, each picking the last letter of the previous song. Some boys remained loyal to their team, and others cheated by helping the girls' team.

Together they laughed, sang, supported in the chorus, and even danced on the final evening at the college. They enjoyed the dinner and relished the dessert. Around ten, shortly after dinner, the girls bid *adieu.*

The boys, who were early to arrive at SAC, did not feel like going back to the hostel still. They continued to sing and dance. Those who had been shy and conscious of the girls' presence before also opened up. Now there was no tune in the songs and no rhythm in the dance moves, only joy. The laughter was now uncontrollable and bantering uninhibited.

Back in the hostel, at midnight, all the half and quarter-filled old bottles were taken out and the leftovers consumed. Boys sipped and drank and offered them to each other, going from room to room.

The most iconic songs dedicated to alcohol and drinkers, the likes of "*Chhalkaaye jam aaiye aap ki aankhon ke naam,*" "*Yeh jo mohabbat hai,*" and "*Nadiya se dariya, dariya se sagar*" were sung.

Someone mentioned Professor PK's idiosyncrasies, another one talked about Professor Pranav's carelessness. Some mentioned the trauma of the Spring Lake incident, others brought up the suspense of the inquiry committee. Someone talked about the pressure of ragging, another recalled the anxiety of exams. Some mentioned the list of companies that had visited, while others remembered the funny top ten list of girls based on the Hotness Quotient.

Jokes were made, tears were shed, hugs were exchanged, and more tears rolled to honor the last night at the college. A night to remember.

THE BEGINNING

Third Button

Here I am today, on the Kalinga Utkal Express Train, Coach S5, occupying Birth 60, the lower birth, heading back to my home.

I look at the formal white shirt I am wearing, noticing the small round buttons, and gaze at the third button. I look back, thinking of the tears in Mommy's eyes when I left for college, of the journey that Dad and I embarked on, of the admission day at college, of my first day in the hostel, of my many other days, of laughter and pain, of rejection and acceptance, of friendship and togetherness.

I think of that wise man, my elderly neighbor back home, who had pronounced my college tenure as an experience of life, whose words of wisdom I had then dismissed due to my ignorance and naivety.

He had said, "*A new city and hostel life! Congrats! Your life is going to start now. Get ready to learn the lesson of life.*"

So, what is life? What is the lesson of life?

I think of my friends.

Golibaaz Ranga, who convinced with his stories.

Supercharged Sushant, who laughed and wailed with equal vigor.

Nonchalant Pyare, who made crass and hilarious jokes.

Outspoken Bhuvi, who blatantly spoke his mind.

Mischievous Dhanjeet, who applied balm on his brittle ankle only during the ragging period and never after.

Dejected Bholu, who shook his head at the drop of a hat.

Timid Dispensary, who slept in bow and arrow positions.

Loud Ganjoo, who would offer us help with buying soaps and toothpaste, only to use it as an excuse to roam in the market during the ragging period.

Stone-faced Jashan, who always warned us of the worst.

Lost Sunny, who would struggle to keep up with the bantering in the group and would ask Ranga softly, "*Kiski lee?*" (Who is being made fun of?)

Friendship. You do not just get it. You must earn it.

Respect. Respect from the juniors for treating them as no less. Respect from peers for being cordial. The respect from seniors for being humble.

You must earn respect.

Earn the trust of a friend, a friend like Ranga who found your shoulder to cry on in a vulnerable state.

Forgive people, people like Sandhu, who tortured or mistreated you, as there is no reason to hold any grudges against a person who does not matter to you. There is no place for hate that holds you back from moving on. Learn to forgive.

Remember the memories of good and bad times, for good ones give you fulfillment, and the bad ones keep you grounded. Remember the first Lohri, the first Diwali, the first Holi celebrated with friends. Remember the day I got my first job. Remember the fun-loving, bubbly nature of Rinki. Remember the sparkling eyes and infectious smile of Sanaa. Learn to remember.

Learn that there is no shortcut to success, be it in the examination hall or on a job interview panel. And plans for cheating in an exam do not work, even if done for a friend.

Earn and learn. Earn wisdom and learn from mistakes. As I look back, I think I did okay. I earned, and I learned, for this is the lesson my precious four years at the National College of Engineering taught me. The lesson of life.

TRING! TRING!

Engrossed in my train of thoughts, I don't realize that my mobile has been ringing for some time, until Ranga points at my pocket.

I answer the call from an unknown number. "Hello?"

"Hi, is this Aahan?"

"Yes, Aahan speaking."

"Aahan! This is Sanaa!"

"Sanaa? Sanaa, is it you?" I say, bewildered, suspecting if it is really her.

"Yes, it's me."

"Oh... Hi, Sanaa. Hi. Oops!" As I suddenly rise from my berth in excitement, I accidentally bang my head against the upper berth.

"Are you alright?"

"Yes. I am fine, Sanaa! I just can't believe you called." I say, trying to compose myself.

"Are you okay to talk?"

"Absolutely! More than okay! How are you?" I say, struggling to find a quieter corner in the hustle and bustle of the coach.

"I am good! I guess you are traveling back?"

"Yes. Yes, Sanaa! On my way! On the train," I say, now at the door of the coach, next to some guy smoking.

"Okay. I called to tell you something."

"Tell me, Sanaa."

"Do you remember the day, that day, when you asked me for tea?"

"Mmm… Yes, I remember, Sanaa."

"I wanted to… Wanted you to know…" Sanaa pauses.

"Tell me, Sanaa. I am listening," I say, unable to bear the silence.

"I just wanted you to know that when you asked me to go for tea…I really wanted to go with you."

XXXX

About the Author

Rohit Dharupta was born and raised in Shimla, India, where he did his schooling. He completed a qualification in engineering from the National Institute of Technology (NIT) in Rourkela, India, in the year 2005.

Presently, Rohit works for a global company and lives in Montreal, Canada.

His passion for storytelling inspired Rohit to write *Third Button*, about the nostalgia of his college days. The story is loosely based on his memorable four years at NIT.

He describes this experience as a journey which took him from a boy with hope to a man with belief.

Thanks for reading. If you enjoyed this book, please consider leaving an honest review on Amazon or on the website of your favorite store.

Made in United States
Orlando, FL
01 October 2024

52204184R00136